LILITH'S CHILDREN

RACHEL PUDELEK

CITY OWL
PRESS

LILITH'S CHILDREN
Wild Women, Book 2

CITY OWL PRESS
www.cityowlpress.com

Cover Design by Mibl Art and Tina Moss. All stock photos licensed appropriately.

Edited by Heather McCorkle.

Map by Dani Woodruff.

For information on subsidiary rights, please contact the publisher at info@cityowlpress.com.

Print Edition ISBN: 978-1-949090-30-7

Digital Edition ISBN: 978-1-949090-29-1

Printed in the United States of America

To my readers.
May you embrace your inner Wild.

Huldra—Forest women, able to cover their skin in bark and grow branches from their hands and feet, created by the Goddess Freyja.

Washington Coterie

- Faline

- Shawna

- Olivia

- Celeste

- Patricia

- Renee

- Abigale

- Naomi (missing)

Succubi—Empathic women, able to manipulate and absorb energy, created by the Goddess Lilith.

Oregon Galere

- Marie

- Heather (missing)

Mermaids—Aquatic women, able to shift their legs to a tail and cover their skin with scales, created by the Goddess Atargatis.

California Shoal

- ~~Gabrielle~~

- Azul

- Elaine

- Sarah

Harpies—Women able to sprout bird-like wings, feathers, and talons, created by the Goddess Inanna.

North Carolina Flock

- Eonza

- Salis

- Lapis

- Rose (missing)

Rusalki—Women tied to nature, able to read minds, practice divination, and cut lives short, created by the Goddess Mokosh.

<u>Maine Coven</u>

- Veronia

- Daphne

- ~~Azalea~~

- Drosera

- Aconitum (missing)

- Oleander (missing)

Nagin—Women represented by the cobra, able to use kundalini energy to manipulate the energy of a person from the inside, created by the Goddess Wadjet.

<u>United Kingdom</u>

- Anwen

- Berwyn

- Eta

Shé—Women able to change their lower half into a snake tale while in the water. On land they maintain their legs and can grow scales on their body for protection as they play their handmade instrument to change the energy, moods, and thoughts of others, created by the Goddess Nü Gua.

<u>China</u>

- Chen

- Fan

Echidna—Women able to change their lower half to a snake tail for

speed, defense, and squeezing their prey, created by the Snake Goddess of Crete, whose name is not uttered or known to outsiders.

Crete

- Calle

- Gerda

PREFACE

In the Garden of Eden, the ultimate tempter was a snake, evil incarnate. But the serpent was once a symbol of the goddess, for females too shed their lining and yet still they live. Soon, though, the Goddess will rise again, and her snake children will unite to reclaim their life of paradise.
These were the nighttime whispers of Faline's mother.
The Hunters told a different tale.

ONE

My day of wine-tasting had not gone as planned, a fact I bemoaned as I flung an elbow at a Hunter's nose and sloshed pinot noir down my white shirt.

The large, blond Hunter who'd advanced on me, and the four other Hunters he'd brought, wore black cargo pants and black long-sleeved shirts, just like the Hunters back home. They also kept a special dagger concealed on their bodies like my oppressors back home. But they were most certainly not Washington Hunters.

I'd just wanted a trip away.

A vacation. Relaxation between hunting the Hunters and annihilating their complexes, one at a time.

Was that too much to ask? Apparently, yes.

My blow to the Hunter's face fazed him for all of two seconds before he reached for my hair to lift me off my feet. Bad idea on his part.

I couldn't tell you how the Hunters found us. How they knew we'd left the state of Washington and ventured into pinot noir country in Oregon.

I could tell you, though, that these weren't Washington Hunters ruining our little vacation. They knew nothing about defending themselves against huldra. Which was one reason Shawna hid in the corner, half-petting the cat and half-covering her ears. Minutes earlier, my partner sister, Shawna, had grabbed the petite grey and black striped winery cat from atop a square plastic behemoth of a wine container to comfort her in the corner of the winery warehouse.

It'd only been a week since we rescued Shawna from the Washington Hunter complex and soon after the strongest drugs they'd given her had worn off we noticed her huldra abilities were lacking. Somehow the Hunters had muted them. Either that or her fear was muting them.

I smiled, happy to play this male's game as he lifted me from the floor by my hair.

I let out a screech and kicked my feet, pretending my toes searched for purchase on the cement floor. And I could be mistaken, but I was pretty sure the Hunter smiled too, which only made the moment sweeter. Nice of him to do that for me.

The Oregon Hunter complex had only sent five Hunters to ruin our wine-tasting excursion. Clearly, they were just responding to a suspicion of Wilds and had no idea they'd find the notorious Hunter-burning huldra. Not that they'd given us that name. In fact, there'd been an eerie silence surrounding it all—nothing in the newspapers about a burnt complex and no emails or summons from the Hunters.

Marcus, my ex-Hunter boyfriend, took on the biggest Hunter of the bunch, and my sisters and aunts shared the other three, while my sister, Celeste, escorted the winery owner and his son into the back offices to distract them and keep them from calling the cops. I took in the sight of Marcus fighting for a few moments. How could I not? He looked oh-so-sexy, with muscles bulging the seams of his blue shirt, a color that set off his tanned skin and dark hair quite nicely. These males had no chance, but it was awfully cute how hard they were trying. Well, maybe not cute. Just awful.

When the blond Hunter was confident enough of my impending death to emanate the scent of vanilla and cherry, I stopped pretending to flail my legs and swiped at him. I shot my right hand up and wrapped my fingers around his arm, above his fist clenched in my hair. With my left hand I wiggled my fingers as though I were cursing him with a spell. Vines discharged from the tips of my fingers and wrapped around his neck. Thin branches poked into his wrist from my right hand, and he shook, struggling to hold on despite his new puncture wounds.

He hadn't been trained to tense his neck muscles. Rooky mistake. Right as Blond Hunter's face turned a light and lovely shade of blue, and his scent took on the musty iron tone of fear, Huge Hunter sliced through my vines and set his brother free. I retracted the burning vines into my hand and crouched to spring onto my newest foe. Blond Hunter fell to the floor, breaking free of my branches and gasping for air.

"Shit," Marcus yelled as his right shoulder slammed into Huge Hunter's back, linebacker style.

Huge Hunter turned to swing a fist at Marcus, who ducked in time to avoid the blow. The missed calculation caused Huge Hunter to stumble forward where my coterie members were willing and waiting to finish him off.

We encircled the last living Hunter in the winery warehouse. He puffed out his chest and tried to force an intimidating growl.

"Leave the growling to the Wild Women," I suggested. "You're embarrassing yourself."

Huge Hunter saved a special scowl for me, one that barely showed the blue of his eyes, and yet overemphasized his stained teeth.

"Let me have him," Marcus seethed.

I answered Marcus by calling the name of my partner sister. "Shawna," I said in an almost sing-song voice. Gentle enough to pull her from her probable fetal position in the corner. "You can come out now, it's safe."

Marcus caught my gaze and nodded his approval of my plan.

Shawna, cat in tow, eased out from behind the row that stretched the length of the warehouse, stacked three barrels high. A compressor hummed outside the roll-up door, ready to do whatever wine makers did with compressors.

Shawna neared us with slow footsteps. She watched the Hunter, and I couldn't tell if I saw fear or fury in her brown eyes. She tilted her chin toward her chest, still eyeing the Hunter.

"Your brothers drugged me," Shawna said under her breath as she moved closer to our circle. "They beat me. Called me awful things. Threatened to rape me." Her voice shook on that last part.

I shook, too. All of me. It was a heinous thing, using a body to dominate another's.

Shawna had refused to tell us what'd happened to her at the Hunters' hands. Refused to give us details, other than to tell us they were awful.

She stood within an arm's length of Marcus, outside the circle. "Threatened to rape me," she repeated. "To shatter my temple and leave me to pick up the pieces."

A guttural growl rose from my partner sister's throat like nothing I'd ever heard before. Cold shivers covered the back of my neck. The cat she carried hissed and flung itself from her arms. She didn't notice. She took another step and Marcus moved aside for her to enter the outer circle made mostly of her fellow huldra.

Marcus swallowed loudly and clenched his fists—tell-tell signs that Shawna was setting off Marcus's Hunter red flags. You could take the Hunter out of the complex, but you couldn't take the Hunter out of the man. While he was on our side, he still had his instincts—instincts that reacted to our kind in a negative way. Huge Hunter twitched and clenched and opened his hands. Whatever my sister was putting down, these two Hunters were picking up.

Shawna's timid steps morphed into those of a lioness seconds before the deadly pounce. She drew up close to the Hunter and my coterie quickly moved behind him to restrain his arms. I stood to one side of Shawna, and Marcus covered her from the other.

"It's not like in the movies, you know," Shawna said lightly. "They show the captured woman scared. But fear isn't a big enough emotion for it."

She leaned forward and sniffed him. "You don't wear powerful cologne like the Washington Hunters. Can succubi not smell your emotions?"

I watched my sister in awe. We all did. She hadn't woken this morning as the same woman we'd rescued a week ago, no, but she'd still been timid and reserved. That's why I'd planned the coterie trip to go wine tasting. What better way to loosen up and remember what matters? Apparently, a tall glass of Hunter was what my sister needed, not a red blend.

Huge Hunter gave one response to my sister's question. He spit in her face.

Wrong answer.

Shawna sprang at him. "I'll kill you!" she shouted in a voice I'd never heard before. Her legs wrapped around his waist. Her hands pushed his head sideways, toward his left shoulder. And then my sister did the thing I'd never thought possible of her.

Shawna sank her mouth into the Hunter's exposed trapezius, bit down, and pulled away with a mouthful of flesh. Her mother, Abigale, screeched and leaned away. Standing behind the Hunter's right side, she'd gotten the best view of her daughter's retribution.

Huge Hunter knocked his head into my sister's and fought to be free. Marcus punched him in the face, leaving him bleary between the impact and the blood loss. My coterie members released the male and stepped back, allowing Shawna the freedom to do as she willed.

"Finish him," Marcus commanded through gritted teeth.

I shot him a look, but he was too focused on my sister to notice.

Tears streamed down Abigale's face.

Blood dripped from Shawna's jaw.

"Do you think he would have helped you?" Marcus asked Shawna. "Do you think, if he were there at that cabin, holding you against your will, he would have been kind?"

I thought back to the day we rescued my sister, to the large Hunter at my sister's bedside, in control of the IV drip attached to her arm, the one in the white lab coat who made jokes about growing a Hunter/huldra hybrid within my sister, about personally inseminating me with one.

The Hunter I bit. Repeatedly.

"No," I warned. "Don't Shawna, it'll only make your huldra harder to control." I spoke from experience. I couldn't tell if my sister had blacked out the way I had, but it didn't matter.

"What huldra?" she screeched. "They took her from me. They stole my wildness!" She zeroed in on the Hunter whose body she clung to.

"*You* took my wildness." She shoved his head to the side again. "I'm taking it back!"

I didn't know whether to stop my sister from making a huge mistake, or to join her. She ravaged the huge Hunter like the Washington Hunters had no doubt threatened to ravage her. In a second of clarity I peered around the warehouse in search for the winemaker and his son. They were gone, thankfully.

The Hunter's tirade of obscenities toward my sister and our kind lessened as my sister's light green shirt turned a deep red. The scent of blood filled the warehouse and my huldra yearned to be let loose.

But this was Shawna's battle, a war I'd witnessed her fight since the day she came home from the Hunter's complex with ash on her face and the seed of revenge in her heart.

Seeds are funny things. You never know, just by looking at the seed, what it'll grow into. If it'll even take root, or wither and die. Shawna's seed was sprouting in a hurry. And despite its inability to cause vines to grow from her fingertips, I had no doubt it took root and pulled her huldra from wherever she hid deep inside my sister.

Shawna clung to the Hunter's back as he hit the floor with a thud. Marcus distanced himself. Smart.

I, on the other hand, moved closer to my sister. Maybe not so smart.

A low growl vibrated in her throat and she paused, not taking her eyes off her prey.

"I'm not trying to take him from you, Shawna. He's dead. You did it."

She pulled her head away from his chest and turned to look at me.

I'm not easily scared. But the huldra who looked back at me through Shawna's eyes scared the shit out of me. My huldra tried to rise to the surface, to meet the one staring at me, but I urged her to let me handle things my own way.

"You stopped him," I said in an even and firm tone. "He'll never hurt another Wild again. You did that."

She looked back down at her prey, measuring her accomplishment.

I wished desperately that she'd blacked out, that I were shaking her into consciousness rather than placating her huldra. I shoved every worry of how this would impact my sister into the crowded "future problems" portion of my mind and called my sister's name.

"Shawna, I know what you're feeling." Except I didn't. Yeah, I'd experienced attacking a man and a Hunter, and each time coming to with blood on my lips. But that was as far as our shared experience extended. "Slow, deep breaths will help you control yourself. Once you've got your breathing down, imagine roots growing from the soles of your feet, anchoring you to the earth."

She didn't nod or say anything to confirm she'd followed my directions, but her chest rose and fell a little slower.

"Good," I said. "Keep going."

Her fingers unhinged from his neck and shoulder.

She took a few more slow breaths.

Her legs straightened and she stood over the dead Hunter.

Abigale ran to her daughter, sobbing, and before I could warn her against it, she wrapped her arms around Shawna and squeezed.

Shawna released the longest exhale. Her eyes closed and she leaned her head on her mother's shoulder. Abigale's crying quieted. "It's okay. It's going to be okay now."

Olivia leaned back against a barrel and Patricia bent forward to rest her hands on her knees. Seeing as none of us had experience in subduing a rogue huldra, we all sighed in relief.

I made my way to Marcus and kept from smacking him in the arm. "What was that?" I whispered, knowing full well the only people in the warehouse that couldn't still hear me were the human males probably holed up in the restroom or an office.

"It's how she'll heal and move forward," he answered unapologetically.

"By losing control of herself?"

"By taking back control, which is exactly what she did." Marcus rubbed the back of my bicep. "They took her and drugged her and there was nothing she could do about it. Today she got to fight back. She got to release the anger and hurt onto a Hunter."

"You just shook a bottle of soda and popped the top off. We won't be able to get it all back in. What's out is out." I shook my head. "Her huldra is out."

Marcus cupped a hand to my cheek and leaned in toward me. "There's nothing wrong with that."

His comment caught me off guard and I reassessed my thoughts. My huldra had saved my sister and just now my partner sister accessed her own wildness to save herself. There was nothing wrong with that. Nothing to be ashamed of. It's not like she killed an innocent human, or even another Wild Woman. This huge Hunter tracked us down to either take us in or kill us while trying. We defended ourselves.

Shawna defended herself.

"I hate that what they taught us still hides in my thoughts," I confessed.

Marcus pulled me in for a hug and rested his head on top of mine. "Welcome to the club, babe. Welcome to the club."

TWO

FIBERGLASS SKYLIGHTS LIT the messy warehouse, made messier by our little scuffle. We didn't set out to end the lives of five more Hunters today, but that's what had happened. And all before dinner. Which gave me an idea.

"Anyone else hungry?" I asked while heaving the largest Hunter onto the pile of his brothers.

Marcus dropped the arm of the Hunter he'd been helping to move and wiped his hands on his dark khaki cargoes, now stained with blood, dirt, and...was that wine? Well, didn't we make a wine-stained pair. "Seriously?" he asked. He glanced from me, to Shawna, and back to me.

"What?" I said, unafraid to talk about the elephant in the room. "Just because *she* had a snack, I shouldn't be hungry? The partner sister bond doesn't work like that." I went back to work hauling the Hunter, but without the help of my coterie and Marcus, the body didn't move an inch.

Abigale stifled a gasp. Shawna went back to coddling the skittish cat who'd found her after the fighting ended. My coterie members fidgeted and wiped dirt from their hands.

I dropped the leg I'd been tugging on. "Oh, come on."

Olivia spoke up. "You're being insensitive, Faline."

"Really?" I wiped sweat from my brow. "How so? I attacked and killed a human man, then watched a rusalka kill a mermaid friend of mine with a snip of her birch scissors, and then I killed a bunch of Hunters. So excuse me if being present to my sister taking a few bites of her enemy didn't leave my stomach in knots and my appetite on the fritz."

Shawna laughed. "I know I shouldn't be, but I'm hungry too."

I wanted to fist-bump my partner sister right then and there, but I withheld the urge. Instead, I smiled at her.

Her words changed the energy of the warehouse and my coterie relaxed—brows un-furled and arms uncrossed.

Celeste peeked from the hallway leading to the restroom and offices, leaving the wine owner and his son behind. "I have to get back in there. Don't want them worrying enough to call the police. Just, let us know when it's safe to come out. It's not like they can live in that tiny office." Celeste rested her hands on her hips and took stock of the almost-pile of Hunters.

Don't ask me why we'd decided to pile them up; it's just what they do on TV.

"No one's getting anything...else...to eat until we deal with this mess." She retreated back the way she came.

"Why don't you call Marie and see if she knows of a good service for something like this," Marcus suggested.

I had no idea why a peaceful succubi leader, who only used her energy manipulation powers to heal others and have fantastic sex, would have contacts for a body-removal service, but I doubted the human winery owners could point us in the right direction, so it was worth a shot.

Renee scoffed. "No, thanks. We'll be just fine without the manipulating succubi. Especially that one."

Old xenophobia dies hard.

"No, he makes a good point," I said, speaking more from a desire to fill my growling stomach than actual logic. My coterie had gotten accustomed to Marcus, though I wouldn't say they liked having him around by any stretch of the word. Abigale appreciated him. Shawna needed him. And I had the hots for him and still waited on bated breath for the moment we could spend a full night together rather than midnight rendezvous while Shawna slept. The others weren't too keen on the male. Not that they didn't like him; they barely made an effort to get to know him. I couldn't blame them, though. If I were in their shoes, I'd probably feel the same way.

"This isn't our territory," I added. And maybe Marie would know of someone who discretely disposed of bodies. She might be peaceful, but she was also highly sexual, and I could imagine how many secrets were spilled between the sheets with a succubus. "Most of you have never even left Washington until yesterday. How will we know what to do with the bodies? We don't even know our way around without a GPS."

"So we're in agreement?" I said, pulling my for-now-phone from my back pocket. I inspected the screen for cracks while I waited for a unanimous response. Not one crack. The heavy duty case had been worth its expensive price tag.

"Fine," Renee said with all the grace of a toddler whose opinion had been overruled.

My sisters and other aunts nodded, and I called Marie. We hadn't spoken since the Wild Women left our home to go back to theirs the day after we leveled the Washington Hunters' complex. I'd been meaning to call, to discuss the dates for the next Wild gathering in North Carolina to overrun that Hunter complex. But honestly, I'd been putting it off. I needed to rest and unwind before playing mind games with Marie again.

"My favorite huldra," Marie answered with a smile in her voice.

"I have a favor to ask," I said, cutting to the point. The quicker we cleaned up our mess, the quicker I could sit down to a table and order food.

"What? Did you lose another sister?" Marie laughed and a man moaned from her side of the call. Was she ever by herself?

"Nope, all huldra are present and accounted for. Your Oregon Hunter complex is missing five members, though."

The phone rustled and a door shut. "You killed Oregon Hunters?" Marie asked with a whisper. It interested me what Marie deemed private versus what she deemed public.

"My coterie, Marcus, and me, yeah," I answered.

"You still have that Hunter dropout hanging around?" she said with contempt.

I almost told her to watch her mouth, that Hunter dropout was my boyfriend. But then I realized Marcus and I had never actually had that talk. That morning before I met with the harpies, when we'd spent the night together in the dank hotel, I'd promised him we'd discuss the topic of us after I got my sister back. A pit formed in my empty stomach. When would Marcus collect on that promise?

Thankfully, Marie didn't have the ability to read my emotions over the phone. "What should we do with the bodies, Marie?" I asked, changing the subject from Marcus to dead Hunters.

"How should I know? Succubi give life, not death."

If she were standing in front of me, I'd shoot her a level gaze. Come on. "Seriously, Marie. I know you know people."

The line was quiet for a few breaths before she answered. "I'll send a crew out. Once they arrive, you should leave. Are there humans present?"

"Celeste is keeping them company in the back room," I said.

"Perfect. My sisters will wipe their memories. Where are you, exactly?"

I eyed the line-up of wine bottles that were supposed to be our selections for tasting, six bottles that ranged from a dry chardonnay to a sweet dessert wine and a few different pinots and red blends in between. The gold label read Sass. "We're at Sass Winery. It's a small winery, in a warehouse overlooking vineyards. You have to go up a gravel road to get here and their only sign is an old oak barrel with their name on it."

"Okay, my sisters are on their way." The line went dead and I slid my indestructible phone back into my jeans pocket.

"I think," Shawna said in a far-off voice, "that whatever the Hunters gave me to suppress my huldra had something to do with me being able to carry a child with Hunter DNA. They were trying to suppress my body's nature to only birth females." She set the cat onto a huge square plastic vat of wine. The cat walked back and forth under Shawna's hand for pets, arching its spine with each pass.

We all shot each other looks as though one of us could explain what the hell was going on with Shawna.

"That would make sense," Marcus said, nodding. "Wilds only give birth to females. Hunters can only be male. If they're making hybrids, they'd need to come up with a way to bridge that gender gap. Suppressing the huldra probably wasn't the goal as much as suppressing the female-only Wild genes."

Yeah, what Marcus and Shawna were saying made absolute sense. But what shocked my sisters, aunts, and me, was the fact that Shawna was even saying such things—discussing her experience with the Hunters. It was as though fighting back today cracked open a scab and now she processed the pus flowing from the wound, wiped it away to reevaluate the damage.

"Do you think I could be pregnant?" she asked calmly, gazing at the purring cat.

Renee's chin snapped up and she shook her head. "Let's hope not. But either way, we won't know for a few weeks. It's too soon to tell."

"Do you remember them doing any other procedures to you, rather than inserting the IV?" Olivia asked.

Shawna thought for a moment. "No. But there were times when I woke up from a drug-induced sleep and hadn't realized I'd fallen asleep. So I wasn't coherent the whole time."

Renee, always the nurse, prodded, "Faline told us the substance in the IV was green. Do you remember anyone coming in with a syringe to put something else into the IV drip? Something that wasn't green?" She turned to address the rest of us. "They could have given her a numbing agent via the drip and completed the procedure without her knowing."

Whether the "procedure" meant through her abdomen with a long needle or vaginally, I shivered at the thought.

"When we leave here, I'll find us an herbal market and pick up some black cohosh. It's powerful stuff and can induce a miscarriage. Just in case." Patricia, the acupuncturist, pulled her phone out to browse herbal shops within driving distance.

And that's how the next hour played out. Long stretches of silent minutes, followed by an uncomfortable truth spoken from Shawna's trauma, followed by more silence, followed by someone's attempt to fix it. How Celeste kept the two winery workers occupied in the back, I had no clue.

Shawna was my partner sister—not partner as in the same sex relationship kind, but as in we were born at the same time on purpose so we'd have someone to help us raise our children. Huldra didn't marry, for many reasons. Her health, both mental and physical, meant the world to me. And if talking helped her, I'd sit and listen for days on end, no matter how hard it hurt to know that while I was trying to build a Wild Women army, my sister had been enduring her own personal hell. I wished they'd taken me instead.

She quickly shut up, though, when a black van full of succubi parked directly outside the open roll-up door to the warehouse. Eight succubi jumped from the van. Gravel crunched beneath their combat boots. They all wore black and each had some sort of snake tattoo on their bodies. Even if I couldn't see it all under their black tank tops and tube tops, I knew it was there. It was the symbol of their Goddess.

I didn't have to tell them anything. Despite our teaming up only a week ago and having fought a battle together, they didn't act like old friends. The blonde succubus with the thick braid and a snake tattoo weaving from the back of her neck and around her left ear seemed to notice Shawna for the first time and offered a lingering smile. Shawna smiled back.

"Where's the humans?" the blonde succubus asked my partner sister.

Shawna lifted her hand from the cat and pointed to the short hallway beside the makeshift tasting area made up by one black countertop with bottles, crackers, and a stereo resting atop it. "Back there, with Celeste in the office. It's the last door on your left, I think."

"Thanks," the blonde said before ducking into the hallway.

The others quickly went to work loading the bodies into the back of the van. They allowed Marcus to lend a hand and soon the rest of us joined in. Couldn't let the ex-Hunter make us look bad, even if he did weigh enough in sheer muscle to make two of us.

Once the bodies were loaded, a raven-haired succubus brought out a bucket of powder from one of the van's side doors and a short-handled broom. She poured the powder onto every blood spot, waited a few minutes, and then swept the clumpy, red powder into the bucket.

"What should we do about the stain?" I asked. Yeah, the substance of blood was gone, but traces of red remained.

"We don't usually work with blood," the succubus responded as she heaved the filled and now cumbersome bucket to the van.

Succubi may not deal with blood very often, but huldra most certainly had these days. I grabbed the open bottle of merlot we hadn't gotten around to tasting yet and poured a little on each blood stain, letting the liquid splash and splatter the nearby areas.

"Genius," Olivia said as she walked to the counter and grabbed a stemmed glass. She held it out for me and I poured merlot into her glass.

I shook my head with a laugh and went back to work.

The blonde succubus reached her head around the corner to the hallway and eyed me making a wine mess. "Um, so this doesn't fit with the story I gave them to remember." She disappeared back down the hall and returned only minutes later. "Okay, the guys believe that you'd just started your tasting and the cat freaked out, saw a mouse or something, and accidentally knocked over a couple bottles of red wine. You guys helped them clean up the glass."

Within seconds of her hurried explanation, the owner and his adult son moseyed toward us without a care in the world, followed by Celeste, whose smirk filled me with questions. The blonde succubus must have gifted them with happy energy when she wiped their memories and gave them new ones. Did she also give Celeste a little energy hit? The owner didn't seem to notice the blood stains a few of us carried on our clothing. He either assumed the stains were caused by spilled wine, which some were, or the blonde succubus had kept him from noticing somehow.

"I am so sorry we were detained," the older man said. He hurried to the tasting counter and began pouring full glasses of pinot noir as though it were a perfectly normal afternoon. "This is usually a favorite of guests."

Before the last glass sloshed with light red liquid, the succubi group were in their van and barreling down the gravel driveway. The winemakers behaved as if they'd not even seen the extra women. I wondered what would become of the Hunter bodies and made a mental note to ask Marie when I saw her at our upcoming meeting at the harpy complex.

I took a sip of wine and decided this varietal was a favorite of mine too.

Shawna held the cat in one arm and drank wine with the other. "It's delicious!" she exclaimed, happiness filling her eyes in a way I'd yearned to see since she was taken.

"I'm glad you like it." The owner motioned to his son. "Grab some fresh oyster crackers for our friends here."

The son reached into a nearby cabinet and pulled out an unopened bag of little white circular crackers. I admired the tattoos covering both of his arms as he did so. He poured the crackers into the recently emptied—hey, I said I was hungry—wooden bowl and pushed the bowl toward me. Hint taken.

Ready to go eat actual food, I finished my glass and expressed my thanks to the owner and his son for a delicious tasting. "How much do we owe you for the tastings?" I added.

"Nothing. I appreciate you helping me clean up the place. We love that cat, she's a great mouser, but sometimes she lets the hunt take over her mind."

I knew what that felt like.

"Here," the man said as he searched a shelf behind him. "Let me give you a gift, for your troubles." He didn't find what he was looking for, so he told his son to grab the magnum. Whatever that meant.

The younger man returned with a 1.5-liter bottle of pinot noir. He handed it to his father, who handed it to me.

"I appreciate it," I said, feeling more than a little guilty that the winery owner was handing over a hundred-dollar bottle of wine to people who'd stained his cement floors with Hunter blood. I decided to send him a check in the mail for his troubles.

I held the cool bottle and another thought pushed the guilt out with a swiftness. I wondered if Salem had any restaurants with bottle service. Another thought followed that one. I'd just promised Marie a favor, and knowing her, she'd call in a doozy at the worst possible time.

THREE

SALEM, Oregon did, in fact, have a restaurant with bottle service. Marcus and my coterie made quick work of the magnum-sized bottle of pinot noir. While finishing off the last drop of red deliciousness, we decided to head home after dinner. Yeah, we'd forfeit the amount we'd paid for our hotel rooms, but it was a small price to pay to avoid another unprepared Hunter run-in.

Marcus wiped his mouth with the white cloth napkin and placed it on the empty plate in front of him. "We need to figure out how they knew where to find you."

I automatically looked at Shawna to gauge her reaction to the topic. Nothing. She took a bite of mashed potatoes and gave me a closed-mouth smile when she noticed I was staring.

"You'd know better than us. You've spent more time with them," I said.

"I do have a couple ideas," Marcus answered.

I raised an eyebrow.

Marcus looked around the table and then leaned in. "I don't know a whole lot about the other complexes. I did a short trip with my father, before going to the police academy, and toured the complexes of the

United States. But we only spent a day or two at each location, so I can't tell you anything about their tactics or training."

"Then what *can* you tell us?" Celeste asked. She pulled lipstick from her purse and slowly applied the color like an expert—no mirror needed.

"Our women don't work outside the home," Marcus started.

I bristled at the term "our women," and he noticed.

Marcus grabbed my hand under the table and squeezed. His way of giving a tender apology without letting the coterie know. They accepted him for Shawna's sake. Not for my sake. "Sorry. The women of Washington Hunter families don't work outside the home. And the men usually take jobs that suit the brotherhood. But what if the Oregon Hunters don't operate that way?"

"What are you suggesting?" Celeste asked. She pushed her glass of water away from her. After a new coat of lipstick, smudging was not an option.

"What better way to monitor the coming and going of out-of-town visitors than to pour wine at one of the many local wineries? Especially a popular one?"

He had a point. The first winery we visited was huge. It sat atop a hill, overlooking rolling hills covered in vineyards. The open tasting room, complete with a fireplace, brown leather couches, and water stations, led to a terrace where people ate meals from the winery kitchen while taking in the spectacular view. A definite tourist stop. Hell, we'd made sure to stop there. The front desk woman at our hotel suggested it, said they'd just finished a multi-million-dollar remodel.

Renee called the waiter to our table and asked for the check. He took a few plates and left to follow her request.

The dark wood walls and floor-to-ceiling windows gave the restaurant the feel of fancy meets relaxed, if that was even a thing. Upside-down wine bottles filled with twinkle lights replaced chandeliers. Framed cork art decorated the walls.

"You think we were served by a Hunter or a female from a Hunter family?" I asked. "Did any of you talk Wild speak at that place?" I canvassed my coterie.

Wild speak wasn't a scientific term, exactly. More like my own way of explaining the act of discussing topics that aren't appropriate to be mentioned around humans. Stuff like back bark, and finger vines, and oh I don't know, burning down the Hunter complex.

I received a bunch of noes and head shakes. Someone must have said something without realizing.

As though on cue, my phone rang.

I didn't want to look at it.

"You going to get that?" Renee asked.

Bossy pants.

"It's probably Marie," I answered.

"Then answer it. She may have hit a snag with the bodies or something."

I doubted it. Marie had a pretty tight handle on things, which was probably why she was calling.

I pulled my phone from my pocket, and sure enough. I cringed and swiped the screen. The woman was going to hit on me, I just knew it. The more I had to talk to her, the more inevitable it was. She didn't care that I'd made it clear I wasn't interested or available. No wasn't in her vocabulary. "Yes?"

"You aren't very good at hiding your excitement," Marie responded.

"Excitement?"

"No one will know. You can admit it."

"Admit what?" I asked, knowing full well Marie was pulling me in like a fish to a worm-covered hook.

"My voice. It calls to you. I assure you, my moans are better."

Ah, yes. Sexually free succubi leader. That's Marie.

My whole coterie overhead Marie, but only Celeste laughed. I covered the receiver. "Wait 'til she hits on you. Then tell me how funny it is."

"I hope she does," Celeste quipped. Did not see that coming.

I returned to my phone conversation. "What can I do for you?" I waited for her to make a joke, or maybe not a joke, about doing me.

"You owe me a favor," she said, which happened to be the other response I was expecting.

"For earlier today?" I asked.

The waiter handed Renee the check and she promptly gave him the total in cash.

"And for the help we gave your coterie last week," she answered.

"No, no, no. We've already discussed this. All of us came to an agreement." I looked around the restaurant and then lowered my voice. Marcus's theory made too much sense for me to ignore. "They'll be expecting us to hit the Hunter complex in your area next. Probably why they were so quick to catch up to us today. Thought we were here to attack them. The east coast complex won't be expecting us. We go there next. We rest and regroup. Just like we planned."

The waiter gave Renee the receipt and removed an armful of dirty dishes from the table. My coterie pushed their chairs out and stood. I followed them out of the restaurant and toward the minivan we'd rented. Hunters would never look for a group of Wilds in a minivan. Also, that's all Enterprise had on short notice.

"Come, stay at my home tonight," Marie offered. "We can discuss it here."

I waited for Renee to unlock the van. "Absolutely not," I said. "After what happened this afternoon, we're heading home."

I sat on one side of Marcus, on the middle row bench, and Shawna sat on the other side. So, she was feeling better, but still needed Marcus. Good to know. This last week I'd noticed myself taking Shawna's emotional temperature on a nearly constant basis. I hoped she didn't notice. I couldn't begrudge her needing him. He was the first person she'd seen when we came to, her rescuer in her eyes. And if it made her feel more secure to have him close by, I was good with that.

"Put me on speaker," Marie insisted. And I did. Not because she told me to, but because my coterie deserved to have their say.

"Welcome to Portland, Oregon, huldra coterie," Marie announced like she hadn't just demanded a return favor.

"Thank you for sending help," Patricia responded. "We owe you."

I gave her a hard head shake. Not the smartest thing to say to a succubus.

"I was hoping you'd feel that way," Marie said, a smile in her voice. "I realize we had a plan, and I am still willing to continue with it, but in the meantime I need your help here."

"What kind of help?" Olivia asked.

"I'd prefer not to discuss it over the phone," Marie responded. "In person is better."

"You offered your home to us earlier when you spoke to Faline," Patricia said in an even and assertive voice. "Which was very kind of you, but I fear that may be dangerous for you and your sisters. Five Hunters were sent to detain a group of possible Wild Women and they never returned to their complex. I wouldn't want your local authorities to think your kind had anything to do with it."

Marie snorted. I didn't even know Marie was capable of snorting. "Returning to your home would be the bigger mistake, much more so than visiting mine."

Patricia rubbed her temples. I kept my I-told-you-so to myself. "Yes, we've already thought of that. But all our records were destroyed in the fire. And as far as them locating us by our last name, we've already begun the process of getting that legally changed; one of my aunts knows a guy. Also, where would they detain us? Their complex is gone."

A long moment of silence hung in the air. The name thing was a big issue for us. Legally changing it would take weeks. Weeks we didn't have. And the only way to keep this change out of public record was to count on an ex-lover of Renee's, who happened to be in the FBI and able to pull a few witness protection strings, which was tricky in and of itself. But Marie didn't need to be privy to our concern.

Marie let out a long sign. "Your coterie isn't the only non-human visitors in the Portland area."

"Other Wilds?" I asked.

Marie answered on a heavy breath as though her façade had slipped and she was finally leveling with us. "No."

I took the phone off speaker and pushed it against my face. "What do you mean, Marie? What type of creature outside of Wild Women and Hunters exists?"

Marcus closed his eyes and shook his head.

"What?" I asked him. "What aren't you telling me?"

"I can't say more over the phone," Marie answered.

"Fine," I said. "I can't speak for the others, but I'll have them drop me off on their way home." I'd figure out the next step from there.

I ended the phone call, anxious to hear what Marcus had failed to tell me earlier. I leveled a gaze at him. "Fess up."

He rubbed his barely-there five-o-clock shadow and let out a groan. "You remember the front door to the cabin where your sister was kept?"

I thought I saw Shawna shiver. She scooted closer to Marcus.

"Yeah."

"Remember how it had symbols for all the different Wild Women and then some extras you couldn't quite place?" he went on.

"Mmhm."

"Yeah, there's more out there than just the Hunters and the Wild Women."

"Who? What?" I asked.

He shook his head. "Too many to know. We didn't regulate the male species, only the female."

My chin dropped. "There's males out there, like Wilds?"

"Yes and no," he said. "I don't know. We had like a day or two of training on them, at best. And it wasn't something we discussed. We just knew they were out there. We left them alone and they left us alone."

His exposure baffled me. So many questions ran through my mind. "But what about what you told me in that hotel room before I met with the harpies?"

"Excuse me?" Renee cut in. "You two shared a hotel room?"

I held back a groan. "Not what's important right now," I commented, and got back to business. "Marcus, you said the Hunters have always wanted power, and controlling the most powerful kind, Wild Women, gave them that power. So there's others out there like us, who are just as powerful?"

"No, I didn't say that. You're assuming I lied to you." Marcus turned his body to face me and took my hands in his. The cat was out of the bag now anyway. "I know that look. You're building walls against me as I speak."

I ground my teeth and looked away. I hated that he studied me so well, sometimes.

"I didn't lie," he continued. "Wild Women are the most powerful non-human species. Period. They create life. They grow baby Wilds. The males can't do that, males of any species. They need a human woman to carry their offspring, which weakens the bloodline in a way. Some aren't even sure, when they impregnate a human woman, if their offspring will be human or not. Wild Women have the purest bloodline and are most powerful."

His ego-boosting words knocked down any semblance of an emotional wall I'd unconsciously tried to build. "Okay," I said. Because that's all I could think to say. "Okay." I allowed him to lean his chin onto my head, despite my coteries' stares.

I ignored Renee's gasp.

I pressed my hands into his thighs in resolve. "Okay," I said again. "Let's go see what type of male, non-human creatures can rattle the leader of the succubus galere."

FOUR

OUR GOODBYES outside the succubi's apartment complex didn't last long. By the time my aunt pulled the minivan to the curb in front of the white brick apartment building everything that needed to be said had already been said. Some good. Some not so good.

On the drive from the restaurant we'd decided throwing Shawna into a building "infested" (their words, not mine) with succubi, would likely pull her two steps back. Of course, during this decision-making session Olivia blew up my phone and Marcus had a few things to say via text too.

Olivia worried that Shawna's response to the Hunter was a bit over the top—not exactly a step in the right direction as some of the others voiced during the drive. She was definitely pro taking-Shawna-home. But she also didn't want to accompany her.

Shawna had no input to share as we spoke of her. She sat contently with a half-smile on her face, or maybe a smirk—I couldn't tell. I assumed she was still riding high from her earlier attack.

Marcus didn't want to return to Washington without me either. He sat beside me, our arms touching one another, not speaking audibly, but rather through our phones. His texts were fewer and farther between compared to Olivia's. If he had an opinion about Shawna, he didn't say so. One thing he did make very clear, though, was his desire to stay with me. A desire I had no say in and I told him as much through text. Shawna didn't seem to need him too terribly the last couple days, but she was only a week out of her traumatic experience and susceptible to losing ground on her recovery.

"I want to say goodbye in a more private space," he'd whispered before I opened the car door. It was the first thing he'd said since begrudgingly agreeing to stay with Shawna and head back to Washington. He's a grown man and could do what he wanted, but he agreed that his presence had probably given Shawna the safety to fight her inner demons and he wanted to help her to continue her fight to emotional stability.

When the decision for my aunts and Shawna to return home was solidified, Marcus said he'd accompany Oliva, Celeste, and me. To which Shawna's smirk dropped and she wrapped her arm around his bicep and squeezed. Her wide eyes begged him to rethink his decision.

My sister was strong as hell, but everyone needed a helping hand when healing—be it physically, mentally, or emotionally. Ever since Marcus lifted Shawna from the Hunter's bed and carried her to my aunt's car amidst the Hunter/Wild battle, Shawna had chosen him to be that helping hand. Her trauma mindset linked Marcus with safety and protection. And the link was of titanium grade. I couldn't blame her, either. Every minute I spent with Marcus made me want to spend an hour more.

Separating from him and Shawna gave me another reason to be irritated with Marie. I was sure she'd give me ten more reasons within the first few minutes in her home.

Marcus followed me from the car and shut the door behind him, giving us the semblance of privacy. I thought to lead him to the alley beside the apartment complex, but remembered it was a Hunter's hand I held. Marie wouldn't be too pleased knowing a Hunter stood within arm's reach of her home. And we didn't need more drama today. Another reason he should go with Shawna.

I walked with Marcus, hand-in-hand, to an enclosed bus stop nearby. Thankfully it was empty. And due to the rain, if we whispered we were just out of earshot of the car full of huldra. The sun had set hours ago. Orange halos illuminated the ground around the bottom of each streetlight.

Marcus released my hand to wrap his arms around my waist and pull me close. "I don't like leaving you here to face supernatural males without me."

"You said we're stronger than them," I reminded, partly to ease his worries and partly to ease my own.

"You are, but it doesn't mean they can't still do plenty of damage." He shook his head. "Just the thought of one of them touching you..."

Well, then. I'd never seen this jealous side of Marcus. I kind of liked it.

"I can hold my own," I said.

"Yeah." He leaned his chin onto my head. "That doesn't help."

I took in Marcus's scent, wishing I could wrap it around me like a blanket wherever I went. I didn't have the energy to check in with my heart and my head on this whole Marcus thing, so I promised them we'd do it later. For now, when it came to him, I'd just live in the moment.

His breath on my head and the gentle beating of his heart drew me deeper under his spell. "I'm afraid," I found myself admitting. I dropped the briefcase I'd taken with me from the car and let it lean against my calf so I could wrap both arms around Marcus's waist.

He smoothed a hand over my hair. "Of what?"

"Afraid that I won't be able to keep up. There was no training or election. I just fell into this whole saving the Wilds thing. But there is so many to save, and they're all so different. It's like, I'm trying to deal with A while thinking and planning for B and then C, D, and E pop up. The moment I make a mistake, drop a letter, everything will go to shit and it'll all be my fault." My confession slipped from my lips and took with it the weight of worlds.

Marcus leaned back and cupped his hands onto my cheeks. His eyes bore into mine. "How did I get so lucky?"

I couldn't help but laugh. "Is that what we're calling it?"

He didn't crack a smile. "That's what it is."

I expected him to say more, to explain his thoughts, but he showed them instead. With his fingertips at my temples and his palm at my jaw, he leaned in and rocked my world with his lips. My hands crawled up his back and pulled him into me with urgency.

I hadn't expected to leave Marcus again, now that my coterie had accepted his existence, let alone his contribution. I guess I'd always just imagined that he'd be with me every step of the way from here on out, that we'd work together and sleep together, and when this was all over, then we'd decide what came next.

Having to say goodbye so soon, even if for a short time, stabbed at my heart. This concerned me. Huldra don't marry. Our partners in life are our sisters. We are expected to raise our children together, run a coterie together. Men are not part of the lifelong equation. And yet here I stood, at a bus stop, rain falling around us while streetlights lit the night. Kissing. Not wanting to let go. Not wanting to part.

Words stirred in my heart, words that should never be spoken from my lips. I pulled away from the only male whose embrace made me want to melt into him. I treaded on dangerous territory.

"I'll keep you updated, let you know what type of creatures we're dealing with as soon as I find out," I said, trying to fill the space between us with less dangerous words than those filling my mind. It didn't work. I grabbed the leather handle of my briefcase and let it hang from my straight arm against my leg.

Marcus nodded and ran a hand through his thick hair. "Yeah, okay." I didn't need mind-reading skills to know he felt me pushing my emotions away and assumed I was trying to get rid of him as well.

He turned to walk back to the car, but I caught his hand and held it tightly. I refused to move forward and he turned back to see why.

"My issues about us have nothing to do with you," I assured him. Since a day or so after he came to stay with us, we'd been discussing the topic of us off and on—more off than on. I gathered that he wanted a label for "us," and I still wanted to clear my own confusion about what it meant to even be an "us."

Marcus licked his bottom lip and looked up at the streetlight. "I'll try to force myself to believe that."

I refused to let go of his hand, but we walked back to the car in silence.

When we neared the minivan, Celeste and Oliva jumped from the car with their travel bags, ready to get to work. I dropped Marcus's hand. He slipped past my sisters to fold himself into the car and buckled his seat belt. My own suitcase waited for me beside the back tire.

"Don't worry," Abigale said from the back seat. "We'll take care of her. Hold up the fort at home. You girls stay safe down here."

"Will do," I said before hugging Shawna goodbye and shutting the car door. "Hopefully this'll take a day, two at the most, and then we'll all be flying to the east coast together."

The three of us stood in the middle of the street watching our coterie and Marcus drive away. When the red tail lights turned a corner and were no more, we headed toward the apartment building, dragging travel bags and rolling suitcases behind us.

"Why are you carrying that thing like it's handcuffed to you?" Olivia asked, pointing her chin at my brown, soft-leather briefcase. "I noticed you've been storing it beside you in the car and not in the back with the other bags."

I lifted the thing to examine it as I spoke. "I wasn't planning on working during our wine-tasting trip, but I figured it wouldn't hurt to bring a couple skip files just in case I had a few minutes of down time." I added another option I'd considered while packing for our Oregon trip. "Or if I ran across one down here."

"Is it the human-trafficking ring?" Celeste asked, the first to step onto the curb in front of the succubi's apartment building.

I nodded. "There's been a couple developments that've leaked that may help me make sense of who's really on top, if I could get some time to work on it."

Dale had called me the other day, asking why I hadn't contacted him in a while, although he knew I only check-in when I needed something, so I'd figured he was just checking to make sure I was all right. He'd used rumors that he'd heard Brian was offed by a deal gone wrong as his excuse to call. The same Brian I offed at the Westin in Bellevue, though I didn't mention as much to the guy who paid me for picking up bail runners.

After I'd assured him I was fine, Dale had told me my early hunches that the human traffickers were targeting the women in online amateur porn had been proven correct. It had been a theory I'd been working on, and even trying to get in front of, until that day in the cabin at the Washington Hunter's complex when Clarisse mentioned something about Samuel Woodry having ties to the trafficking ring. The victims he'd chosen didn't fit the profile and threw a huge kink in my chain of a theory. Even if his earlier victims were just for him, and his trafficking involvement was a newer development, that didn't explain the young barista he'd been trying to snare when I'd caught him. I'd checked and found nothing online that led me to believe she was a secret porn actress.

"I know I promised the Hunter's daughter, Clarisse, that the rusalki would get their revenge on her for killing their sister, but she's also a part of the human trafficking ring in Seattle. If I could get some alone time with her, I'm sure she'd point me to the key players and help me find the puzzle pieces I'm missing. Taking them down would ruin the ring and save so many lives. I can't let it go. She's a skip I'd make good money on if I took her in, but more than that, I want what she knows."

"Why?" Celeste asked. "Marcus even said that women within Hunter families aren't allowed to know or do much outside of the home. How'd she know the ins and outs of a whole damn human trafficking scheme?"

We made it to the apartment building's door, but didn't move to open it, or knock to get buzzed in.

"Because," I answered my sister. "I think she did their book keeping. She had to have. She took the fall for them, claimed to be the leader of the whole thing, which we know she couldn't have been. But to make those claims and have lawyers and cops believe her, she had to know a lot about their operation, give them enough to bring up charges against her. I've been reviewing her file. The stuff she said during interrogations couldn't have been made up or coached into her. What she shared came from personal experience."

My sisters grew sullen. "What did she share, exactly?" Olivia asked.

I didn't have a chance to answer before a red-haired succubus flung the front apartment door open.

"Come in," she said. "Marie is upstairs in her apartment."

"Thanks," I said slowly, shocked that Marie hadn't sent an entourage to walk me up to her place like last time. Maybe she needed me a little more than I'd thought. But why? She had a whole galere at her disposal.

Succubi stood along the stairwell watching the three huldra ascend the stairs. Some closed their apartment doors, shutting us out. Others peered from their homes. Old ways die hard. You'd think we hadn't just fought beside these Wilds a week prior.

My sisters stood behind me as we entered Marie's apartment. Her door had been left open and she lounged on her red couch. Alone. I'd fully expected to see her in a tiny robe, but she wore silk sleep pants and a tight tank top. The pink fabric looked bright against her tan skin.

"Please shut the door behind you," was her greeting.

I peered around. No succubi flanked her. And she wanted to be left alone in a room, behind a closed door, with three huldra?

"Go ahead," she urged. "We have a lot to discuss."

Celeste shut the door and stood to my right. Olivia stood to my left. I didn't feel any threat, but it was wise to stay alert.

"You're sad," Marie said, eyeing me. "Love can do that to a person."

Her reminder caused my shoulders to slump for half a second before I realized they were giving me away and I righted them again.

My sisters shot me a look. Thank you, Marie, for putting words to emotions I hadn't dared to sift through yet.

"We're not here to talk about me," I reminded. "This visit is all about you."

"Yes, well." Marie leaned forward and poured red wine into four glasses, then gestured for us to join her. Olivia and I sat in separate chairs facing the couch. Celeste eased onto the couch beside Marie with hesitance before grabbing a glass of wine. "I've found myself in a bit of a predicament."

"With supernatural males?" Celeste asked before taking another sip of wine.

Marie turned to her and I saw the exact moment her eyes twinkled at my sister. A smile lifted half her face as she took Celeste in. My sister's dark hair, light skin, and almond eyes made Marie sit up straighter and smooth the wrinkles in her silk pants.

"So, tell us about these males," I interrupted Marie, who was clearly taking in the sight of my sister. I'd come for a reason and wanted to get that out of the way so I could leave.

Marie snapped to attention. "Oh, yes, excuse me. Lost my train of thought." She cleared her throat and took a drink of wine. "Last time you visited we discussed a younger sister of mine. Her disappearance."

I remembered. "I'd visited the mermaids to get her back."

"But she wasn't with them," Marie added.

"And so we figured she could be with the Hunters," I said. At least I'd assumed as much. Not sure if there was an actual discussion about it, not with everything else going on and Marie's secrecy around the whole thing.

"But she's not with the Hunters. She never was." Marie paused and looked up to the ceiling while nibbling her lower lip. Her voice barely cracked as she said, "She ran away."

"With the supernatural male," I added. Thoughts of Marcus and how being with him would mean leaving my coterie filled my mind.

Marie took a deep breath. "Yes. An unfortunate situation I have tried to rectify. But it's gotten past the point of my being able to fix it on my own. She won't come home, feels more thoroughly protected living with the males." Marie glanced at Celeste before directing her words at me. "Our check-in is in three days."

"Shit, Marie." And now I knew why she'd insisted I come. "You don't think this is just a little last minute?"

"I know, I know. But I believed she'd listen to reason." Marie exhaled and her shoulders slumped forward. "I was wrong."

Celeste comforted Marie by rubbing her thigh. "It's not your fault. You can't hold yourself accountable for what your sisters choose to do, who your sisters choose to love."

Was that comment directed at me? I controlled myself, held my mouth shut and didn't call my sister to the carpet. I'd do that in private, not in front of the succubi leader she was making googly eyes at.

Marie rested her hand on Celeste's. Their eyes met. "Thank you."

I stood to pace. Yet another letter was being thrown at me to deal with. "If she doesn't show for check-in, the Hunters will be even more suspicious that you all may have had something to do with the destruction of the Washington Hunter complex." I spoke my thoughts as I worked them out. "If they grow too suspicious, they'll imprison you at their compound." I shook my head at the impossibility of all this. I was a huldra. A young, scared succubus would never listen to me. That is, if I could even get past the big, bad, protective males to get to her. "And if they imprison you, that'll jeopardize our whole plan. You won't be able to fly out to help us take down the east coast complex, and the other Wilds won't have enough time to be here and ready with a plan in three days to take down the Oregon Hunter complex. We need every Wild if we want to pull this off. All of this."

Yeah, we were screwed.

I paused my pacing to stare at an orange and red tapestry almost covering a whole wall. I had no idea what the geometric design represented, but I assumed it had something to do with energy. Crystals tied to a string hung from each top corner of the tapestry.

If the succubi were detained, trying to take down another Hunter complex would be too risky. That meant the other already-imprisoned Wilds would have to suffer even longer. Including my mother. They'd already waited for our help long enough. And hadn't the Wilds as a whole already waited long enough for the freedom to be wild?

"You have no fear of attending check-in?" Olivia asked. "Despite using your abilities last week during our Washington complex battle?"

Marie shook her head. "We've figured out a way to use just enough of our energy-manipulating abilities to not give us away at check-ins, but that'll also prove effective when combined as a group. If we each use a little, at the same time and in the same way, it appears as though we're using a lot."

"Smart. Makes sense," Oliva stated.

This succubus sister of Marie was really irritating me. First, she pulled me away from my much-needed time with Shawna and Marcus, and now she threatened the safety and happiness of every United States Wild. "All right. Well, where can I go to find her?" I wanted to meet this young succubus causing me all this trouble.

"You're skipping the male part of this equation," Olivia reminded me.

Of course. Why did there always have to be a male in every difficult equation?

"I've set a meeting with them for tomorrow morning," Marie said. "It's better that way—to wait. Your energy is all over the place. They'll see you as unstable and won't trust you enough to give you access to my sister. They may even immobilize you, somewhat like my sisters did the first time you visited us. If you're still feeling this way in the morning, I am more than happy to work on you before we leave."

Only succubi saw and manipulated energy. And succubi were female. Not male.

A headache formed in my right temple and grew with each breath. "What type of male creature has succubus abilities?" I asked, turning away from the tapestry and focusing on the three Wilds.

Marie slowly drank her wine and carefully set the glass onto the coffee table, leaving her hands free. She didn't need her hands to manipulate energy, but they seemed to help. I suddenly became super-aware of everything I felt, in an effort to know if Marie was shifting any of those emotions.

"Some would call them the cousins to succubi," she answered. "Some would call them our brothers."

I suppressed a groan. "And what do *you* call them, Marie?"

"Before they showed up in Portland, I hadn't called them anything. The humans, though, they call them incubi. Incubus. Our male counterparts."

Well, shit. Males with all the power of a succubus and twice the size. I'm such a lucky lady. Now I wished Marie *had* softened the blow with a little energy manipulation.

FIVE

When Marie opened the door to a first-floor apartment, four succubi were finishing up cleaning the place. After quick hellos, the four left with a broom, rags, buckets, and a mop in tow. Marie didn't have to say the words for me to know that her giving us the bottom floor apartment was her way of showing us we were free to come and go. I appreciated the sentiment.

"There are two bedrooms," she said as she stood in the doorway and the three of us moved around the small living room-kitchen combo, taking in our surroundings. "One has two twin-sized beds and the other has a double."

I leaned on the white-tiled kitchen counter. "That won't work. We need to sleep in the same room." I trusted Marie...to an extent. But I didn't trust her with my life. Or more importantly, the lives of my sisters. Sleeping apart from one another was unsafe.

"It'll be fine," Celeste said, brushing off my concern. "I'll take the double bed so that my sisters can share a room. Thank you, Marie, for giving us our own space."

Marie's smile warmed until her eyes smiled too. She gave Celeste a slow nod. "It's that one." She pointed to a closed door across from the entrance to the apartment.

Celeste peeked into the room.

I assumed Olivia's and my room was the next door over, but I was wrong. Still, I toured the little bathroom with its single sink and claw foot tub. The next door over belong to us, our temporary bedroom. Dark tapestries made up the bed coverings and curtains.

"There's microwavable meals in the fridge. You know where to find me if you need anything. I'll be around tomorrow morning at seven to pick you up." Marie left the apartment and shut the door behind her.

After a more snoop-centered tour of the place to check for cameras and anything of the sort, my sisters and I convened on the dark green couch beneath a wall painting of Lilith. She stood tall and proud, her white eyes glowing against dark skin. Snakes wound around her naked forearms and calves like jewelry.

I folded my legs beneath me and rested my back against the couch's arm. "What do you guys think?"

"I want to help them," Celeste said. She pulled her knees to her chin and faced me. Olivia sat on the middle cushion, between us.

"Of course you do," I uttered under my breath.

"What's that supposed to mean?" she asked.

"Did you feel your emotions shift at all while we were up at her place?" I asked. "Like, one minute you felt one thing and without a reason that feeling went away and was replaced by another?"

"No, Faline, Marie did not manipulate my emotions. She's a good person."

"How do you know what kind of person she is?" I asked, offended that my sister took offense to my protectiveness. "You've barely talked to her."

"Marie and I trained together at our house," Celeste informed me with a raised voice. "We ate meals together. I've taken more time to get to know the succubi leader than you've taken to get to know any of the other Wilds."

Olivia raised her hands between us. "You two are getting too loud. They'll hear us."

I spouted off, "Well, according to Celeste, it shouldn't matter if another Wild group hears us, right?"

"We're all on the same side," Celeste reminded.

"We. Don't. Know. Them," I stated through a clenched jaw.

"Because of the Hunters. We don't know them because of the Hunters, Faline," Celeste countered. "Not because the other Wild Women are bad or unsafe to be around. The Hunters fed us lies to keep us apart, to divide and weaken."

"Yeah, the Hunters lied to them too, about us. What do they still believe? We don't know. And until we do, they aren't safe. They don't have our best in mind. They have their own in mind." I let that little fact sit with Celeste for a moment.

"And whose best does your Hunter have in mind?" Celeste scoffed. "You're lecturing me on connecting to a succubus when you're sleeping with a fucking Hunter."

Olivia shot Celeste a shut-up glare.

"No, she needs to hear it," Celeste insisted. "Marcus is the huge male elephant in the room, even when he's miles away. I get why Shawna insists on having him around, in a weird and twisted way. But you? Why do you insist on having him around, Faline? Does he make you feel more powerful or something? Because I don't get it. None of us get it."

My sister's words knocked the wind from my pipes and I stuttered to give her an answer. Except, I had none to give. Her concerns echoed my own private thoughts. Why Marcus? Was it some seduce-the-oppressor crap I dealt with mentally to make me feel more in control than I actually was? No. "I liked him before I knew he was a Hunter," I heard myself saying.

I'd forgotten. Our jail-house chats and argument of superheroes and heroines over dinner seemed like lifetimes ago. When I thought he was human and he assumed the same of me. When life was so much simpler.

When life was so much more laid out for us, chosen for us by the Hunters.

With self-empowerment came layers of personal truths, some messier than others—all foreign and in need of close examination. That's the hard part. Examining my own heart.

"He has proven his loyalty." I closed my eyes before speaking the words begging to come out. I couldn't look my sisters in the eyes when my true feelings saw the light of day. I couldn't stand to see their disappointment in me. "I have feelings for him. Deep feelings."

Olivia sighed and touched my knee. I opened my eyes to see Celeste's filling with tears. She bit her lip and shook her head. She had to have known. Wasn't it obvious? But maybe the confirmation was too much.

"But he's a Hunter," Olivia said gently.

"You guys keep saying that," I said. "Don't you think I already know? Don't you think I hate it a thousand times more than you do? But he betrayed his own kind for our cause. That counts for a lot."

"It's just, his past is his past. He can't help who he was born to," Olivia said. "But, Faline, we know close to nothing about Hunters, other than they are supernatural. What if something in him is triggered, something he doesn't even know about? And he can't control his strength, his urge to dominate you, to control us, physically, mentally, and however else they do it? What if he gives us up to the Hunters by following an order he can't deny?"

I thought of the night I'd blacked out and killed a man. How I'd thought my huldra had taken over without my consent because I was born that way, evil to my core. But I had been wrong. My huldra protected me, strengthened me, because I worked with her and not against her. I shook my head. "I have to believe they aren't born with the uncontrollable urge to hurt and lord over us. I have to believe it was ingrained in them, like fearing our abilities was ingrained in us."

"Would you risk the safety of your coterie for that belief?" Celeste asked.

I swallowed the burning lump in my throat. Of course I wouldn't risk their safety.

"I support you. I love you," Celeste said in a softer tone. "I just worry you haven't thought this through all the way. I don't want to see you get hurt. I don't want to see any of us get hurt."

Neither did I.

I leveled with my sisters. "You're right, I haven't thought about this in detail. I don't want to, if I'm being honest. I don't have the headspace for it right now. I'm thinking of the survival of our kind. I'm thinking of the future for the next generation of Wilds and the one after that. I want our daughters to grow up loving the skin they're in rather than suppressing their strength to gain acceptance from their oppressors—literally having their skin marred with a number as though they're nothing more than branded cattle. I want them to be whatever profession they desire and not have to cower down to some asshole Hunter telling them that their thoughts don't matter, that their life and happiness is not equally important." My voice cracked. "I'm thinking about things like having my mother back in my home someday, in the room next door to me, safe and proud of what her coterie accomplished."

"We realize you've done a lot for us. And we appreciate it," Olivia said.

"Really?" I asked. "Because it doesn't feel like it." It had been a while, since before the night I'd blacked out, that I'd had an honest and open conversation with anyone other than Marcus. And it felt cathartic to get it all out and on the table. "I don't like the role I've been put into. I don't want it. But I want what's best for my coterie, for all Wilds, so I've accepted it. But every day I struggle with uncovering the real me, who I would have been without the Hunters governing our lives, which parts of me are products of their brainwashing and which are my own."

"We're all going through that," Olivia said.

"So are the succubi," Celeste added. "Marie is trying to lead a galere of succubi who can see and feel the emotions of others, with a confidence she's not sure she has. Consider how challenging that is."

"But is she trying to lead a war?" I started to say, but then realized the words came from a place of hurt. "I shouldn't compare struggles."

My sisters nodded. Celeste and I scooted closer to Olivia until the three of us met in the middle of the couch. We held hands like little girls, like best friends.

"I know this is hard on all of us," I whispered.

"It is," Olivia said as she squeezed our hands. "Thankfully, we're not going through it alone."

"But if we don't talk about it, compare notes and support one another, it's as if we are going through it alone," Celeste added. "So can we be more open, talk through it with each other without fear of stepping on toes and hurting feelings?"

"I'd like that," I said.

"Me too," Olivia agreed.

Olivia pulled us in for a group hug before standing and stretching her legs. "In one day we tasted wine, beat up a group of Hunters, and found out incubi actually exist. The sun is down and I'm ready for this shitty day to be over."

Celeste gave me one last squeeze before hopping from the couch and heading to her bedroom for the night. She shut the door behind her.

Olivia made her way to our room and stopped at the door. "You coming?"

"In a minute," I answered.

Olivia shut the bedroom door behind her, leaving me alone, standing in front of an altar to Lilith. I rubbed the Freyja pendant hanging from my necklace as I watched the candle's firelight dance. The succubi who'd opened their home to us prayed to a Goddess in the same way we did. Burnt incense lay in the hollow part of an upturned turtle shell. A small snake skin lay atop a dark velvet runner across the back edge of the altar.

Like the snake, as we grow, we shed our old ways of thinking and beliefs, our old skin, to don new selves. Lilith has been demonized by many for having the attributes of a snake. But according to my mother's whispers, before the Hunters came to be, people revered the snake for her ability to grow and change despite the discomfort it entailed. "They honored the snake," she'd say during bedtime stories. "For the snake conquered death to live anew each time it lost its skin. Much like we women bleed monthly and do not die. This is why the Hunters demonized Lilith. Because Lilith could do what they could not."

I kept the candle burning and let my mother's words sink in as I made my way to bed. Had I demonized the succubi because they had abilities that I didn't? Was I also guilty of fearing the unknown?

And if my answer was yes, where did that leave me in regards to the horde of who-knows-how-many incubi who currently lived within the same city I slept tonight?

SIX

I SHOT from my temporary twin bed with a start and canvassed the room. Olivia rolled in bed to face me. "What is it?" she asked.

The sun hadn't risen yet and a nearby streetlight sprinkled light through the window into our room.

"I heard something, movement, outside our door," I answered.

Olivia flung the sheet out of her way and stood beside me, at the ready to burst through the door. She stood in a t-shirt and panties, not bothering to throw on her shorts she'd draped across the foot of her bed. I held three fingers up, then two, then one, and swung open our bedroom door.

I knew it was unwise to sleep in separate bedrooms, especially while staying in an apartment building full of succubi. A huldra can never be too careful.

The hall was empty. We hadn't even crept out into it when we heard another noise from our sister's room. Celeste was in trouble. Shivers ran up my spine. I couldn't lose another sister, not even for a moment. My coterie had suffered too much already; our hearts couldn't handle another blow. I motioned my head toward Celeste's door and Olivia nodded. At once we both ran for her room. Olivia reached the door knob first and gave it a turn before I could smash through the wooden thing that kept us from our sister. I stumbled forward into Celeste's room, set on rescuing her from a galere of succubi, or at least helping her to fight them off.

But only one succubus lay in Celeste's bed, her naked body beneath my sister's. Candle light flickered across their skin; shadows of their intertwined bodies danced across the wall farthest from me. Celeste paused from running her lips along the tattoo of three snakes interwoven to look like a belt under Marie's breasts, around her ribcage, with Lilith in the middle.

"Can I help you two?" Celeste asked, still straddling Marie.

Marie only smiled at us, her fingers still woven through Celeste's dark hair.

Awkward silence hung between Olivia and me until she excused herself and padded back to bed as though we'd just interrupted Celeste reading a book or something. And normally I would too, except the story my sister read was printed along the skin of a succubus with every ability to manipulate her emotions enough to invite the huldra to bed without realizing fully what she was doing.

"Your concerns do not belong here," Marie said with a raspy voice. "Our affections for one another are organic." She kissed the top of my sister's head and leaned back onto the pillow.

Celeste caught my gaze for all of a second before scooting up to plant her lips on Marie's. "You can shut the door behind you," she offered between passionate kisses.

I backed out of the room, a little jealous and a little in shock. I hadn't pictured Celeste and Marie together, with Celeste more of the controlling Type-A personality and Marie a leader who didn't like to be questioned. But, since tapping into her huldra abilities, Celeste's characteristics seemed to have found their stride, her nervous need to control rested into a comfortable sense of knowing what she wanted and sticking to that. Apparently, she wanted Marie, which brought me to my feelings of jealousy. While falling for another Wild hadn't been done before, that I knew of, it'd be much more accepted than falling for a Hunter.

I shut the door behind me like I was told.

By the time I'd gotten a drink of water and crawled back into bed,

Olivia was sleeping peacefully on the other side of the room. I thought to text Marcus, ask him how the drive back had been, ask him if he was still angry at me for pulling away when he left, but I couldn't bring myself to open that can of worms, not when a wriggling snake lady lay two doors over from me, under my sister. Not when I currently attended my own pity party of one, wishing I didn't always have to take the hardest road possible to get to my goals.

Exhaustion gnawed at me, made my mind weak. No, talking to Marcus would be better left for the morning. At least I hoped so because whether or not I was ready, I had to have a phone conversation with him before seven o'clock, bright and early, before my visit to the incubi.

SEVEN

SEVEN A.M. CAME TOO EARLY. Or maybe too late. The fogginess clouding my head made it too hard to know. I'd tossed and turned as though worry concerning the incubi resided on one side of my body and fear for the future of Marcus and I lived on the other. And then there was the guilt. The United States Wild Women were prepared to follow me into battle. Hell, they already had once and eagerly waited to do it again. My mind should be on working out the newest kinks in my plan to take down the east coast Hunter complexes—the runaway succubi kinks. Should be. Yet I lay here concerned what my sister's newest romance said about my own.

As I shuffled from the bedroom and down the short hall to the small kitchen beside the dining table, I was thankful succubi couldn't read minds. My two sisters and Marie sat at the table, enjoying coffee and making small talk. The talk of friends and lovers, not new allies. Why did that bother me so much?

I chalked it up to lack of sleep as I poured my own cup from the half-full coffee pot and mixed it with a splash of creamer. I took the fourth and last empty chair at the table and drank a few swigs of the java before nodding to my sisters.

"Allow me to give you a tad of energy before we go," Marie offered.

She wore that red silk robe I'd seen her in the first time I'd met her. The time she'd propositioned to have a threesome with me and the strange man on her couch and then later propositioned just me.

Maybe that was it. Maybe I didn't like my sisters being so friendly with Marie because I knew more about her than they did; I'd seen her more manipulative side. I got to be at the receiving end of her ability to manipulate energy when she had her sisters pin me in place, when she thought me a threat. My sisters only met her once Marie had agreed to join our cause. I met her before, when we were still on enemy terms.

"No, thank you," I said before taking another sip.

"Come on, Faline, let her help," Celeste urged.

I shot my sister a look from above the rim of the mug. I didn't need Marie messing with my energy. To be honest, at this point, the only other Wilds I trusted, besides my coterie, was the rusalki, and I hadn't heard from them since we attacked the Washington Hunter complex. They lived completely off the grid—no cell phones or even email addresses. Although, a couple of times, I could have sworn I'd seen them out of the corner of my eye in my room at night. But no one was ever there. To me, the rusalki seemed like ancient women in the bodies of young women. There was a reverence to them I respected.

The mermaids kept secrets. The harpies were jumpy and usually assumed the worst. And the succubi were...what were the succubi? I couldn't place my thoughts.

"Have you talked to Marcus yet?" Olivia changed the subject. "About the incubi?"

I regarded my sister with a smile. A little piece of me felt like all this Wild Women reunion stuff was pushing our coterie apart, not pulling us together. But then again, maybe the presence of Marcus in my tree home most nights was doing the job just fine.

"No," I answered. "Not yet. I was waiting 'til he got up and 'til I had a cup or two of coffee."

Marie scoffed. "She's afraid."

I shot her a glare. "Not today, Marie. I'm not in the mood."

"No," she answered. "You're in fear. A great amount of fear. And

I'm sorry, but your energy is too draining for me to just sit here and ignore."

"Well, Marie." I set my mug down. "If you're so keen on hashing things out, I wasn't exactly thrilled to walk in on you screwing my sister when we're supposed to be here on business." I regretted the words the moment my sister's face twisted from hurt to disbelief.

Celeste gasped. "I cannot believe—"

Marie placed her hand on my sister's to gently quiet her, and then she spoke to me. "Technically, I wasn't screwing your sister." She smiled and it even reached her eyes. "And who said business and pleasure do not mix well?"

I replayed the old saying about just that in my mind, but based on Celeste's pissed-off expression, I knew not to actually verbalize it. I shook my head.

"But seriously," Marie said. Her smiled dropped and she let go of my sister's hand. She turned her body to face me fully. "I will not allow you to go into the incubi lair with your current energy. In fact, I refuse to take you; I will not be responsible for your safety, and I do not wish to start another war with another group of males once they feel your fear and assume it's caused by them. They would enjoy the power too much."

She and I just stared at one another.

"For Freyja's sake, Faline!" Celeste stood and walked over behind me. She placed her hands on my shoulders where I sat. "Go ahead, Marie. We need to leave soon; being late is not a great first impression to a whole species we're trying to keep peace with."

I fought the urge to shove her off and jump up. She was right. The succubi were our allies and this interaction with these incubi had to go smoothly. The faster we were in, the faster we could convince Marie's sister to leave with us and show up to the next Hunter check-in as if the whole succubi galere were innocent Wild Women with no clue as to what the evil huldra did to their own Washington Hunters.

Still, Marie waited for my permission. And I couldn't exactly level with Celeste that the Wild she held a proverbial candle for had instructed that her sisters energetically detain me against my will. The desperate feeling of helplessness wasn't one I wanted to risk reliving.

"Fine," I said. "Go ahead and zap me."

Marie didn't bother to correct me. She scooted forward in her chair until her knees almost touched my own. Her hands slowly descended onto my thighs. She closed her eyes. I felt the urge to do the same as I exhaled. Warm tingles started in my thighs and spread throughout my body. My shoulders rolled back and down. My jaw unclenched. My arms fell away from my side.

I wasn't sure why Marie chose to use touch this time in performing her energy work, but I didn't care. I hadn't noticed how tightly wound I'd been until I was unwound. I let out another exhale as Marie pulled away.

"You have a lot to think about, to weigh you down. Don't let your sister's and my relationship be another weight," she said softly.

My eyes fluttered open.

She answered my gaze. "Her energy attracts me like none other in a way I am still trying to explore. But know that what you've seen from me in the past was a desire for pleasure. I realize I joked earlier about business and pleasure, but with your sister, it is neither. It's so much more." Marie stood and made her way toward the door of the apartment. "I'll call and let them know we're on our way. Meet me out front in ten minutes. And Faline?"

I looked at her in a bit of a daze, still relishing in the energy bath she'd doused me in.

"Stop putting off calling Marcus. We may not agree with his assistance, but when it comes to getting my sister back, I'd like all the information I can ascertain."

Marie closed the door behind her. Celeste sat back down and started up an unrelated conversation with Olivia. I stood with a groan and made my way to my temporary room to make a phone call that for some reason caused the pit in my stomach to drop out once again.

EIGHT

MARCUS PICKED up on the first ring. "Faline?" he asked right away.

I nodded and realized he couldn't see me. I blamed exhaustion. "Yes."

His voice changed, laced with concern. "Everything okay?"

I answered on auto-pilot, "Yeah."

Before I had the chance to correct myself, he filled the silence. "Good, because we have a new development over here."

"Oh yeah?"

"Another Washington Hunter approached me at my apartment when I stopped by to pick up my mail and grab a few things," he said. "He was waiting outside my door."

"Is he going to tell the others that you're fine and well? Did he tell you that you have to go back?" I asked, a little more awake than moments earlier.

"No, that's the thing," Marcus explained. "He left the brotherhood and needed a place to crash, to get away from everything and think. Said he came to me because I've left before."

"Why did he leave?" I asked because inquiring minds and all.

"He said he's tired of pretending he's not gay."

"What?" I said, shocked. "What's wrong with being gay?"

"Nothing in my book," he said. "Everything in the Hunter's book. But hey, I told him I was going out of town for a much-needed vacation and that he could stay at my place. I did a quick sweep before I left, made sure he couldn't find anything incriminating."

"Why? Is he snoopy or something?" I asked, rubbing my eyes.

"He could be a spy," Marcus answered mater-of-factly.

Damn, this exhaustion crippled my bounty-hunter brain.

He paused on the other line. "You don't sound like you're firing on all cylinders."

"I need some information," I blurted.

"You sure you're okay?" he asked a second time.

I let out a sigh and mulled over the best way to explain my thoughts. "Yes and no."

"You know how the missing succubus is with males of the un-human persuasion." He kept quiet, so I continued. "Males that I have no experience with and was hoping maybe you would know a thing or two about them. Because I have to leave in a couple minutes to meet them in what Marie is calling their lair, whatever that means. She's being secretive about them."

"Okay," Marcus responded. "You going to tell me what kind of beings we're talking about?"

I just spat out the word. "Incubus."

I pictured Marcus shaking his head and rubbing his chin stubble as he exhaled and said, "Shit."

"Is that a good 'shit' or a bad 'shit'?" I asked.

"It's a don't-go-within-a-mile-of-these-guys shit," he said.

"Well, that's not an option." I stopped pacing and stood in front of the dresser, examining myself in the mirror on top, leaning against the wall. I ran my fingers through my red hair to straighten the wavy fly-aways. "If every succubus doesn't show up for check-in in two days, the Oregon Hunters will have enough reason to think they were involved in the Washington Hunter complex being destroyed and they could detain them. They're probably on edge as it is. They don't need something like a missing succubus to push them over."

"My dad called while we were at one of the wineries. I returned his call when I got back to Washington and stopped by my apartment to grab a few things and listen to my voice mail," Marcus said.

He carried a throw-away cell phone for him and me to get ahold of each other, but he gave the number to nobody else. He didn't want his phone tracked to us Wilds. His excuse to the others was that his phone must have burned when the complex burned down, seeing as they always kept their personal phones in a locked box while on Hunter duty. In reality he took the battery out and canceled his service. "He said it was to check up on me; he knew I'd been hurt in the battle with the Wild Women at the complex and stopped by my place, but I hadn't been home. He said he was worried." Marcus scoffed. "I call bullshit."

I paused from my self-grooming. "What do you think he wanted?"

"To sniff around."

"Do you think he suspects anything?" I asked.

"He's a Hunter official; he suspects everyone and everything." Marcus paused. "But no, he's not on to me. I asked if I needed to report to him or anyone else and he said they were still sorting things out. That they were calling in what's left of the Hunters, but not the new recruits, which, since I'd left and then re-joined, they see me as new. They'll call in the new recruits last."

I sighed in relief. What little plan we'd created before storming into the Washington Hunter complex, Wild Women fighting, did not include the aftermath for Marcus—if he'd stay a member or not and what that'd look like either way. So far, he thought it best to stay, to keep his ear to the ground, so to speak. He didn't think the Hunters knew where us huldra resided, but it wouldn't be too hard to find out, even with most of their files burned in the fire. He figured if there was an effort to storm our homes, they'd call him up to do the storming. But in my mind, and his heart, he was an ex-Hunter. I just wished my coterie could see it that way.

So far though, he'd been given a leave of absence from his police job for the time being—Hunters in high places and all. I suspected the higher-ups wanted to make sure the surviving Washington Hunters who were present during the attack didn't turn tail and run. They'd eventually need all the man-power they could get with so few remaining, so treating them like war heroes made sense. We just weren't sure how long that'd last.

"You can't go meet with the incubi, Faline," Marcus said, circling back to our discussion. "What if there's Hunters watching them?"

"Is that why you're so against it?" I asked. "We'll be careful. I won't be seen." I didn't know where we were going exactly, not enough to make such a promise, but I trusted Marie in her skills to go unnoticed. The first day I'd met her, before I'd even entered the succubi apartment complex, Marie was there without me knowing. Even spoke to me and I couldn't find her.

"They're males with the ability to entice women and manipulate energy to their will," Marcus said. "Manipulate you to their will. And they don't have the history of allegiance you Wild Women have. There's nothing to keep them from trapping you like they've trapped Marie's sister."

I almost laughed. "They won't trap me. And when I'd first met Marie, she had no reason to treat me fairly either." I peered at the door and wondered if Celeste was listening from the dining table. "And she didn't...treat me fairly. She had her sisters hold me in place against my will, use my energy against me. But I made it fine through that." I didn't mention I'd already gone over this scenario in my mind, that I'd already considered the risk of being taken out of the game much too early. The other Wilds were counting on me to save their sisters and mothers. And not because I was special or anything. But because so far, the only Wilds who were on the Hunter's radars and able to miss check-ins were the huldras. And of the huldras, I was the only bounty hunter, well-versed in tracking folks, thinking battle strategy, and kicking ass.

But none of us would be able to take down another Hunter complex without the succubi galere. And none of them would be able to help us if they were all detained because one of their sisters missed the check-in. "I'll be fine," I assured him.

"Damn it," Marcus ground the words through clenched teeth. "Why don't you trust me? Just this once, can you listen and trust me?"

"Whoa, wait a minute," I countered. "Do you realize you're telling me that by me not doing what you want, I'm not trusting you?" Before he could answer I answered for him. "Of course I trust you. I wouldn't share a bed with you night after night if I didn't trust you. I wouldn't let you anywhere near my sisters if I didn't trust you. But I trust me too, Marcus. And seeing that at the end of the day *I* am all I'm left with, my own gut instincts on this far outweigh your advice, trust or not."

"You're all you're left with? What's what supposed to mean?" he asked the moment I took a breath.

I stared at the ceiling for a moment before leveling a gaze at myself back in the mirror. I shouldn't have said that. It was just, after the whole battle with the Hunters, watching my Wild sisters fall in combat, almost losing Shawna, death had been on my mind. If they all died in the next battle, I was all I had left. I could only protect those I love so much. They were dark thoughts, but they were my thoughts. I couldn't tell him that, though. I didn't need him worrying any more than he already was. I'd just told him I'd be fine. He couldn't know how unsure I was of that.

"It means..." I couldn't come up with an answer for the life of me. "I don't know what it means."

"Well, it's a pretty strong statement to have no basis," Marcus retorted.

I said the first answer that popped into my mind. "It means I need to be responsible for my own wellbeing. It's not like we're married or in a committed relationship or anything." Clearly the wrong thing to say.

Marcus's voice deepened, but somehow grew louder at the same time. "You don't see our relationship as a committed one?" I pictured his eyes lit with anger.

That hadn't at all been what I'd meant. But I only made it worse by trying to explain myself. "Huldras don't do committed relationships," I stammered out, trying to get my brain to catch up with my mouth. I was trying to lay out the facts of my kind and that relationships and sharing didn't come natural to me. It'd take lots of work and practice. But damn if my lips refused to express this truth.

"Wow," he said sarcastically. "Well, I guess I've got a lot to think about then. What with me putting my life on the line to act as an undercover agent for a woman who's not in a committed relationship with me and never plans on changing that."

"Hold on." Now I was pissed. "Are you saying you're only doing this because of me? Because that's not at all what you told me that night at the hotel in North Carolina and the next morning, when we discussed aligning. You said it was because you knew what the Hunters were doing was wrong. You said you weren't doing it for me." I remembered that conversation vividly.

"I've got to go," was all he said before the line went dead.

"Damn it!" I stopped myself mid-swing before plowing my fist into the dresser top.

"Everything all right?" Olivia asked, her voice muffled through the door.

No, everything was not all right. Not that it mattered. I pulled my long hair into a pony tail at the back of my head and wiped bits of mascara, smudged from sleeping, from under my eyes. "Yup."

I swung the bedroom door open to see my two sisters ready and waiting. "Let's go," I said, walking from the apartment to meet Marie out front.

NINE

I'D SEEN shows about the Portland Shanghai Tunnels, the underground that once operated on vice with no room for virtue. It is said that from the late 1800s to the early 1900s men were kidnapped from bars in the area and taken to the underground where they'd be sold off to ship captains to work as crew with no pay. Of course, prostitution ran rampant in the tunnels as well. Visiting the Forbidden City of the Wests underground had always interested me, but seeing as leaving the state would require more than a little difficulty concerning the Hunters, and Portland was my prior enemies' territory, I'd figured watching it on TV was as close as I'd get.

Those worries and prior restraints seemed like a lifetime ago.

Now I stood in the damp tunnel, the scent of mildew and rot all around me, with the addition of rats and mice scurrying about and cobwebs covering the top corners like draped curtains. Only, we didn't enter the tunnels like I'd seen in the shows, or like basically any human tourists had. At least, I assumed as much. With a black fabric bag over my head it was hard to tell, exactly.

A human man had met Olivia, Celeste, Marie, and me in an alley, carrying the head covers. A transient man slept under a wet cardboard box and when our guide told the man to leave in a particularly gruff manner, I had pulled a Subway gift card from my back pocket to give to the homeless man for his troubles. The man with the head covers gave me a strange look, but I didn't care. Homeless or not, people were people and they deserved to be treated with decency. The fact that his man clearly didn't agree ticked me off right off the bat.

We'd taken the black bags freely, as the man promised it was for our own protection. If we wore them, we would be guided back out of the incubi's lair once our business was done, no questions asked. I opted to do it. No fabric bag could stop my vines from growing and choking a guy out if he made a wrong move against my sisters or me. Still, as I'd placed the bag over my head, Marcus's words of caution rang through my mind.

And here I stood, after moving through unknown doors that creaked open and shut, after a couple sets of stairs, numbering forty-seven steps. Or had it been fifty? Following the man, I'd kept track of his flashlight beam through the fabric. The human told us to stop and left us alone in the tunnel, bags still over our heads. Through the fabric I saw nothing; the area was pitch black, without so much a candle flame to light the way.

"Should we take off the bags?" Celeste whispered when the only sounds left were created by trickling water and rodents.

"No," Marie said under her breath. "They need a show of submission from us, I think."

I bucked at that idea, but she was right. Never show your cards, and as a female in some cultures, that also meant never show your strength and independence—at least not until the time is right. It was our wild card, our tactical advantage, to be underestimated. Not that my heart didn't still argue with her plan.

"Now will you give us more information on these guys?" I asked the succubi leader, who up until this point had been too secretive for my comfort.

"They are called our brothers, but they are not," she started. "They are like distant cousins sired by a cheating father."

"Care to explain?" I asked, not knowing how much time I had to collect intel before the incubi arrived and wishing she'd stop talking in riddles.

Marie spoke after a few moments. "Incubi are not born, they're created."

Call me a purist, but I didn't like the idea of anyone not born into their current species. Being born into a species is natural, organic. Being changed leaves too much open for question. Are they able to manage their new abilities? Do they misuse them? Do they hate their new self and want to take down any other creature they come across? And that's just the tip of the iceberg. A few months ago I wouldn't have even known such beings existed, and now I stood in their hidden, underground lair with a bag over my head, hoping they either knew how to control their incubus abilities or hadn't yet learned how to use them in the first place.

"Where do they come from?" I asked, hoping to get an idea of their species' cultural background.

"The product of a night of passion between a succubus and a vampire," Marie answered. "At least, that's how the first incubus' maker came to be. Succubi only give birth to females, which leads me to believe the original maker, or sire, was female. The vampires were nearly extinct and the union was their last-ditch effort to preserve their kind. They nearly worshipped my kind for our generosity. Up until the last vampire walked the earth."

Unholy shit.

"And you didn't think to give me a warning of this in advance?" I asked, forcing myself to not rip off the head covering and run my ass out of there. I'd thought vampires were nothing more than legend, or maybe a species the Hunters had killed off in their early days.

"I didn't want to chance you not joining me. This is what's best for all Wild Women." She paused. "And control your fear. They'll feel it before getting within arm's length. And they may use it to their advantage."

"Do they bite?" Celeste asked.

Celeste sighed and I figured Marie was calming my sister with her touch. "They do not. They do not have fangs that I am aware of. They received their energy abilities from the succubus and the ability to change humans into their own kind from the vampire. From what I've heard, when they lie with human women, the women are unable to conceive their shared offspring. So all incubi have been changed, not born that way."

I thought to ask her more about their inability to procreate, but decided it wasn't important. I wasn't planning on taking an incubus to bed. The thought of Marie's sister staying here, with these incubi, popped into my head, but I was sure Marie had already contemplated the possible outcome of a succubus sleeping with an incubus. She didn't need a reminder of the possible pairing and what could come of it. But her insistence that we get her sister now made more sense than ever, considering what I'd just learned.

Heavy footsteps with a wide gait entered my hearing and we silenced. What appeared to be a lantern came into my line of sight, its orange flame dancing as the man walked. The bark at the small of my back ached in a good way, readying to spread across my skin in protection. I took a deep breath to calm my protective instincts.

"As beautiful as you ladies look right now, I'm more than curious to see what's behind the masks," he said, his voice deep and smooth with hints of an accent too rough to be from any classical romance languages.

None of us moved.

"I know full well each of you is capable of tearing those bags to shreds in your own way. Playing the damsels won't work with me. I know your capabilities." He scoffed. "Plus, you'll need your vision down here. You didn't think I'd force my guests to discuss business affairs in such a cold, wet place, did you?"

I broke the rope tying the bag loosely around my neck and removed the fabric from my head. Before I could drop it to the ground, freeing up my hand, the man spoke again.

"Oh, wait, no, hold onto that, please. You'll need it to leave here. Sorry, should have mentioned that." Now that I could see the man behind the voice, I could see how well his looks *matched* his voice. He stood six feet tall and then some, his dark brown hair combed smooth atop his head. He wore dark suit slacks and a button up, with a couple buttons at the top open and his sleeves rolled over his forearms.

His eyes caught mine looking him over. "You are no succubus," he said, peering me up and down in a way that intrigued me more than offended me.

I preferred to keep my species to myself. At least for the moment.

"No," he went on. "Your energy carries different signatures, warrior signatures. Hmm, I can't exactly place it, but I've felt such energy before, a long time ago."

"So then you are very old?" Marie asked, her bag clutched in her hand. Celeste stood between Oliva and Marie, with Marie and me being the Wilds on the outside of the line we formed.

The man bowed his head for all of two seconds. "I am," he said with a smile when he met her gaze. "Please, call me Aleksander. Come." He turned and began walking deeper into the tunnels. "Follow me."

I mentally pocketed another fun fact about the incubi: they were gifted or cursed with either a long life or immortality from their vampire side. Fabulous. We were potentially dealing with beings that couldn't be killed. Then it hit me. A human male had retrieved us from the streets of Portland. Could these incubi also not go in the sunlight? Is that why they lived under the streets?

We followed Aleksander through the tunnels lined with brick archways, some narrow and some wide, leading to other parts of the unground system. A hundred years' worth of dirt and pieces of old tools and shoes and various objects littered the ground. Based on the stories of these tunnels, I wondered if Marie felt an energy hanging around, one of fear or great sadness, because while I couldn't feel actual energy like the succubi could, I definitely sensed an air of desperation down here.

Aleksander turned one last corner before propping open an old steel door and motioning for us to go inside. We entered a quaint room with two red Victorian style couches and a black velvet chaise lounge within it. A closed door occupied the wall opposite us. The tall incubus closed the door behind him. "Please, sit," he said, waving toward the furniture.

The other Wilds and I exchanged glances before accepting the invitation. My sisters and I shared a couch while Marie chose the lounge, facing us at an angle, but off to the side a bit. Candles burned in large sconces attached to the walls and on shelves and end tables beside the couches. Aleksander stood at a dark wooden floor-to-ceiling cabinet and opened a glass door to retrieve four tumblers.

"You're probably wondering how I got a *schrank* all the way down here," he said as he removed the stopper from a crystal decanter and poured the caramel brown liquid into a tumbler. He turned toward us with glass in hand. "It wasn't easy, not by any stretch of the word." He took a sip and shook his head. "I am so sorry. I rarely get visitors these days; I forgot my manners. Would you ladies like a drink?"

I looked to Marie to answer for us. She knew more about this man and his kind than we did.

"That would be very hospitable of you. Thank you," Marie answered, with no inflection of her normal mischievous self.

The male poured a finger of what looked and smelled like brandy into each of our glasses, and handed them to us before taking a seat on the couch facing my sisters and me. "Now that the pleasantries have been taken care of, let's get down to business," he said, his inviting smile no longer present. "I understand you're here to retrieve one of your own—Heather."

"You would understand correctly," Marie said. She sat straight with both her feet firmly planted on the ground. What I wouldn't give to be able to read his energy like she no doubt was currently doing.

The incubus leaned back and rested his right ankle on his left knee. He sighed and glanced at me with a twitch in the corner of his lips before his focus rested back on Marie. "Then while I wouldn't call your visit a complete waste—sharing drinks with beautiful women is something of a passion of mine—I do regret to inform you that you will most certainly not be leaving with Heather."

TEN

EVERYTHING in me wanted to spring from the chair and demand that the incubus return our Wild sister to us, but I reminded myself that Heather was here of her own volition. That fact was all that kept me on the couch, squished between my huldra sisters. I clenched the cushion beneath my legs to hold me back. My fingers ached with want to grow vines from their tips and wrap the green ropey plants around his neck.

"Now, now," Aleksander crooned directly at me. "There's no reason to get angry."

He gave a short, deep laugh. "She really is a powerhouse, isn't she?" he asked Marie.

The succubus gave no response.

"It's just come to me!" Aleksander said, slapping his knee, and still not spilling his brandy. "Why hadn't I realized it sooner?" He peered at Marie. "I'm losing my sharpness it appears." He turned back to me. "You've got the energy of a shield maiden. Powerful and fierce in your own right. It fits you like a glove, by the way." He tapped his finger on the glass he held. "You must be huldra then." He waited for my response, an expectant half-smile on his lips and a gleam in his eyes.

Was this a game to him? I shouldn't expect anything different, really. Marie loved playing mind games, why wouldn't an incubus? Except, something told me he wasn't playing games. This was Aleksander, and he relished in...whatever this was. The incubus piqued my interest, his ability to exuded masculinity without any of the traditionally masculine behaviors like aggression and dominance. Marcus wasn't dominant either, but the Hunter in him held onto the aggression living just beneath his surface. I didn't fault him for it. As long as he didn't use that aggression against me or my kind. Except, hadn't he a little this morning, when he'd demanded that I not meet with the incubi? When he'd thrown around the "trust" word as a means to get me to do what he wanted? Had he been trying to control me? No. Marcus wouldn't do that. Would he?

I scolded myself for comparing the two supernatural males and responded to Aleksander's assessment. "Yes, I'm a huldra. And you're an incubus. So why isn't Heather here telling us she refuses to come home with her sister? Why are you the one relaying the message, seeing as you're neither a huldra nor a succubus?"

My curt response did nothing to dissuade his friendly demeanor. "She's young, you know," he said to me, like that explained everything. "An adult, yes, but young by my standards anyhow. She still cares what her leader thinks of her, doesn't wish to let her leader down." He jerked his head toward Marie a fraction of a second before she began talking.

"While it's easy to believe what you say, how can I leave without seeing my sister first? Without ensuring her safety?" Marie asked. She crossed her legs and sipped her drink. I couldn't be sure if her relaxed confidence was real or not. I supposed that was the point.

In a way, I felt like a child watching the adults discuss matters above my head. Except they weren't exactly discussing these things verbally, I assumed. I was at a disadvantage in that I couldn't read energy the way those two were probably currently doing. I had no idea what kind of energy messages were flying back and forth. My methods of getting information were more physical and, like a child, I didn't know how much longer I could sit still.

Aleksander considered Marie's words as he rubbed small circles with one finger on his tumbler. He didn't look my way, but I sensed he saw me watching his finger. A smile rose on one side of his mouth and too late I realized he felt the sexual energy building within me. It had been a while since Marcus and I had had any kind of good sex, and I don't mean quiet quickies. If I really thought about it, the disconnect between Marcus and me had started before the Oregon winery trip, though I couldn't put my finger on exactly when.

Speaking of fingers, I pulled my gaze from Aleksander's and pushed all thoughts of sexual pleasure from my mind. Wrong time. Wrong place. Wrong male.

The incubus's half-smile dropped and he gulped down the rest of his drink before standing to set his glass on the cabinet counter he'd pulled it from. "I've got an idea," he said, turning to face us.

My legs itched to stand, to be at eye level with him, but I did as Marie and stayed seated.

"Do tell," Marie said not too quickly so as to seem needy, but not too slowly so as to seem suspicious.

"Well, the way I see it, you need to know your sister is here on her own accord and faring well before you'll feel comfortable enough to leave. Yet your sister fears telling her leader that she wishes to stay with a kind that is not her own," he said.

Marie nodded.

"Middle men tend to work well in these situations. And I've got one on standby for such an occasion as this." Aleksander ran his fingers through his brown hair, just long enough to give way to his hand, but still keeping it tidy.

Before Marie gave an answer, Aleksander landed three loud knocks on the door we'd entered through and stepped back. It opened and a younger looking man with blond hair entered the room, shutting the door behind him. Still, I balked at Marie's lack of vehement rejection to the idea of not seeing her sister, not checking to make sure she was okay.

"You called, my king?" the baby-faced man said.

"Yes, thank you for joining us. Please," Aleksander said, motioning to the couch he'd been sitting on earlier. "Take a seat."

With both men on opposite sides of the room, I wasn't sure which to keep an eye on. But Aleksander quickly relieved my little problem when he stood behind the younger incubus. "Mason," Aleksander said. "These are our neighboring Wild Women. I'm sure you can feel the succubus, you're well acquainted with such energy, but the other three are huldra, if you were wondering."

Mason's eyes widened as he took in my sisters and me. I made a mental note to ask Marie if they could see energy too, and if there was any way to hide mine from view. "Thank you, sire," the young man uttered.

"Mason, these women are concerned for Heather's well-being. Will you please explain to them why their succubus has chosen to stay with us?" Aleksander requested.

Mason nodded. "Yes, of course, sire." He spoke mainly to Marie. "We are in love."

Marie's control wavered for a millisecond before she regained it again. "I'm uncertain how this is even possible," she said with the diplomacy of a queen.

"Your sister respects your place in the galere and is thankful for your concern," Mason went on to explain. "But we wish to be together, not separated. And her safety is my top priority."

His words hit a nerve and I accidently spoke up. "Her safety is *her* priority, how she stays safe is *her* choice."

He regarded me. "Yes, and this is her choice."

Marie gave one nod and pushed her hair back from her shoulder. "Then you may come stay with us temporarily, if she cannot be separated from you. But all sisters of mine must live under one roof."

Marie's judgement may have seemed harsh, but I knew she did so with the best intentions. Succubi are stronger with numbers. Their group is the largest Wild group, outside of the mermaids, for a reason. They can't flee by swimming into the sea, flying away, vanishing, or tree-jumping, like the rest of us. Their option is to stand together and combine their energies to overpower their foe. They need each other. The absence of one weakens them all.

Aleksander answered Marie, the two leaders discussing what seemed like young love, but in reality was the basis of a political relationship. "She has heard the latest news in the Wild Women war, and she chooses to stay out of it."

Marie blinked her eyes and cleared her throat, obviously taken aback. "I do not accept this." She flexed and then folded her hands on her lap. "She is one of us and would never choose to betray us with such disloyalty."

Aleksander gave a quick nod to Mason, who bowed his head before removing his long sleeve shirt. His stature was smaller than Aleksander's, but still lean muscles lined his chest and abs. A dragon tattoo wound up his bicep, twisting around it. But our focus was the ink freshly needled into his skin, on his right pec, where a dragon and a snake were knotted up with foreheads touching. An outsider of the succubus/incubus world, even I knew the meaning behind such body art.

Marie's breath hitched. I didn't need energy reading skills to translate the shift in the room from tense to battle-ready.

"Please," Aleksander said with hands open, palm out. "We are not your enemy."

"Clearly you are not my friend either," Marie spat.

"We have no place in this war of yours, and only seek to offer a place of refuge for those who desire it. Nothing more. We will not get in your way."

"You will not help us either," I said.

"You misunderstand me, huldra." Aleksander paused. "I am sorry, I should have asked your name much earlier. I would prefer to address you properly, if you don't mind."

"Faline. My name is Faline of the Washington huldra coterie. And if you're not for us, then you're against us."

"I do beg to differ, Faline." Aleksander came around the side of the couch to sit beside his fellow incubus. "We support your cause, but not in the way you prefer. We have nothing to lose by standing down and everything to lose by taking up arms. Supporting someone does not necessarily come from a place of agreeing with them, only recognizing their plight."

"Seriously?" I scoffed. "You think you understand what we've gone through? You don't, or else you'd be standing beside us, not behind us."

"Technically," Aleksander said with an infuriating twinkle in his eye. "We do not stand behind, or beside, or in front of you. We stand beneath you, in the underground."

"Why the hell is this so funny to you?" I said, unable to contain my anger any longer. I jumped up from the couch. My sisters quickly joined me. "If Heather doesn't return to her galere, they'll all be imprisoned. And without them, we have no—"

Marie shot up and sent me a harsh glare. I shut my mouth. Shit, I'd done it again, let my temper get the best of me and showed our cards.

Aleksander stood and took a step toward me. He reached his hand out to plant it on my arm, but Marie quickly stood between us. "Do not touch her," she seethed, finally showing her true feelings.

He stepped back. "I was only trying to help."

"Your methods of helping us have yet to inspire any amount of trust on our part," Marie warned.

"You cannot doubt that the young incubus and the succubus are in love. She too has a matching tattoo," Aleksander said, taking two more steps back until his legs hit the couch Mason still sat upon, shirtless. "But beyond that, we'd like to prove our support."

"Oh? And how do you plan to do that?" Marie asked, nearing the door to leave. We followed, at the ready for anything.

"I hear you have a check-in coming up," he said.

I almost asked how he knew that—was it what I'd just said or had he already known?—but didn't want to interrupt him showing his cards.

"Rather than attend the check-in and risk never leaving the Hunter complex," Aleksander offered, "come stay with us. All succubi are welcome. Our presence is unknown by the Hunters and they've never taken much notice of our existence anyhow. Come. You will be safe and free here."

Fear shot through me. If Marie took Aleksander up on his offer, the rest of us Wilds would not succeed in rescuing our mothers and sisters from the Hunters. Without the succubi galere, we wouldn't be able to take the other Hunter complexes. The harpies were few in numbers, as were the rusalki, who'd just lost a sister at our last battle and hadn't contacted us since. I couldn't count on them to show up to the next battle. That left the mermaids. And after the rusalki uncovered some of the mermaids playing double agents, I trusted them about as far as I could see their sneaky scales. The harpies and the huldra were in no way able to take down whole Hunter complexes on our own. And my mother could still be out there, suffering whatever foul plans the Hunters were concocting. I'd made a promise to myself to get my mother back. I refused to accept anything less.

Marie opened the door to the dank, dark tunnels and left the room, with us huldra flanking her. "I will think on it," she said.

Aleksander caught up to us, moving quicker than any other being I'd seen, and pulled a business card from his pocket and handed it to her. "Call me any time, day or night, with your answer. In the meantime, know that your sister is safe. You could be too, if you chose." He spoke smoothly as though he'd just casually walked right up to us.

Marie turned on her high heel and walked back down the tunnels, the way we'd come from. Aleksander snapped his fingers and the two incubi who had stood guard outside his chamber door hurried to walk in front of us, leading us out of the maze. One handed us the black fabric head coverings.

Marie gladly took the bag and placed it over her head, as did I, happy to be free from the claustrophobic underground. And I didn't have to be able to feel energy to know she was even more ticked than I was about the outcome of this meeting.

* * *

We convened as we briskly walked back to the apartment complex down the busy Portland streets. The morning sun barely shone through the clouds, but even the small amount of daylight made me wish I'd thought to bring sunglasses after spending an hour underground.

"Bullshit," I murmured as my boots pounded the pavement.

"Which part?" Celeste asked.

"All of it." I let out a huff. "Of course they want to be Switzerland in all of this. Why would they mess up a good thing? The Hunters keep their every watching eyes on us, which means the incubi can just slink through the night, unnoticed, as they drain human women of their energy and create new incubi."

"Maybe the Hunters don't know the incubi exist," Olivia offered.

"No, the Hunters know," I said. "Marcus didn't want me meeting with them because of their reputation." I wondered if the Wilds walking with me bristled at how I connected Marcus to the Hunters, but I didn't look to find out. I hadn't meant to do it. From what I'd seen, he'd been wrong about the incubi being overly dangerous. Or maybe he had just overreacted out of jealousy. I wasn't sure what to think of that.

"And I thought for sure bringing you three would do the trick," Marie muttered.

"Why would you think that?" I asked.

Marie's heels clicked the pavement in rhythm as she spoke. "I wanted him to see the succubi united with other Wild Women, to know that he'd be outnumbered if it ever came to a fight."

Apparently, Aleksander didn't think it'd come to that.

A blue-striped city bus rumbled by and my pony tail whipped at my face. I spit strands from my mouth. "They think that cheering from the sidelines is helping us to destroy the opposing team. We don't need cheerleaders; we need those who'll stand beside us and join in our fight for freedom. But the free get great comfort from believing everyone else enjoys the same freedom as they do. Admitting that someone is oppressed almost forces anyone with a conscience to help the oppressed group, and so it's easier to tell yourself they're fine."

We rounded the corner, within sight of the succubi's white brick apartment building. Trees lined the sidewalk, full of orange leaves, but not nearly mature enough for my taste. Their thin trunks told of life in a city that only recently began appreciating nature.

"What are you thinking, Marie?" Celeste asked.

When the succubus didn't answer, only stared ahead at her home, I added, "You've been awfully quiet. Don't tell me you're actually considering Aleksander's offer." Or was she too angry at her sister to speak? Pissed over her sister's selfishness in endangering the galere by insisting to stay with her incubus rather than attending check-in together?

I waited for a reassuring answer, but got none. "Marie, if you and your kind forsake the Wilds, we're doomed." There, I'd said it. I didn't want to, didn't want to reveal how much we needed her and her sisters, but her silence bore into me the way impending doom twisted one's insides into knots.

Marie bounded up the apartment stoop ahead of us and through the front door. At the base of the stairs she paused and turned toward my sisters and me. "Feel free to rest in the apartment we've loaned you. I must meet with my sisters and discuss our next move." She took the steps up to her top-level apartment, two by two.

All we could do was stand there and watch as the threads of hope for our kind potentially unraveled.

ELEVEN

WHEN I FINALLY TOOK MY throw-away cell phone off airplane mode, it buzzed repeatedly with messages from Marcus. I called him back, filled him in, and listened to him warn me repeatedly about the risks of dealing with a kind of creature I hadn't wanted to deal with in the first place. It didn't go well. Even more frustrated than before, I ended the call to join my sisters at the small table. Olivia called our coterie to let them know the latest news.

"Marie won't abandon us," Celeste insisted. "She's got a good heart."

"In all honesty," Oliva said, "you've only spent a night with her. You don't really know what Marie will do."

I fought the urge to openly agree, but my sister didn't need salt poured on her wound.

"Either way, we're going to have to leave our homes soon," I said, changing the subject for Celeste's sake. "We know that despite the records burning in the Hunter complex fire, it's only a matter of time before they find out where we live and our name changes won't happen soon enough. We need to think about where we want to go. The mermaid's island is out. They've already abandoned it for who knows where. We obviously can't stay here. The rusalki live in a literal hole in the ground, so that's out of the question. And the harpies have a nice place on a mountain cliff, but it's not very big, so it'd be cramped."

"I need a time out from all of this," Celeste said, covering her eyes with the back of her wrist. "I can't do this right now. It's too much."

I softened my voice, "Okay. We can pick this up later."

"I'm going to lay down now. Let me know when Marie returns." Celeste stood and made her way to her bedroom.

"A nap is a good idea," Oliva agreed, standing to stretch.

I followed her into our shared bedroom, eager for an hour of catch-up sleep.

* * *

"Marie wants to talk to us," Celeste said, her head peeked through the bedroom door. Afternoon sun streamed through the window and settled on my bed. Celeste left the door open and waited on the threshold, arms crossed, looking impatient.

Olivia sat up and yawned. "Seriously? She literally just slept in a bed with one of us last night. And now she's summoning us?"

My thoughts exactly.

We rose and followed her out. Celeste refrained from responding as she urged us to move quicker up the steps. When we entered Marie's apartment déjà vu hit me like a branch to the face. More than ten succubi stood, crammed into her living room so tightly they spilled into the kitchen. Each of them sported some kind of snake tattoo, seen or unseen. All of them watched us, waiting for Marie's signal. Uncertainty crawled through my mind. Marie wouldn't use energy against us the way she'd pinned me the first time we'd met, would she?

Bark tingled to the surface of my skin and spread up my back, wrapping around my waist. A succubus, let alone more than ten of them, would not be stopped for even a second by my bark. But my inner huldra didn't know or care.

"Thank you for coming," Marie said.

She patted the cushion on her red couch beside where she sat. Celeste shook her head no. Despite my aggravation with her, the sight caused pride to swell in me. The two of them may be lovers, but huldra are always loyal to one another.

"Very well then," Marie said as she sat up straighter. "My sisters and I have taken a vote and come to a decision." She canvassed the room before setting her gaze back on us. "We will pack our things and leave tonight to stay with the incubi."

"You've got to be joking," I exclaimed.

Two succubi stepped closer to where Marie sat, one on each side.

I regarded them with a glare, "Don't get all in a huff. I'm not going to try anything."

Marie gave them each a nod and they stepped back.

"I am not joking," she assured. "This is a decision we made for the safety of our galere. You are more than welcome to join us."

Celeste bit her bottom lip and clenched her fists. Bark sprang from the skin on her arms, no doubt caused by her perceived disloyalty of Marie.

"Of course we won't join you," I spat. "We had a plan. I will not sacrifice the safety of other Wilds and their missing loved ones to hide like scared incubi. What about our agreement? You agreed to help. We took out the Washington Hunter complex. The huldra are on the Hunter's radar now!"

"And you retrieved your sister in the process," Marie reminded. "You have no more reason to fight."

The possibility of getting my mother back gave me every reason to fight, as did saving the mothers and sisters of other Wilds. None of them deserved to live under Hunter oppression. None of them.

"How could you betray us like this?" I said in exasperation.

"Why would we continue to fight?" A blonde succubus leaning on the kitchen counter asked. "We have no pawns in this game. They have taken none of our sisters."

I shot her an icy glare. "That doesn't mean they can't or won't."

"It does when we have a place to hide," she retorted. "It means exactly that."

I shook my head and turned my attention toward Marie. "The huldras are outed. It's only a matter of time before we'll be found and have to flee. For all we know, the United States Hunters could be planning an attack on us all, locating our homes and planning to take us all out in one fell swoop." We didn't have time to hide and hope things worked themselves out.

"Then gather your coterie and come with us, underground. You'll be safe," Marie answered, looking at Celeste as she spoke.

"Are you kidding? What about the other Wilds, what about the harpies, and the mermaids, and the rusalki?"

"I will argue with you no longer. Out of our alliance and friendship, I allowed you to be privy to our plan. But now my sisters and I must prepare; the incubi will be here shortly after the sun sets. But Faline," Marie added, "I do still see your kind as friends to mine. And because of that, I would like to help you."

I threw my hands in the air, exhausted by her games.

"Aleksander," she continued, "took a liking to you. He tried to hide it, but I could feel his desire and intrigue radiating like heat from a raging fire. He is an old incubus, I suspect many hundreds of years. But he has yet to learn to hide his tells."

I sighed and rubbed my temples. "I don't see how that can help me."

"The incubi live in the dark, in the shadows, watching those who do not know they're being watched. And at times, they sleep with the most powerful people in the world, people who know things, who utter secrets in the height of the kind of passion only an energy weaver can bring." Marie stood and walked to the back of the couch, between the furniture and her bedroom. "Befriend Aleksander when he comes tonight, preferably in an intimate way, and receive more than the most pleasurable night of your life." She rested a tear-filled gaze on Celeste. "When a succubus, and I assume an incubus, finds someone who embodies more than a conquest to them, but rather an interest and something deeper they can't quite understand, they are likely to give much and ask for little in return."

Marie moved to stand inside her bedroom with her hand on the doorknob. Deep red and orange tapestries hung on the walls behind her. Gold and red fabric, covered in gold embroidery, lay across her four-poster bed. Incense burned from an unseen corner and twisted its way past flickering candles, around her, and out toward us. "Please," was all she said to my sister as they locked eyes. And that's all she needed to say. Celeste took a deep breath, slouching her shoulders as she exhaled, as though releasing her anger for Marie on a breath. She went to the succubus.

The two Wilds closed the bedroom door behind them and Olivia and I made our way downstairs. I didn't know if I'd pretend to flirt with Aleksander for the sake of helpful information. But I did know I had a few phone calls to make. And that whether or not I chatted up the incubus, I was screwed.

TWELVE

"I'VE BEEN TRYING the rusalki and the mermaids for hours, still nothing." My aunt Renee released a heavy sigh. The line went quiet as we both considered our options. We'd called our sisters back home after leaving Marie's apartment. We'd given them thirty minutes to talk and make a few phone calls before calling us back.

After Marie's heart-bashing news, Olivia and I regrouped in our temporary apartment and came to multiple conclusions. First, we weren't hiding anywhere. Wilds had done enough hiding, and clearly that didn't work out so well for them. So, no thanks.

Second, our sister's infatuation with the succubi leader was way more than infatuation—a quickly growing bond we'd do well to respect, however hard that was going to be. And no, the difficulty wasn't in the part that most may think we had issue with, the idea of a succubus and a huldra together long term. No, it was the idea of a huldra and anyone together long term. Before I ventured out of my huldra territory and into the great big world of Wilds, we Wilds never came into contact with one another. Not that I knew of anyhow. And though maybe mermaids were into hooking up with their shoal sisters, huldras weren't. It's one reason why being with Marcus felt so foreign, outside of the whole Hunter issue. Huldra do not do long term. And yet here Celeste was, falling head over heels for another Wild, a woman who could quite possibly be her perfect match.

And here I was...fighting my feelings for Marcus. Because even if the rules had recently changed, which I didn't doubt they had, they hadn't changed enough to allow a Hunter and a Wild a happily ever after. A revolution may be able to happen in a day, but changing minds about who can be with whom—yeah, that takes much longer.

This led me to my next question of Renee. "Have you and the others there had a chance to discuss Marie's advice on my befriending the incubi leader?"

Renee huffed again. "Of course Marcus had no part of this discussion," she assured me. I'd figured as much, but was still thankful she'd said so.

I nodded my head as though she could see, then stopped when I realized she couldn't. "And?"

"Well, we think it's wise to gain any information possible, especially in such dire circumstances," she said, adding that last part as though it were an excuse to tell myself to keep the guilt at bay. Or maybe she had no idea how already the guilt of even considering such a thing as to seduce an incubus gnawed at me. "But, as usual, it's up to you, seeing as you're the one who'll be doing the deed."

"I'm not going to have sex with him," I countered. As if I even had to remind her of my appreciation for loyalty above all else and how terribly I felt that I was becoming a hypocrite. Although, I had to remind myself, before Marcus came to me in harpy territory, I would have assumed the same as my aunt. A fabulous night of sex with an energy worker? Yes, please.

Renee scoffed. "Well, why the hell wouldn't you?"

Before I could answer with some smart remark about keeping my head in the game or not being into tall, sexy Norse supernatural males, my aunt changed the subject. Or rather, she made a noise that changed the subject.

"Huh. You hear that, Abigale?" I heard from the other end of the line.

"I do, like tires on gravel," my other aunt answered. "Odd. Let me see."

Renee regarded me again. "No one comes to visit us. No one even knows we're here."

The sound of the front door opening followed her statement and then another, of boots running across gravel. "Go, go, go!" Marcus yelled and then the door slammed. "Now! They're here. Is there a back entrance?"

"Who?" I asked quickly. "Who's there?"

"Oh Goddess, Shawna, grab the dog," Abigale yelled.

I heard the dog yelp right before what sounded like glass shattering.

"Olivia," I called from our bedroom. She was already waiting at the door; she'd heard my earlier frantic question. She raised her eyebrows as if to ask what was going on.

I verbalized her expression. "What's happening?"

Renee finally answered after the sound of three gunshots blared through the phone. "The Hunters," she said on bated breath. "They've found us. They're here." I picked up the sounds of nature, the forest, across the line, branches snapping, boots thudding. Marcus's boots.

My heart thudded with fear.

Another gunshot sounded, followed by Abigale's scream.

Renee panted into the phone, "We're on our way to you."

And then the line went dead. I dropped to the floor and prayed to Freyja to keep my loved ones safe.

The Hunters were on my property, going through our things, maybe even destroying those items we held most sacred, those pieces of our foremothers passed down—all we had left of our lineage. They were there to arrest us. Our time of reckoning had come and if my next move wasn't the right one, we may never get the chance to take them down.

THIRTEEN

ANXIETY WOUND and unwound within me. Anxiety and rage. How dare they. Olivia looked to the ceiling and bit her lip. I sprang from my kneeled position on the floor and paced. We were too far away to help. We were helpless.

"You have to do it," Olivia muttered, not looking me in the eye. "I know you have feelings for Marcus. I know, and I'm sorry we're asking this of you. But there's no other choice."

She didn't have to tell me. I already knew. I guess I'd known since Marie suggested it, suggested I seduce Aleksander. When my aunt agreed, I'd toyed with the idea of letting Marcus know beforehand, to keep it from being disloyal, to clear my conscience. Now I wished I could tell him, and I very much couldn't.

The room darkened with the setting sun, the light traveling across the wall and vanishing altogether as Olivia and I stood there, planted in shock and worry, waiting for a phone call from our coterie.

"What if they didn't make it out?" she whispered. Tears burst from her eyes and her head slowly rose to gaze me in the face. "What if it's just us? Oh, Goddess." Her knees buckled and she leaned against the door frame for support. "We can't do this alone, Faline. We can't get them back without help from the others."

"I know," was all I could say because she was right, all of it.

"What if the rusalki and the mermaids have already been captured? What if that's why they weren't answering their phones? They may already be locked up on Hunter compounds." She took a ragged breath. "Or worse."

I shook our shared thoughts of doom away. "We can't...we can't think like that."

"Oh? Then how should we think?"

I didn't have an answer for her, so I kept silent. My bounty-hunter brain kicked in, being as I was in an impossible situation. Giving up never helped anyone. We were huldra, fighters, protectors. "We should think like huldra," I finally answered. "Stand up, dust our knees off, and push forward."

Olivia wiped the back of her hand across her cheeks. "Does that mean you'll try to get answers from Aleksander?"

"No, that's not enough anymore," I said, throwing my shirt off and rummaging through my suitcase for something low cut and tight. I had nothing fitting that description. "If the Hunters have taken the rest of our coterie, I need more than intel to get them back. I need the backing of every incubus and succubus in this town. I'll convince him to help us."

Olivia nodded her head and a shadow of a smile pulled her lips upward. "All right then, let's go."

She led the way as we left the apartment and made our way upstairs to Marie's apartment.

Celeste met us half-way on the stairs; she'd been heading down to talk to us. "Aleksander is almost here, so I figured it was time for me to go. Marie said we can use the apartment complex for as long as we need it." She peered down at my bare chest and then back up at me. "If you've changed your mind and decided to take Marie's advice, I don't think this is the most subtle way to go about it."

My current dark emotions allowed a hard laugh to sneak through. "I don't have any shirts that'll do the job. Neither does Olivia. I figured Marie might."

"Come with me," Celeste said, turning on her heel and leading us upstairs.

Olivia climbed the stairs beside me, behind Celeste. She shot me a glance that I knew all too well. I nodded.

"Um, Celeste," I started. "Before we're surrounded by a bunch of succubi, we have something to tell you."

Our sister stopped on one stair higher than us and turned to face us. "Does it have to do with you changing your mind with the incubus? Because Marie said she felt heavy energy from down on the first floor. I thought maybe you were arguing with Marcus about it or something."

"No, I was on the phone with Renee when the Hunters came to our home."

Celeste's eyes squeezed shut and she pulled her lips into her mouth. She tightened her fists before taking a couple breaths and letting them go. She opened her eyes. "Are they okay?"

"I don't know," I answered. "I heard them run into the woods behind the common house, all together, but that's all I know."

Watching my sister experience the pain new and fresh, after Olivia and I had sat in it a while allowing it to fester around us, was like experiencing it all over again. Tears sprang to Olivia's eyes and I blinked a few away from my own.

"This can't be happening," Celeste said, shaking her head. She took a cleansing breath and straightened herself. "So then this is why you're in need of a sexy top."

I nodded.

She turned and continued up the stairs. "Okay then, let's get that taken care of before the incubi arrive."

As usual, Marie's top-floor apartment included at least five succubi milling about. I wondered if she just enjoyed being surrounded by sisters or if they were more of a protection team, at the ready to combine their energy-bending abilities to make sure their leader stayed safe.

Marie breezed past the four succubi at the table playing cards and the other in the kitchen wrapping up food with only a nod of her head.

Olivia asked the succubus in the kitchen if she needed help with anything and was quickly put to work chopping vegetables. Celeste took a seat at the table and asked to be dealt in. Marie and I made it to her room where we stood in front of her small, narrow closet. I didn't know why I'd assumed she'd have a walk-in closet, it's not as though she wore more than a robe all that often.

"This apartment building had been built in the early nineteen hundreds," she explained when she noticed me searching for another closet door. "They didn't have much need for large storage spaces, and neither do I."

Marie studied each top for a moment before pushing it aside to view the next. "I admit, I didn't expect you to come around."

"On the Aleksander thing?" I asked.

She made a sound, as though she were concentrating on the contents of her closet too heavily to speak an answer. Her gaze rested on a red chiffon button-up, clearly see-through. She pulled it from its confines and held it up to my chest. "Clashes with your hair," she finally said before returning her focus to the closet.

A question popped into my head and nagged at my thoughts. Her current distraction seemed to create the perfect timing to gather information from the succubi leader. Why not? She was picking out a top to help me do just that with the incubi leader, get information.

"So Marie," I started.

"Hmm?" She kept on task.

"Why weren't you truthful, about Heather, when I first came to you looking for my sister? You'd sent me to the mermaids and even led me to believe she may have been taken by the Hunters."

"Oh, no, succubi are not untruthful. If you believed she could have been taken by the Hunters, that was your own assumption, not placed there by me. I knew she'd run off, I just wasn't sure where to. Of all the Wild Women, the succubi are the most honest, I believe."

Marie lingered on another red top before shaking her head and moving to the next. "Our original foremothers were created by the great goddess Lilith." She paused to glance at a large stone statue of the Goddess Lilith with her arms stretched out, holding circular symbols, with a snake wound up her body, hanging on the wall between her closet door and a shelf. "Within our foremothers she gifted her attributes of a thirst for knowledge, the ability to sense, read, and manipulate the energies of others, and the deep desire to live by truth. This is why we live by our own truths."

I found myself nodding, though I doubted she noticed as she went back to working what she seemed to deem the important task of locating the most seductive shirt in all the world. I hadn't learned much about Lilith, but I could already see why the succubi worshipped her.

Marie continued and it seemed that the females in the living room listened intently too, as though we were gathered for a bedtime story. All sounds of food-chopping and card-playing ceased. "Before the Hunters, we used our gifts for good. We pulled out the negative energy from humans, absorbed their hurts you could say, recycled their pain into the earth, and from the soil, drew positive energy to fill their void. We healed humans, and sometimes other Wild Women."

"I bet townspeople didn't much like that after the Inquisitors rode through," I remarked, thinking of my own huldra history.

"No they did not. They asked us for help, but behind our foremothers' backs they whispered, calling us demons, saying we'd sucked the life out of the people we couldn't save. And of course, those rumors quickly became the village men's excuse for being unfaithful to their wives; it became a seductive succubi's fault for luring them and removing their free will. It wasn't long before the Hunters took the upper hand and forced us to stop healing people." Marie paused her perusal through her closet. She didn't look at me and she didn't seem to be studying the shirt she'd stopped on either.

"Do you know what happens when healers can no longer heal?" The succubus with the snake tattoo on her scalp asked, standing outside Marie's open bedroom door. "When empaths must live among hurting humans, but can do nothing to help them?"

I shook my head. Huldras never healed. We fought for the weak, protected those who needed protecting, but none of our abilities including healing, outside of learned trades.

"We gradually absorb the hurt. We become emotionally unstable, depressed, sometimes worse." Her voice cracked and I wondered how many sisters among their ranks fought the battle against depression. "Our Goddess brought truth and knowledge to all of humankind, and how do they repay her? They make up stories about her, call her a snake, align her with negativity, the devil. Why? Because she believed everyone had the right to live their truth and be free of inner hurt?"

Marie cleared her throat. "That's enough for now," she said. "And anyway, I think I've found the perfect top for you. It'll turn up the desire of your incubus."

By the time Marie placed the black silk top against my chest, the succubus at the door had left and returned to playing cards. She scrutinized the shirt where she held it up on me and nodded in approval.

"Is that why Heather left, do you think?" I asked. "Why she left her galere? Because of emotional instability?"

Marie removed the top from the hanger and handed it to me. "You say the words as though they are an easy diagnosis when in fact they are as layered as this earth."

"I'm asking because I want to know, because Heather's choices have clearly affected us all." I unbuttoned the front of the top and put it on, buttoning it back into place. The V-neck dipped low between my breasts. I thought to mention my own coterie's current status, running from the Hunters, but while the worry plagued my mind, voicing the news to a non-huldra didn't feel right, not until I received an update of some kind.

"You would not know the difficulties of running a matriarchal home within a patriarchal society," Marie countered, moving to her open suitcase upon her bed and placing items from her closet in it. "You have no children or younger generation within your ranks. You cannot fathom the confusion they must endure in their raising, their questions as to why those outside their home do not operate like those inside their home, their immature assumptions that the world will accept and respect their personal truths the way their galere does. And then their backlash when you must create boundaries to keep them safe from a world they feel they do not need protecting from. You cannot imagine the difficulty in these things."

"Is Heather your daughter?" I asked in shock and yet in a sudden understanding as to why Marie decided to join Heather with the incubi underground.

Marie placed a small statue of Lilith in her bag and zipped it shut. She stood the suitcase beside her. "None of us have one mother. The galere mothers each daughter so that each succubus has many mothers."

She only answered my question partly, but seeing as it was Marie doing the answering, partly was more than I expected.

"Is Heather a minor?" I asked.

"No, she is eighteen," Marie answered. "And yes, her choice to be with her heart's desire over her galere is naïve, one she will grow to one day learn was unwise. But her feelings, her desire for safety and fear of the unknown future, those are shared by others in this galere."

I sighed. "Of course we're all afraid. It doesn't mean we should hide away while other Wilds are being picked off. That's what courage is, the ability to stand up to something despite our fear."

Marie placed a hand on my shoulder. "I know something has happened very recently to those you love. I felt it earlier, and can feel the fear and worry draped like a heavy cloak on you now."

A succubus peaked her head in and regarded Marie, "They're here."

Marie nodded. "Good, bring them up, invite them in."

The shaved-head succubus left the apartment to fetch the incubi.

"But," Marie continued with me. "Courage is an emotion that wells up within a person, urging them to walk a difficult path, to make a hard choice. And as with any emotion, it cannot be defined in one way, but takes on the definition of the one experiencing it. You may believe standing against the Hunters is a courageous act. But we do not." She left the bedroom and sat on her red couch in her living room, waiting for the incubus leader.

The sudden urge to argue with her, to make her see her huge error in judgement, welled up within me. I stomped into the living room. But before I opened my mouth, the front door opened sharply. In an instant Marie flicked her hand toward me and my anger dissipated, replaced with desire for the tall man who now stood in her hall. My whole body tingled as Aleksander's eyes found mine and bounced to my chest. A smile grew across his face. I followed his gaze to see what delighted him so much and then groaned inwardly.

Now I knew why Marie had chosen the loose silk top. She'd planned to make me nip like a braless woman in the frozen food section of a grocery store. And at the moment, she executed her plan perfectly.

"Aleksander," I greeted the incubus with a nod.

His eyes found mine again and this time they sparkled. "It's good to know you're happy to see me, Faline." He spoke through his smile, his accent stronger than earlier.

His voice did hot things to me that made standing in the frozen food section in only a silk top seem like a really good idea. And his body...it was a tower of muscle that went on forever. This may be a lot easier than I expected. While I wanted to hate that, part of me didn't. Not at all.

FOURTEEN

MARIE WASTED no time in leaving the apartment. With her head held high, she made her way from their brick building, through dark alleyways, while trailing a red, wheeled suitcase, her galere silently following behind her like a funeral procession. Except, instead of all black, most of the female members of the group wore ripped jeans and tank tops. Only a few incubi joined us. Aleksander walked alongside Marie at the front, and others sprinkled throughout the group. Us huldra brought up the rear, which was fine with me. I'd rather not have a bunch of unknown supernatural males at my back.

I wondered if it was trust the succubi gave the incubi, or some other emotion yet to be seen. Did they feel a familial bond to the men? What must that be like?

"So," Aleksander spoke to Marie for the first time since leaving the succubi's home. "Tell me about the huldra leader." I couldn't see them, of course, through the group of succubi and incubi in front of my sisters and me. But I'd been listening for their voices since we left the apartment, because while I was sure Marie knew huldra had impeccable hearing, I assumed Aleksander had no clue. An advantage I clung to.

"The huldra don't have a leader, not like us," Marie retorted quickly in monotone. "And she has a name."

I'd never heard the woman speak so...unemotionally. Maybe this decision to go into hiding was as she'd said, not of her making.

Aleksander's voice showed no offense to her remarks. "Excuse me cousin. I will endeavor to do better."

Oh, what I'd had given to see Marie's expression. I'd only ever seen her angry, mischievous, and whatever else one would call her behavior around Celeste—I never claimed to be an emotional guru. But I'd never had the pleasure of experiencing annoyed Marie.

The parade of supernaturals into the more bustling parts of downtown Portland took well over ten minutes, though my antsyness kept me from counting exactly how many minutes. The moment I'd realized this, I chided myself for being sloppy. I'd been too wrapped up in waiting for Aleksander and Marie to finally talk and then listening for information in their conversation, that I'd let my attention to detail slide. If a group of Hunters sauntered out of an alley at this very moment, I wasn't sure I'd know my way back to the apartment complex.

I leaned over to barely whisper in Olivia's ear. "You haven't been keeping track of the time or which streets we've turned down, have you?"

She grimaced and shook her head.

Well, shit. I took stock of our surroundings. I didn't know Portland like I knew Seattle and Everett, but the empty park we currently passed got my attention, or at least its trees. I inhaled their pine scent to memory and glanced at the time on my phone. That's when I saw the GPS app. Duh. My mind had to be out of sorts in a major way for me to forget about my GPS.

Too much was going on at once. I still hadn't heard from my coterie and Marcus. I had no idea if the Hunters had them or not. Neither the mermaids nor the rusalki had returned my phone calls. Only the harpies texted to say they were just waiting for the Wilds to show up in their territory. They still thought the plan to attack their Hunter complex was on.

So yeah, no pressure or anything.

I opened my GPS map, the screen's brightness messing with my night vision, and put a pin at my current location to reference later. I glanced at the map each time we turned a corner and placed another pin to mark the spot.

Humans passed us on the sidewalk, some gawking at the interesting procession, others clearly unfazed by Portland's newest oddity. I assumed Aleksander chose the night hours to escort the succubi through the city for this very reason, fewer humans to take notice.

Marie finally responded to the incubi leader she walked beside at the front of the group, "Believe me, Faline won't take it well to you calling her 'huldra' rather than her name. It won't start you two off on the right foot."

"I appreciate the advice." Aleksander waited a breath before speaking again. "I wonder, would you have any other advice for me regarding Faline? She intrigues me so. I've met Wild Women over the centuries, but never one quite like her. I'd like to get to know her better, spend some...quality time with her. How should I go about arranging that, do you think?"

Olivia shot me a look. I rolled my eyes.

There had to be another way to go about getting Aleksander to join our cause and in turn convince the succubi galere to change their minds about going into hiding. I was a huldra for Goddess's sake! Instead, I felt like a helpless being prancing around in her bikini—or in my case a low-cut silk top—for the attention and affection of some male.

Aleksander was handsome and all, but no. Just no.

I stopped walking. "I'm not doing this," I said aloud to my sisters. "This is bullshit and I'll take no part in it."

"What's bullshit?" Celeste asked after taking two more steps and turning to see me.

"All of it." I motioned to the crowd ahead of us, walking and furthering the gap between them and us. "I had a moment of weakness. That's passed." The dread I hadn't realized I'd been feeling dissipated, a new sense of urgency taking its place. "I'm not going to roll over, belly-up, and lower myself for some male just because he's lived a life of privilege and thinks we ought to too, like we even have that option outside of fighting for our freedom. They're telling us to go into hiding when they will still get to walk around the city whenever they choose. To them, hiding is just living in a place that no one knows about. For us it'll mean being shackled to a place no one knows about. Huge difference."

I hadn't noticed the succubi procession stop until Celeste's gaze bounced from me to Marie as Marie walked through the center of the galere who'd been following her and made her way to us. "Why have you stopped?" she asked, probably unable to hear our earlier discussion. Aleksander joined her.

Celeste reached to Marie who clasped her hand and kissed it. "My sisters are discussing a change in plans," my sister answered her lover.

Marie slowly nodded. "I see. And are you in agreement with this change in plans, of which, I assume, include not joining our galere for the time being?"

Celeste eyed me and then Marie again. She exhaled and bit her lip. "I am."

Marie dropped my sister's hand and backed away. She closed her eyes and opened them again with a tight smile, clearly fighting to rein in her hurt feelings. I expected her to try to convince us, to shift our own emotions enough to follow her into the underground. But she didn't. She only whispered, "Stay safe," to Celeste and turned on her high heel to walk off and lead her galere once again.

Aleksander lingered by my side. "This is quite a disappointing change of events," he uttered, tipping his head as though we lived a hundred years ago and not in the twenty-first century.

I saw no need to respond. What he deemed unfortunate, I saw as the first clear-headed decision I'd made since Shawna and Marcus pulled away from Portland.

I would, I decided, show politeness to a fellow supernatural being that wasn't currently hunting me or mine. "It was good to meet you, Aleksander. Be well."

"It is disappointing," he continued, as though I hadn't just stated the equivalent to a socially acceptable dismissal. "But I have set a contingency plan in place."

He paused, as if waiting for me to ask about this plan of his. When my response consisted of only a stare, he explained, as he pulled a folded paper from his pocket. "I have secured a safe house for you and your coterie."

He held out the paper. "Here's the address. The key to the front door is in a lock box on the knob. You'll find the code to that box below where I've written the address."

I made no move to take the paper from him.

The semblance of a smile he'd been sporting dropped, leaving pure seriousness in its place. "I realize my feelings mean nothing to you, but whether we like it or not, your feelings, your safety, mean everything to me. If you refuse to join us underground, at least for now, stay in a home unknown to the Hunters."

I considered his offer for half a second. "Here's my problem with all of this," I started. "I don't know you. How can I be sure this house of yours isn't bugged with cameras in the bathroom or something?" It was a legit question. An even more legit question rang through my mind: what would this incubi leader expect in return? I had no interest in being beholden to him or anyone else.

The slight smile returned to Alexander's face, framed by his five o'clock shadow. "Because it is not my home I am offering. It is a nightly rental, large enough to ensure your coterie's comfort and procured under a name the Hunters will not recognize."

The man seemed practiced at hiding others, a little too practiced. I wondered how many types of people he'd done this for throughout his many years on the earth. How many supernatural secrets were buried behind the incubi leader's smile? But now wasn't the time for questions and I wasn't in the mood to give him any indication that I was interested in anything about him. I took the folded paper from him and stuffed it into my jean's pocket with no intention of opening it. His intensity made me uncomfortable and if accepting the address appeased him enough to leave me be, then so be it.

A look of relief washed over his face.

The tall incubus smiled, that gleam once again in his eyes suggesting that he knew something I didn't. This time it didn't bother me. We all know things others do not. Doesn't always mean they're useful things.

"I do hope to see you again," he said as he took a half step and bowed toward me, not fully committed to the choice. He righted himself and left my sisters and me to continue at Marie's side, leading the procession. The little smile and glance over his shoulder gave me the distinct impression he hoped I was watching him walk away.

When he was out of earshot, I hugged Celeste. "You okay?" I asked.

She shook her head into my neck.

"They might change their minds," Olivia consoled our sister, wrapping herself around Celeste's back.

"She's just doing what her galere wants," Celeste huffed into my neck. "She knows it's a mistake."

So they had talked about this in their alone time. My respect for Marie rose another few points. She remained loyal to her galere, despite her opinions or her desire.

My phone vibrated in my hand and I swiped to answer. Celeste and Olivia pulled away to give me my space.

"Hello?" I answered, unfamiliar with the phone number.

"Hey." His voice sang to me like leaves on a breeze. "You okay?"

"Marcus, seriously?" I laughed, happy to hear him. "You guys were the ones running from the Hunters. Of course *we're* okay, just incredibly worried."

He gave a deep chuckle. "True. Yeah, we're fine."

I ached to wrap my arms around him. How had I ever thought I could seduce Aleksander? How had I ever thought I could bring myself to flirt with, or even touch another man in that way?

Tears trickled down Olivia's cheeks. She nodded, staring at my phone like it was her lifeline too. Our coterie was safe. They were safe, thank Freyja.

"Did you ditch your cell?" I asked.

Bed springs groaned through the line. "We all did. We're at a hotel, calling you from this phone. Shawna and the others want to talk to you, too, but I had to hear your voice, know that you're okay."

"I'm fine. We're fine. The succubi went into hiding, left their apartment complex. They offered to allow us to stay in it, but I don't think it's safe, so we'll need to find another place. If the Hunters found our house, they'll easily locate the succubi's." I paused, deciding to save the shop talk for later. "Where are you guys?"

"We're in the south Sound area," Shawna said, past Marcus. "Outside of Tacoma."

My ex-Hunter chimed in. "We didn't want to stop, not even to make a phone call, until we were well out of the area."

I fought the urge to throw my face into my hands and bawl with relief. "Good, good," was all I could say past the lump in my throat. I swallowed it down. "Where should we meet up?"

Renee spoke up now, though Marcus still breathed into the receiver. "We're only two and a half hours away from you. Let us get a few hours of rest and we'll meet you there in the morning."

"Perfect." I put them on speaker and pulled up my GPS. Let me give you the coordinates to where we're at. Let's meet here...what time?"

"Seven in the morning," Renee answered. "We'll be there at seven."

Seven felt like a lifetime away. After the way we had left things, I couldn't get to Marcus and my sisters fast enough. The world grew wider and more dangerous with each passing moment and we were stronger together. I may not agree with Marie's decision, but the succubi had gotten that part right.

FIFTEEN

I WOKE to the quiet creaking of a door being carefully shut outside of our apartment, to the sound of someone trying not to make any sounds. I jerked up in bed. Bits of morning light filtered through the curtains. My sisters and I had first thought we'd sleep in the park, the spot we'd said we'd meet our coterie and Marcus, but after an hour of trying to get shut-eye with humans wandering around, unknowingly alerting us to their presence, we gave in and decided to take Marie up on her offer. Only for a night. I mean, we'd rationalized, how likely were Hunters to choose this one night to storm the succubi galere?

Pretty damn likely, as it turned out. Except, they weren't storming, they were sneaking. I rushed out of bed and pulled my jeans on.

"Olivia," I whispered, buttoning my pants. "We've got company."

Olivia jumped out of bed, ready to go, her jeans already on.

I eased the bedroom door open. No one had entered our temporary domicile yet, so I hurried to Celeste who already had her ear to the front door.

I gave a nod toward the door and followed suit with my sisters who were allowing bark to sweep across their arms.

We silently counted along with Celeste's fingers. One. Two. Three!

Celeste swung the door open and bolted into the entryway of the apartment complex, hands out, attack ready.

I pushed out behind her. Squeals of delight met us as my aunts and Shawna gathered us into a group hug. Shawna's little white dog yapped in excitement at our feet. Relief swept my bark away. I had my coterie again. Finally.

Marcus hung back, waiting for his turn with me, which he'd eventually get, but not before I squeezed every member of my coterie in a thankful embrace. I almost lost them, and if the Hunters had taken Shawna, again, it would have killed me. But I didn't have to worry about that anymore. Shawna was here, rubbing my arm. My whole coterie was here.

"You said seven," Olivia declared, pulling out of the group hug.

Marcus took that as his opportunity to wrap his strong arms around me from behind and I turned in his embrace to face him. I relished the moment, breathing in his scent. He moved and smiled with ease, as though he felt perfectly fine. I checked his neck, moving aside the black collar on his cotton shirt, and looked his hands over for wounds anyways. I thought to press my lips into his skin, kissing each spot my eyes grazed for signs of a bruise or a cut, but with my coterie nearby, I figured it wasn't a good time. *Later*, I told myself. *I'll give him a more thorough inspection later.*

"I know I said seven," Renee countered Olivia's declaration of what time the members of our coterie said they'd arrive in Portland. "But we couldn't sleep. We had to get out of Washington and reunite with you three. When you weren't at the park where you'd said you'd be, we came straight here, remembered the way from when we'd dropped you off."

"It's so good to see you," Celeste sighed, looking a little less heartbroken than she had yesterday.

"So," Patricia said, taking a look around the quiet apartment complex. She smoothed her hand over the ornate banister. "They're all gone?"

"They are," I said, gazing around. The place didn't seem right sitting nearly empty like this, almost eerie. "Their check-in at the Hunter compound is today, and once they don't show, the Hunters will probably be out in force, trying to keep what happened in Washington from happening here. So we should probably go too."

"The incubi leader, Aleksander, got us an Airbnb, but Faline is being stubborn," Celeste tattled. I felt like we were little kids again and she'd caught me trying to explore the woods beyond our property line.

Marcus flashed me an unsettling look.

"We should take him up on it," Olivia added. "There's no way the Hunters will find us there and it'll give us time to plan what's next."

"Can we eat breakfast first?" Shawna asked. "We haven't had a decent meal in days. Unless they took their food with them." She paused. "I just realized they may have done that."

I stayed in Marcus's arms, trailing my fingers up and down his bicep. "Not all of it, they traveled light. I think there's eggs and bacon in the fridge. And while we eat we can fill you all in on everything that's been going on." I ignored the whole Airbnb thing.

* * *

I wasn't particularly proud of it, and when I saw Marie again I planned on letting her know I'd used her bed, but after the happy reunion with my sisters and aunts, I took Marcus upstairs to the top apartment, to Marie's apartment. I'd told my coterie he and I would be back down when the food was ready.

I wanted to be alone with him. I needed to be alone with him.

After the swing of emotions the last couple days had brought, and my inner uncertainty about any kind of future Marcus and I had in store, I just needed him, to be with him in the moment. I needed everything else to wait its turn, to lie on the floor while this beautiful man and I created a heavenly existence elevated on the bed.

"What are you doing?" Marcus asked in a low voice, acting like the innocent man I knew he wasn't.

"We're in a succubus's lair, so I'm seducing you," I quipped playfully as I led all six feet and however many inches of him through Marie's front door and into her bedroom.

Marcus's attention shifted from me to the walls covered in draped tapestries and burned-down candles. "It looks like a sex temple."

I let out a laugh. "That's exactly what I thought when I first came here!" I thought to rephrase that. "When they first brought me in here."

"Is that Lilith?" he asked, pointing to the stone statue of the Goddess standing proud, holding circular objects in each hand.

I nodded. And then, because his eyes belonged on me and not a stone carving or colorful fabrics, I climbed onto the queen-sized, four-poster bed. On my knees at the edge of the bed, I was at eye level with Marcus who was still standing, except of course, his eyes were pointed elsewhere. Never mind. A woman always has her tricks.

I unbuttoned Marie's black silk shirt from my chest one...button... at...a...time until he noticed from the corner of his eye and delicately unfastened the last two buttons himself. The top fell away from my shoulders like liquid. Marcus lowered his mouth until soft kisses quickly covered my shoulders and collarbone. Chills ran through me. His touch did things to me, good things. And I wanted so much more than his lips.

As if he read my mind, his strong hands gripped my waist and pressed upward, cupping the undersides of my breasts. He stepped as close to the bed as possible, until his thighs pushed into the side of the mattress. Everything in me wanted to tear his cotton shirt from his chest, but I wasn't going to stop kissing the tops of his tattooed shoulders to ask if he'd brought another shirt with him.

Logic slowed my thrumming heart. He couldn't have brought a shirt; he'd been run out of town with my coterie by our enemies.

No. I couldn't entertain reality. For just a few stolen minutes, I wished that shit would stay on the floor.

Marcus's lips found mine as his fingers went to work unbuttoning my pants.

And for the next hour, the only reality that mattered lay entangled on the bed, breathing each other in, and wishing to the Goddess herself we could be like this always.

* * *

I wouldn't have led him up to our own private sanctuary if I hadn't thought Marie would approve. Based on Celeste's disapproving expression when Marcus and I finally showed up for breakfast forty-five minutes late, I may have misjudged the situation. Although, I couldn't be sure if Celeste believed Marie would disapprove because I'd bedded an ex-Hunter in her room, or if it was Celeste who disapproved that she and I had now both had sex on the same bed. Either way, not an inch of me regretted it.

Okay, yeah, Celeste's upturned brow when Marcus and I walked to the small dining table, hand-in-hand did give me pause. But only because, for those moments upstairs, it felt like those first times we were together, back before we attacked the Washington Hunter complex, back before I'd introduced him to my coterie and the other Wilds. Back before their disapproval of our relationship became a reality rather than an assumption.

And of course, that thought led to another, how Marcus really was on the outside. My coterie had accepted his help in taking down the Hunter complex and his support of Shawna. But just because they approved of him, did not mean they approved of us. Not to mention, the other Wilds didn't approve of Marcus, not even as a helper, or a giver of intel. So if he'd stood back when he and my coterie had first arrived and shared hugs of absolute relief...stood back from a group of Wilds who actually accepted him...then how much worse would it be for him when we reunited with the other Wilds to complete our mission?

If there was still even a mission to complete.

I hated that my mind wandered to Alek and Marie. Aleksander was a male, but because he wasn't a Hunter, he and his pacifist ways would probably be more welcomed by other Wilds than Marcus. Not that any part of me held any type of feelings for Aleksander. It was just that as I sat beside Marcus and scooped cold eggs onto my plate, I realized where the line had been drawn, and that Marcus was not on our side of that line. Which, in my mind, made absolutely no sense, seeing as he'd put himself on the line more often than Aleksander turned that opportunity down.

I caught Celeste's look of discomfort.

"You worried about Marie?" I asked to clear the air and break the uncomfortable silence brewing between the two of us. If she had something to say she might as well get it out rather than constipate herself holding it all in.

"Why? Should I be?" she retorted.

"You tell me," I responded in what was turning out to be a cat and mouse chase with words. Only, I couldn't be sure who played the role of the cat and who played the mouse.

I took a bite of cold toast, wet with congealed butter.

"Everyone is tired and tense right now," Olivia said with arms outstretched over the table. The other coterie members had no way of knowing the bubbling feud between my sister and me, how she clearly felt my being with Marcus was unfair while her love languished underground. A decision Marie made, I might add.

And so I let them all know. "She chose to go, Celeste. Don't blame me for that. Blame her."

"Marie didn't want to go; she did what was right for her galere, for her sisters." Celeste's eyes bore into mine, tears trapped behind lids. "She parted from me, the person she claimed to have feelings for, for the good of her kind."

Shawna and my aunts stopped to listen. One of them gasped at Celeste's revelation.

"And how does that have *anything* to do with me?" I asked.

Celeste shook her head. "That's what I can't stop going over in my mind, that exact question. Because I think the answer is nothing. It has nothing to do with you because I don't think you could leave the person you have feelings for, for the good of your kind."

I sprang from my seat and Celeste mirrored me.

"Whoa!" Olivia yelled, stretching her arms out, one to each arguing sister. "This has gone too far! Celeste." She turned to my standing, dark-haired sister. "It's okay to be upset that you've finally found this special person, this special bond with someone you can actually have a future with, just to have it ripped away. You can be angry about that. You *should* be angry about that."

"Because *she* won't go into hiding with them!" Celeste yelled, pointing her head toward me.

"Oh my Goddess. I cannot believe you're even considering giving up," I exclaimed, ready to rip into her with my words.

"And Faline," Olivia yelled, now turned to me. "It's okay that you feel betrayed by the succubi galere, who promised to help and now they're turning tail and running. But that's their right, to change their minds about what's best for them is their right."

"To leave the other Wilds in captivity should be okay with me?" I said. "Well, it's not. It just put the rest of us in a more dire situation than we were already in."

"You don't understand what it's like to be a succubus," Celeste added, tears rolling down her cheeks. "They can feel everything, all of it, our fear, our hurt. When we all get together, they have to feel all of our burdens. Now imagine if one of them were caught by a Hunter, imagine how that'd feel for them."

Fire burned in me. "I don't have to imagine it. I got to see it through our sister. Our. Sister. And if your precious succubus could feel our sister's pain, then why didn't they help her with it? If they knew, why didn't they do anything?"

"You have no idea, do you?" Celeste walked around the side of the table, and Olivia moved too, to stay between the two of us. "Shawna's PTSD isn't just a feeling, an emotion. The effects of it are, and Marie wished more than anything she could remove the effects, but the relief would only be temporary and then Shawna would know the pain all over again. Marie was helping by stepping back on that one. And yes, our sister is rescued. Marie's sisters helped make that happen. And now that they've seen those effects, they're not willing to risk that happening to one of them!"

"Stop it!" Shawna screamed from the living room. She balled her fists at her side. "Stop talking about me like I'm mental or not here. I'm here. And I'm not mental!"

Abigale rushed to her daughter's side. Shawna's fists loosened.

"I care for Marcus," Shawna went on. "He's helped me a tremendous amount. More than I'll ever be able to repay." She shot a glance to the man sitting near me and then looked back toward Celeste and me. "So if Faline wants him around, I'm all for it. Because shouldn't I get a say in this? He did help rescue me after all." She paused and exhaled. "And if the succubi are scared and want to hide, I don't blame them. No one should have to go through what I went through. And I wouldn't ask anyone to volunteer to risk making that sacrifice."

"But there are Wilds still going through what you went through," I said on a breath, feeling exhausted and somewhat defeated. My sisters were my life, and to know one of them held contention for me...it hurt.

Only Marcus sat at the table. The rest of us stood, in a silent tense state, waiting for someone to make a move, to spew the next accusation that would set another off.

The front door to the apartment burst open, catching us totally off guard, and each Wild jumped into attack mode.

"I'm a friendly, an incubus!" the young-looking male announced before we could pounce, his hands in the air. I recognized him as the incubus we'd met in the incubi underground, lover of the succubus Heather.

Still, the bark suddenly covering my arm stayed put.

"The succubi," he said, panting. "They never returned. They went to the Hunters and they never returned!"

SIXTEEN

THE INCUBUS smartly kept from crossing the threshold into the apartment. And we smartly waited for him to catch his breath and explain what the hell he was talking about before jumping at him for answers.

When he could finally stand straight and breathe at the same time, he looked to my aunts who'd gathered near one another, as he explained, "Their leader—"

"Marie?" Celeste asked, cutting him off.

He regarded her for a moment and then went back to talking to my aunts. I assumed he figured the hierarchy of a huldra coterie resembled that of an incubi hoard—elders were in charge. He figured wrong.

"Yes, Marie, I believe that's her name." He paused as though Celeste had confused his thoughts and crossed a few wires. When he got back on line, he continued. "Their leader took them all to their check-in, to the Hunter complex."

"Wait," I interrupted, now my turn to confuse the poor guy. "Why they hell would they do that? They had sanctuary underground with you all."

The young incubus's blank eyes met mine. He didn't even try to offer up an explanation.

I re-approached my question in a way that maybe he'd understand and therefore answer. "When were they due back?"

"Due back?" he asked.

Damn, I'd crossed his wires again. I peered at the time on the microwave. "It's almost nine o'clock in the morning. What time was their check-in?" I said.

"Oh." The light of understanding lit his eyes. "It was at seven-thirty. I would have been here sooner, but I went to the rental first, where Aleksander said you'd be."

"Their check-in was only an hour and a half ago?" I double checked. He nodded.

"Okay, then." I turned to ease Celeste's worry. "They haven't been gone long. Maybe their lesson session ran over. Maybe a new rule was enacted that they'd have to learn about."

"Who sent you, exactly?" Celeste asked Mason, who now leaned against the door frame.

"Aleksander," he answered, and maybe it was just me, but I thought I heard reverence in his voice when he uttered his leader's name.

"He wouldn't have sent someone if everything was normal," Celeste said to no one and everyone.

"They're incubi," I reminded her. "They've not had to deal with check-ins a day in their lives. They don't know what's normal and not normal. Wasn't Aleksander just saying that dealing with the Hunters was a necessary difficulty for Wild Women? Clearly he's so far out of the loop that any thoughts or feelings he has on the topic are irrelevant."

"He's also a very powerful incubus," the young man added.

We considered him for a moment, and he seemed to finally realize he was standing before a deadly huldra coterie. He straightened from leaning against the door frame and fidgeted with the hem of his shirt.

"Well," I said in an antagonizing tone. I'd had enough of the incubi coming in, acting like they understood shit that was so out of their realm of existence that they assumed they knew all about it. "I do apologize for our obvious ignorance in the ways of the world, but you still haven't told me why the succubi went to check-in at all. And also, what would give Alek any indication that the women were in trouble?"

Mason's eyes shot to me. "Oh, he doesn't like being called Alek."

"I'll take note of that," I answered, mentally reminding myself to call the incubi leader Alek to his face the first chance I got.

"And," the incubus continued. "We feel energy. I can't sense that there's anything wrong with the succubi, but if Aleksander sent me to fetch you then he must be feeling something."

Celeste grabbed her purse from the couch and slipped her shoes on beside the front door. The incubus took a few steps back when my sister got too close. *Is this out of fear of the unknown or something else,* I wondered.

"He's come to fetch us," Celeste said, repeating the incubus. "I'm going to find out why."

* * *

Five more incubi had been waiting in an alley when we arrived. Marcus refused to allow them to place a covering over his head and lead him into their underground home. I quickly agreed, citing that Aleksander could just as well meet us out in the open rather than having us go through the trouble of coming to him. Celeste bucked my opinion a little, but in the end, the discomfort of our fellow coterie members won out and she sided with her kind.

It took another twenty minutes before Aleksander stood before us, his gaze bouncing from me to Marcus and back again. If he was as powerful as his subordinate believed, he was connecting the dots of Marcus and my relationship. I almost wanted to ask him to let me know what he found once we were done, because when it came to Marcus and me our feelings for each other were so clear they confused me. Maybe for a mermaid and a human that kind of clarity would be illuminating. But for a huldra and a Hunter? Not so much.

When the two men, both over six foot and riddled with muscles, were done peacocking, I started in. "So, Alek, what's this about the succubi going to check-in?"

The sun shone in the sky on this crisp morning, but its light failed to touch us, crammed in between two multi-story brick buildings. Wet remnants of boxes lay between a large trash bin and a moss-covered wall.

Aleksander bristled at my title for him, but he didn't openly object. "You were not in the safe house I had secured for you."

Celeste answered before I strung together enough words to turn down his offer. "We will gather our things and go straight there after this."

I rolled my eyes. Apparently, my coterie had made the decision during breakfast while Marcus and I were upstairs. I didn't blame them for wanting to feel secure, and admittedly, that was the exact point of a safe house. But nothing came without a cost, not even safe houses.

"I feel a shift in Portland and its surrounding areas," Marcus started, answering my earlier question about why he thought the succubi were in trouble. He eyed Marcus again before pretending to relax by leaning against a brick wall void of moss. He folded his arms in front of him and kicked a leather shoe up behind him to wedge onto the wall. "An energy shift. It feels heavier around here."

Seeing as I didn't feel energy any more than anyone else, I had to take him at his word. Still, I wasn't gullible either. "Couldn't that be caused by an incoming natural disaster or something?" I asked, thinking about how I'd read that animals can sense impending disasters and run for the hills before it claims their lives.

He nodded. "It can, Faline. Very insightful for you to suggest. And I'd probably allow you to sway me into believing that's precisely what I'm sensing. Except, I've been walking this earth for longer than his grandmother's been alive." Aleksander motioned to Marcus. "And in that time I've picked up a few...helpful abilities. One of which is being able to tell the difference between a flash flood, an earthquake, and a group of scared women."

Now it was Marcus's turn to bristle. My ex-Hunter, who already stood as tall and straight as possible, jerked his head toward the incubi leader and tilted his chin just enough to pop his neck. I almost laughed. And I probably would have if we weren't talking about the safety of a whole Wild Women group. A group I'd come to befriend and trust. A group whose leader my sister had developed feelings for.

"You know," Aleksander said with all the ease of a clear summer day as he pushed from leaning on the wall and dusted the lapels of his dark gray blazer. "If you joined my...group, your neck problems would be a thing of the past, if you agreed to me changing you."

"What did you just say?" Marcus asked, done placating the cocky incubus.

"Oh, no offense," Aleksander added as an afterthought. "I'm sure you're lovely just the way you are. But, how much more lovely would you be joining me, as a near-immortal? I could use your muscle."

I'd never had to hold Marcus back before. Until now. The man gave me no warning. He didn't shake his head or spew assaults. He took two steps and swung a fist at the incubus.

Aleksander ducked out of the way a millisecond before Marcus's fist grazed the tip of his nose. It took me that long to get between the two of them and sprout branch nubs from the palms of my hands to threaten them both. Act right or get tied up. Those were my conditions. Although admittedly, my close-up view of Marcus's pecs flexed under his thin cotton shirt distracted me enough to keep bark from rising to my skin. So my threats weren't exactly backed up by much. Still, they didn't know that.

Of course, my conditions didn't include them playing nice-nice either. So the two men, much taller than me and certainly more muscular, glared at one another over my head while I stood, separating them.

"I would never willingly place myself in a bloodline of vampiric ancestry," Marcus seethed as though the mention of "vampire" turned his stomach.

"Enough!" Celeste scolded. "Why did Marie go to check-in?"

"And," I added, retracting my branch nubs. "Why the hell are you offering to change Marcus for his muscles if your group is made of pacifists?" Something didn't add up, and my bounty-hunter senses told me that somehow this equation could be connected.

I turned from Marcus to face Aleksander, who quickly backed up after making eye contact with the ex-Hunter behind me. Marcus must have mouthed something. Either that or Aleksander felt Marcus's feelings for me.

"We talked about her going to their check-in, at length, and came to the conclusion that it was in the best interest of her galere to go. Heather agreed to join them if they returned, together, back to the incubi home once they were done," Aleksander explained with a shrug of his shoulders. *So he was concerned enough to have one of his incubi come get us, but not concerned enough to actually act like he cared? Was this an incubi thing or an Aleksander thing?*

Or maybe this was a child of Lilith thing. Marie liked to play games too.

Marie. How would her galere survive the Hunters? They already had the misfortune of absorbing the emotions of humans around them, how much worse were the emotions of Hunters?

"Did you actually tell them to go?" Celeste asked with nothing short of disgust. *She had to have some strong feelings for Marie if she was blaming Marie's bad decision on another person.*

Aleksander regarded Celeste. "I did nothing of the sort, huldra."

Ah, yes, he was definitely related to Marie.

The incubi leader went back to leaning against the brick building behind him. "I simply listened to her concerns and her justifications for going."

"Which were?" I asked.

He gave a long sigh as though we were meddling kids and he was the adult we shouldn't question. *I didn't care how old he was, it tested my patience.* Giving him a fierce look, I made bark spring from the tops of my forearms as a little reminder of who exactly he was speaking to.

He began, "Well, if you must know, she was not quite sure about her galere's decision to hide underground." He paused. "We had a leader-to-leader conversation, which, I'm not absolutely sure she'd appreciate my sharing."

"At this point, seeing as it'd help us rescue her galere, she'd be fine with it," Celeste said dryly.

Aleksander gave a nod and continued. "She believed they were making this choice out of fear, which she deemed an unwise foundation for a decision. She felt that if they went to check-in, it would give her galere one more month to be absolutely sure this is what they wanted. She hoped time would ease their fear and help them to think more clearly."

"It makes sense," I added, thinking out loud.

"Which is precisely why I refrained from dissuading her," Aleksander answered. "She also thought that if they experienced what hiding underground would be like, they may change their minds. She wanted to give them the freedom to do that—change their minds."

"But the Hunters are on high alert since the destruction of the Washington complex," Celeste said, putting the pieces of her lover's decision together like a heart-wrenching puzzle. "And she knows Oregon Hunters attacked us at the winery, probably thinking we were succubi. Why would she knowingly walk into that situation?"

Celeste had a good point. If Marie would have just stuck to our plan—if she hadn't asked me to derail my plans to come convince her sister to come back from the incubi—we'd all be heading to the east coast by the time the Hunters figured out the succubi weren't showing up for check-in. She wouldn't have had to deal with any of this.

"She did mention that," Aleksander said, with a slight brow lift.

"Then why didn't you stop her?" Celeste asked.

"Because she'd assured me that they knew what they were doing when it came to the Hunters. If the Hunters tried anything, they'd manipulate the energy. When they work together, they're incredibly strong. She led me to believe that if worse came to worse, her galere could take down that complex on their own." Aleksander pushed away from the brick wall. The four incubi who had been waiting at a distance in the alley walked over to flank him.

It occurred to me that they hadn't joined him when he and Marcus were toe-to-toe. How powerful was this incubi leader?

"Besides," he added as an afterthought. "How bad can the Hunters be?" He waved an arm at Marcus. "This one doesn't seem so vicious."

Probably not the best comment to make. Not to a Hunter, but most certainly not to a Wild Woman. I closed my eyes for a quick moment to steady my emotions and took a deep breath. To make sure the man beside me didn't do the opposite, I wove my fingers with his to hold his hand.

Also, how did he know Marcus was a Hunter?

"All right, then," Aleksander said as he walked away from our group with his men. "I think I've told you as much as you need to know."

He made it halfway out of the alley before I spoke up. "Wait."

He turned on the heel of his leather shoes and cocked his head. "Yes?"

"Did you feel any emotions from Marie before she left? You told us what she said and thought, but not how she felt."

A smile drew the corners of his lips upward. "Very astute. I knew there was a reason I liked you the most."

I squeezed Marcus's hand tighter. He squeezed back.

"She felt unsure, not fear, nothing so basic as fear," Aleksander said. "Most emotions are difficult to explain to those who can't feel them like we can, you see, so this is an impossible question to answer thoroughly. But, if I had to give her emotions labels, I'd say unsure with bits of hesitancy sprinkled throughout, covered in ambition parading as courage."

He began to turn to leave, but I stopped him with another question. "Why did you offer to turn Marcus if you knew he's a Hunter?"

"For no reason other than that it'd make both our lives easier." And with that, the incubi leader in his casual suit walked out of the damp alley and took a hard left, joined by his men.

"What was that supposed to mean?" Marcus whispered.

"I have no idea," I said, thankful Marcus hadn't been changed into an incubus.

As an incubus he'd know I was lying.

SEVENTEEN

THE WALK back to the empty succubi apartments was a silent one, void of words yet full of tension. We knew to be careful when approaching the apartment building; the Hunters could be there waiting for us. But we had to gather our things before high-tailing it to the safe house. Plus, whether or not the Hunters were at the apartment would tell us just how much information they'd already gotten out of the succubi, if they'd questioned them enough to know the Washington huldra coterie roamed their territory. Once we got that bit of information out of the way, we'd know better how to move forward.

Despite our being blocks from the apartments and unable to be heard or spotted by a Hunter waiting to attack us within the building, my coterie remained silent. I couldn't decide if my sisters and aunts kept quiet because of the humans passing by on the sidewalk, or if it had more to do with a lack of answers.

We spread out to approach the three-story succubi apartment building from different directions, slinking around edges of the brick buildings behind and next door to it, crouching behind the tires of a car with Oregon plates parked across the street from it. We waited, unseen from one another, as my coterie took turns giving the all-clear through whistles too quiet for Marcus to hear. He crouched beside the car's back wheel as I took the front.

"Okay," I whispered to him. "That's six whistles."

We stood and crossed the street to make our way to the stoop. "I don't smell anything different from when we left. Can't hear any movement inside either. Is there a way you can sense them?" I asked, figuring it wouldn't hurt to ask.

A smirk nearly smoothed his brow, furrowed in concentration. "No, I can't sense them," he said in an amused voice.

We paused after stepping onto the sidewalk directly in front of the apartment building. I wished we'd thought to bring an incubus, to know if he felt any male energy inside the building. But all things considered, with the lack of movement and sound, I was fairly certain we were alone on the property. I puckered my lips and gave a nearly silent whistle.

My sisters and aunts answered my whistle by joining us on the stoop so we could walk in together. Marcus entered the building first and I followed close behind to secure the first-floor apartments. Olivia and Celeste jogged upstairs to check the second level while Renee and Patricia checked the third. Once we gave the all-clear in our temporary housing and shut the main entry door, I realized the true answer behind my coterie's lack of conversation since we'd left Aleksander. The absence of hope had a way of sealing mouths shut and causing hearts to stammer.

Marcus broke the wordless silence suggesting the end point we all knew needed accomplishing. Except, none of us knew how to actually accomplish it.

"They're trapped and we need to get them out. The sooner the better." His words faded into nothingness when my coterie sat on the couch and chairs as though the weight of the world became too heavy for their knees to bear. "I know for a fact that they won't be coming home without our help," he urged, standing and trying to rally the troops.

When we didn't respond, he paced the living room, still talking, trying to express his urgency to a group of defeated Wilds. "The ambush we experienced at the winery was the Hunter's first retaliation attack. I know their methods. They start out small, quiet and private, and then grow. They took Wild Women from their groups. Then they attacked the mermaid's island where only mermaids would know of the occurrence. The winery was another step up—their way of taking a slightly bigger risk, of feeling things out as they plan their next, bigger blow."

His thoughts about the winery attack got Shawna's attention. She'd been pretty quiet since returning from home, after fleeing from the Hunters' surprise attack. Reserved. "You forgot their most recent attack on our house," she uttered.

"Exactly my point," he answered, pointing to my partner sister, probably glad to finally get a little interaction from us. "It's a tactic. They make small advances to feel out their foes. It's smart really. And proves the different complexes are working together." He paused, in thought. "It's almost like a dance, actually. They take a step forward, partly to gauge the reaction they'll get, and partly to take a small step back and see if there's retaliation. The whole time, while their dance partner just thinks they're doing the waltz, the Hunter leaders are studying their partner so they can know beyond a shadow of a doubt that they'll have the upper hand in their last dance, their last stand in achieving their end goal. They're studying the reactions of you all, of the Wild Women, on different turfs. How will you react in public? They tried that at the winery. How will you react in private, when you're caught off guard? Those were the island and home invasions. Now they've captured the second largest known Wild Women group, for a new level of testing their responses."

"Stop," Celeste demanded. "I can already imagine what they're doing to her. I don't need you to set that picture into stone for me."

Shawna reached over to place a hand on Celeste's thigh.

"The largest Wild group is the mermaids," Renee offered. "If we can enlist them, we may have a chance at getting the succubi galere back."

Olivia turned to answer my aunt. "I've been trying to get ahold of them. Last I heard, they were leaving their island, but that's it. It's like they trashed their phones and dropped off the face of the earth."

"Then they've abandoned us," Renee said. "Probably something to do with their alliance to the Hunters." My aunt, ever the conspiracy theorist.

"I don't think so," I answered. "The rusalki said we could trust the mermaid shoal, for the most part. Only a select few were working with the Hunters. It wasn't a shoal-wide thing. I don't think their whole shoal would get behind them on that. Especially after the Hunters ran them off their island, away from their home."

"The rusalki," Shawna uttered, staring at her hand on Celeste's thigh, clearly lost in thought. I just hoped this talk wasn't triggering her PTSD. "The rusalki can help us. They may be one of the smaller Wild Women groups, but they are the most powerful by far."

"What makes you say that?" Olivia asked from a chair at the dining table.

Shawna finally looked up. Her dreads fell to the side of her face. She looked ashen. "In the Hunter's house..." She paused and took a few breaths. Celeste wrapped a comforting arm around Shawna's shoulder. "In the Hunter's house, the rusalka whispered things into my mind. I felt so untethered to reality, like I was floating through air, outside of my body. But she met me there, spoke to guide me back to my body. She said energy is everywhere, but the energy of water held a higher vibration than air, so to imagine I was floating in water and to swim back to my body. When I opened my eyes, she wasn't in the room. And then all of a sudden, she was there. It's as though they can transcend time and space."

Her assessment of the rusalki abilities reminded me of Azalea, the rusalka who'd pulled me from my huldra rage before I tried to kill Marcus. My heart tightened in my chest at the memory. Seeing my partner sister drugged and unresponsive, and the fact that at any time I could go into a huldra rage and attack the man I was falling for, twisted me in unfathomable ways. The reality of that truth did not escape me. Azalea had been killed in the battle, by the Hunter's woman no less. The woman who Marcus had urged me to leave behind rather than try to arrest and take in for a hefty bounty as the skip who'd been the alleged leader of Seattle's most notorious human-trafficking ring. Azalea didn't deserve such a death. It made me sick just remembering how everything went down.

My head jolted up and my wide eyes found Shawna. "You're absolutely right," I told my partner sister. "The rusalki are our only hope."

"We haven't been able to get a hold of them either," Olivia said dryly, shaking her head in yet another round of defeat. "They've never had phones, but they'd told us they'd be in contact. They're not."

My gaze didn't find Olivia at the table. I stared at Shawna on the couch. "They're busy mourning their sister, Azalea," I said. "And I know where they're doing it."

EIGHTEEN

We threw our suitcases into the bed of Marcus's dark blue truck and crammed into the extended cab. Thankfully, each time he'd parked his truck at our home in Washington, he'd pulled it into the woods behind the common house, so it wouldn't be visible from the driveway. So when the Hunters made a surprise house call, and he and my coterie ran through the back door of the common house and into the forest, they made it to his truck in time and went off-roading through our property to the nearest highway heading south.

We pulled up to the address on the folded piece of paper and gazed at the yellow split-level located in a bedroom community outside of Portland while the truck idled in the driveway. Celeste exited the vehicle first and the rest of us followed. Shawna let her dog, Sepa, down to excitedly sniff the edges of the front yard before locating the perfect spot of grass to relieve herself.

"I'll unlock the door," I announced, making my way up the flower-pot lined cement steps to the yellow front door. I pressed the series of numbers into the keypad of the lockbox hanging from the doorknob, based on what Aleksander had written beneath the house's address. His handwriting reminded me of the fancy ink calligraphy of historical manuscripts.

Marcus looked over my shoulder at the incubus's writing and groaned. "I still don't like accepting his help. I mean, I get it, but I don't like it."

"We'll pay him back when this is over," I assured him. "Every penny."

I opened the door and we stepped in. The house appeared to be a sewer's retreat. Brochures announcing Portland's bi-annual quilting show sat fanned out on the entry counter. Ornate quilts hung on the walls and spread over the tops of beds, of which there were many. Five bedrooms to be exact—three on the top floor and two on the bottom, most filled with two twin beds. Marcus and I called the only room with a queen bed, and those of us who had suitcases, left them in our claimed rooms.

After Shawna set up a mecca of comfort, complete with full water and food bowls and a floor covered in pee pads for Sepa, we locked up the yellow rental. We were met in the driveway by an Uber that Celeste had asked Aleksander to order with his credit card, and got back onto the road for what we hoped would be a turn-around trip.

* * *

The ten-hour flight from Oregon's Portland International Airport to Maine's Bangor International Airport took forever. We finally had a possible plan, one that may just work, but a long-ass plane ride stood between planning and action. It was a hurry up and wait situation. Watching the reactions of my coterie to their first ever airport and airplane experience had kept me slightly entertained in the beginning. But after ten hours of the same thing, nothing is entertaining. Not even my aunt Renee's suggestion to go home to dig up our weapons and bring them with us, just in case, cracked a smile on my face. Although, my response made Marcus laugh.

"No, Renee, it would have been a waste of time anyways," I'd answered her insistent idea as we waited to board the plane. "They don't let you bring weapons, or anything that can be used as a weapon, past those metal detectors we went through. Trust me, I've tried." I'd left out the fact that we were nowhere near our home to begin with.

Marcus scoffed. "You tried to bring your dagger onto the plane?"

I'd rolled my eyes at him. "Of course I didn't get that far." I muttered the last part, "Gabrielle wouldn't let me."

Marcus slapped his knee and laughed. "God, I would have loved to have seen that conversation."

I replayed the discussion with Gabrielle before my first time flying. My stomach twisted. She may have been cavorting with the Hunters, but I still held onto the notion that she'd had a good reason, that she wouldn't have sold us out in the end. Maybe it was wishful thinking. I liked the mermaid, and I thought she'd liked me too. Gabrielle had been my first Wild friend outside of my own kind. In my mind, there was something to be said for that.

The plane's descent into Bangor, Maine brought back more memories. Being back on the ground helped, and it didn't. The drive to the rusalki's forest, the one where Gabrielle and I walked only weeks earlier, gave me a nostalgia more painful than pleasing. This time, though, I had Shawna. This time I wasn't fearing for her safety, worrying we wouldn't get answers, wouldn't get help in time. I grabbed my partner sister's hand and squeezed it tight, thankful to have her by my side.

Celeste, though, she felt all those things. I saw it written along her scrunched brows and in her hurried steps. In the way she scanned the forest with the intensity of a starving wolf on the hunt, her head snapping one way and then the next, her gaze swinging from tree to tree. She was starving, all right, for answers to help reunite her with Marie. And the more time I spent with Celeste in this hurried and worried mode, the more I realized Marie was not going to be a temporary fixture in my coterie's life.

"These trees look familiar," I said, pausing to examine an evergreen that seemed to have separated early on and grown two trunks from one. "I remember this one. Their home isn't far."

We'd caught an afternoon flight, headed to the Portland International Airport shortly after leaving the incubi and gathering a few things from the succubi's apartment complex. The last-minute tickets weren't cheap, but we'd managed by dipping into our emergency cash savings we had tucked away. We'd arrived in Maine in the early morning hours, shortly after midnight and headed straight to the rusalki.

Abigale caught up to Shawna and me, and wrapped her arm around her daughter's shoulder. Shawna slowed her pace to match her mother's until they hung back behind the rest of us, trudging through the dark forest.

Marcus reached to hold my hand, but then pulled away right as I reached back. I narrowed my gaze at him. "What? What's wrong?" I asked.

He shook his head. "I forgot you might need your hands, branches and all."

I accepted his excuse with a nod, but his monotone voice gave me the impression his answer held a deeper layer.

"You doing okay?" I asked. "Being so close to so many Wilds? In the car, on a plane, tromping through the Maine forest around Moosehead Lake?"

He didn't look at me to respond, only kept in-step with me and looked ahead. "I wish you'd stop asking me that."

"What?" I snapped back with a harsh whisper, knowing full well my coterie could hear everything we said. Still, whispering gave me the false sense that our private conversation was just that—private. "Asking if you're okay? I'm sorry that I care."

"Is that why you're asking?" he shot back in a low voice. "Or is it that you're painfully aware that I'm a Hunter and you can't help but remind me of that fact?"

I almost stopped mid-step, but Celeste wouldn't have it, so I kept stepping over ferns, dripping from an earlier rain, and weaving past tangled bushes.

"The fact that you're a Hunter and I'm a Wild Woman isn't my fault," I answered, no longer whispering. Screw it. It's not like my coterie weren't already privy to our heated conversation. "It's a blaring fact of life that we can't pretend out of existence."

"Tell me how you really feel, Faline," Marcus said, shaking his head and looking away.

"What?" I asked, exasperated. What the hell was his problem?

"Is that it?" Celeste exclaimed, running out from behind me, pointing to a pile of dirt and sticks in the distance. "Is that their home?"

"Yes!" I yelled with more enthusiasm than I felt, but happy to change the subject. "They could have moved, but this is where they were last time I visited."

We jogged to catch up to Celeste and stopped short of stepping onto the square shape of stones that made up their "porch." After the stones stood a door made of sticks tied tightly together, covering a hole leading down into the mound, into their den. And I knew from my last visit that in their den sat shelves made from sticks, and chairs and a table made from tree stumps, with moss for carpet. I had no intention of entering their home during this visit, though. One night spent underground had been enough for this huldra.

I looked up to scan the tops of the trees around the rusalki den. They should have made their presence known by now, called out to us, stretched invisible fingers into our minds to see what we were up to, and maybe told a parable or two. That is, if they were here. And from what Shawna had mentioned about them helping her upstairs in the Hunter's cabin, as though they were all in water...and how they'd mentioned the higher energy frequency of water...I figured we wouldn't find them in their home or hiding in trees.

I pivoted and ran toward the lake. The same lake Gabrielle complained about having to wade through in search of the rusalki last time we were here.

My coterie and Marcus stopped at the lake's edge less than a minute after the steel toes of my boots barely touched the water. I didn't need my boots anymore, my vines were more helpful if given free rein to grow, but old habits die hard.

It's as though my accomplices knew not to speak, knew, in the same strange way I now understood, we were encroaching on something sacred.

It didn't take long before the tops of three heads broke the surface of the murky lake, followed by the faces of what was left of the rusalki coven. They stared at us, blankly. I waited to feel them rummaging around my mind, but felt nothing. I shot a look to Shawna and she only shrugged. Apparently, they weren't sorting through her mind either.

"I am sorry to interrupt you," I said cautiously.

"The water takes what she has given, but she also grieves her loss when her creation is removed from her realm," Drosera, one of the rusalki said on an even tone.

"We know you're mourning your sister, and we wouldn't have come if it wasn't an emergency," I continued.

The three rusalki didn't so much as blink.

"You can read my thoughts if it'll help," I offered. Never in a million years did I think I'd request rusalki enter my mind, and now I hoped they would. Mostly because they'd get way more information than by mere words alone. And also there was a part of me that felt unnerved by their morose stillness, their lack of desire, the blankness in their eyes that I'd seen all too many times while interviewing families of murder victims in my hunt for skips. The look of vacancy.

"I haven't the energy," Drosera answered in what was probably the most direct statement I'd heard from a rusalka.

My thoughts stuttered over how that was even possible.

"We need your help in saving the succubi," Celeste blurted, nearing the murky water with hurried steps. The rusalki didn't recoil, or move at all. "They attended check-in and the Hunters detained them all! Probably over suspicion with what happened at the Washington Hunter complex. They're in danger!"

Without so much as a head-turn or a muttering of sounds, the rusalki lowered back into the water in much the same way they'd emerged, the tops of their heads being the last of them we saw and soon even that disappeared seamlessly, not even causing more than a wrinkle in the top of the lake.

"No, they can't just ignore us," Celeste seethed, walking deeper into the water as though set on going after them.

Lake water gathered around Celeste's ankles, soaking her slip-on shoes and the bottom of her fitted jeans. She took another two steps and it reached her knees. "Celeste," I called to her. "You can't go in there. They're mourning their sister. The space, they may see it as sacred."

I doubted they'd do to my sister what they'd done to Gabrielle, but I refused to take that chance. Celeste hadn't seen what I'd seen. She didn't know how quickly they strike and how deadly the snip of their birch scissors could be. Her bravery in confronting the rusalki was partly based on ignorance of their abilities.

A thought bloomed in my mind. I'd figured out that the Hunters had been keeping us ignorant of other Wilds, teaching us incorrect history of our kind as well as the others'. But had they also kept us ignorant for another reason? Fearing other Wilds kept us from joining together for so long. But not knowing the abilities of other Wilds gave the Hunters another advantage. If the Wild Women were to ever war again, we'd be at a disadvantage in not knowing how to protect ourselves, how to counter the attacks and abilities of other Wilds. Hunters lower in their hierarchy probably only knew the truth about the Wild Women in their state, the women they were trained to police. John had specifically stated as much when I'd asked him for help in finding Shawna. But the higher-up Hunters probably knew about each kind of Wild Woman, her weaknesses and her strengths.

Celeste's response pulled me from my plotting. "But they just left us, without answering." She didn't step deeper into the water, but she also didn't leave it for land.

Damn. Love could really fuck with the mind—my love for Celeste and her love for Marie. It had to be love she held for the succubus because why else would I be forced to trudge into the murky lake to retrieve her? I pulled my boots and socks off in a hurry that grew with each thud of my heart. I'd seen the rusalki's response to Gabrielle and me entering their territory of forest. How much worse would they respond to Celeste entering their mourning space? No, I wasn't completely sure that's what they were doing, but I'd made an informed guess and that was enough to freak out about.

"What are you doing?" Shawna asked me.

I didn't turn to answer, only flung my socks to the side and headed into the water a little more than irritated that Celeste had forced my hand. "I'm retrieving our sister who is refusing to come back to land," I grumbled.

I didn't need to see Marcus to know he too readied himself to come in after me. I didn't turn toward the shore as I added, "Don't follow me in. Especially you, Marcus."

Celeste's brow furrowed, first in indignation, and then in concern as her eyes widened. Her torso leaned forward as though she were trying to take a step toward me, but didn't. "I can't...I can't move," she exclaimed.

"Shit," I yelled as I ran to her.

Others in my coterie began moving toward the water and I flung my hand up to stop them. "If one of us can't get her out, all of us won't be able to do it," I reminded, trying to keep my voice and breath steady. Causing my sisters and aunts to fear wouldn't help anything. It'd only distract them and right now they needed to stay alert.

Celeste struggled to move and fell forward, soaking her whole body. I grabbed her arms and hoisted her to stand. She pushed her body to move forward again, disregarding my advice to remain calm. As though whatever chains had held her in place broke in an instant, she fell forward with force and her feet sprang from the water as her chest broke through the surface.

I reached to pull her up and run her to the shore, but my feet now refused to budge. "What the hell?" I yelled.

Celeste pulled herself from the lake, sopping wet, and sprang to grab me.

As though my legs were being pulled out from under me, becoming liquid in the process, my body slipped under water, toward the center of the lake. My coterie and Marcus ran for me, and before my face followed my body below the surface I exhaled sharply, "Don't follow me!"

NINETEEN

I FOUGHT THE PULL, thrashing my arms and legs to make it back to the surface; the surface that grew farther and farther from my line of sight with each second. Cold fingers pressed into my right ankle, pulling me deeper. I kicked to loosen the fingers, but to no avail. I peered down, set on prying the fingers from me, when I stared directly into the glowing eyes of Drosera. Like seaweed, her hair floated around her, bouncing on the waves my movement caused. Nothing short of pure moonlight glowed from her skin and stars from her eyes.

Her otherworldly appearance stunned me into stillness. I watched, awestruck, as she turned her eyes away from me toward where she took us, her glowing fingers still gripped to my ankle. The fact that I could still breathe occurred to me, as though air circulated around my face.

Drosera picked up her pace and rapidly pulled me deeper, straight down now, as I lifted my hand to my face and found what felt like a pliable bubble beginning at my forehead and extending to my chin. What looked like the light of hundreds of yellow, flickering candles glowed beneath a dome below us. I watched in stunned stillness as Drosera maneuvered me through her grasp on my ankle, toward the dome where her sisters waited.

As we neared the dome—its exterior a glowing blue layer of light—its dry contents became clear. The body of their fallen sister, Azalea, lay atop leaves and cut fern branches. Wild flowers created a circle on the ground around her and a crown made of vines and twigs sat atop her head. Flat stones rested over her closed eyes. No fires blazed as I'd thought I'd seen, no candles either. The rusalki lit the bubble with their glowing skin. Only one rusalka, the one laying in the center on the leaves, failed to add any brightness. The pale skin of what was once Azalea reminded me of how ashen and unnatural Gabrielle's skin had appeared after she'd met the birch scissors. So lifeless.

Drosera pulled me through the exterior of the bubble, my exposed skin feeling the lack of moving water the moment it entered the dome. Once my face entered the dryness, the bubble enabling me to breathe burst and I fell toward the ground.

I landed in Drosera's arms as she cradled me for a quick moment before setting me onto my feet. I tripped forward and then back, before gaining my footing.

The questions that should have been running through my mind gained no traction past my repeating thoughts at the sight of Azalea. "I'm so sorry," I whispered.

At the Washington Hunter's cabin, when Azalea had been killed by the Hunter's daughter, Clarisse, her body had disappeared. Now, seeing the reality of her fate brought a heavy pit to my stomach. My throat threatened to close in on itself. "I'm sorry," I repeated, this time to Azalea more than to her sisters. Tears filled my eyes. In rescuing my sister, theirs lost her life. "You didn't deserve this; this shouldn't have happened to you."

"It was a fate I chose freely," Azalea reminded.

I jolted and peered in the direction of the voice. An iridescent version of Azalea, naked, peered back at me. Her lips tilted in a smile. I could barely see the crinkles of skin around her bright eyes. She wasn't see-through, but wasn't covered in flesh either. A glowing violet hue pulsed from her being.

I rushed to hug her. Rather than the feeling of matter pressed against me, tingles vibrated my skin wherever she touched in her returned embrace.

"Are you a ghost?" I asked after pulling away to get another look at her.

"We are all souls," she answered. "Some more hidden than others."

"The huldra coterie and the Hunter have come for assistance in helping the succubi," Drosera told her sister's soul, who smiled lovingly at us all.

Azalea nodded.

"The timing is difficult for us," another rusalka said, Veronia. "The energy of grief is a healing balm to the mind, if used correctly, however it leaves little energy behind for other tasks."

"Such as the one you wish us to complete," Drosera added.

Despite me learning this from the rusalki, this made perfect sense to me.

Tears filled my eyes again. My partner sister stood, whole, living, on land; their sister could not. "Azalea," I said after clearing my throat. "You've given your life for my sister. What can I give to help your sisters?"

Azalea glowed a little brighter. "I am always with my sisters, unseen by others of the outside world. And my soul energy is pure and so very strong. But it is not the energy they lack."

"The succubi are imprisoned," I reminded. "They're the only ones who can help with energy."

I turned to gaze at her lifeless body in the center of the dome, but Azalea's soul placed a violet glowing hand on my arm and gained my attention. Warmth and tingles penetrated my skin and bones. Once she had my full attention, she spoke. "In my more realized connection with our Goddess, Mokosh, my sisters have been forced to lessen their own, due to grief." Her gaze bore into my eyes and my heartbeat quickened. "Bridge that gap."

"Anything," I muttered, transfixed on the depths of everything and yet nothing within her glowing eyes.

She gave a nod and her living sisters stood around me in a circle. At once, all three sets of hands pressed onto my head. My heart skipped a beat and then beat wildly, my pulse thrumming in my ear. My huldra arched and stretched within me, causing an ache to push out from my center, followed by an unnerving strength that pulsed from my center, to my skin and back again, over and over. This pulsating picked up pace until it pinged around my body so violently that it had nowhere to go but out.

I gasped as vines shot from my fingers and roots burst from the soles of my feet and buried themselves deep into the lake bed beneath us. The rusalki began whispering and before I could register their words, my roots traveled through the dirt desperately in search of others of similar kind. One root separated from the rest and latched onto the root of a lake plant; the rest pushed further until they found tree roots and fern roots to tie around.

The deep sigh of what I instinctively knew was a tree reverberated through my roots and into my body. The flash of a battle scene played behind my eyes, of powerful huldra warriors protecting their forests from those who sought to steal its trees to build fires with which to burn human women. Another scene flashed—an aged huldra, wrinkles worn as badges of wisdom from a life fully lived, white hair framing her face like the veil of a high priestess. The old huldra changed her skin to bark and seemed to sink into the oak tree before she disappeared within its bark. Another flash and a black snake coiled up a different tree, wrapping around its trunk in what I oddly sensed was an embrace.

Suddenly my roots released their hold and retreated back into my feet. The vines wrapped around my fingers and wrists and arms receded as well. With a snap they each reentered their exit point and rusalki hands pulled back from my head. I let out a gasp and opened my eyes.

I blinked. "Who was the old woman?" I asked Azalea while catching my breath. "The old huldra? I've never seen a huldra so old. Our lifespans aren't that long."

Azalea only smiled.

"Revelations show themselves when the time is right," Drosera answered. "We are ready to help the succubi."

The rusalki walked toward the blue dome keeping the water out. "Wait," I called to them. "What just happened?"

Veronia held my hand and I walked beside her. Before we hit the dome wall she answered, "You connected to your plant friends who willingly gifted you with the energy of our great mother, of Mokosh, for they live deep within her womb and carry her strength. We extracted such energy from you, and now our bond with Mokosh is reinforced, our abilities partly returned."

So I'd connected with my roots, literally. The revelation was humbling. If only I knew exactly what they'd shown me. Within the vision lay answers to questions I'd never thought to ask. If I could only figure out what they were, I had a feeling it would change everything.

TWENTY

As soon as I came up from the lake floor and walked onto the shore, all of my sisters spouted questions at me. I brushed off their queries when I noticed a lack of Marcus on the shore and realized he'd jumped in after me and had been searching the lake the whole time I was under. Amazingly, I hadn't even noticed while I was down there. Not amazingly, he could have gotten himself killed. I doubted the rusalki's birch scissors only worked on land.

When the ex-Hunter finally surfaced and spotted me, he swam hard and then ran once his feet hit land. He wrapped me in his arms and picked me up, into the air, raining kisses onto the top of my head. I allowed it for a minute, but then pulled away to scold him for interfering in Wild business, which the moment the words left my lips I realized my mistake in speaking them. I didn't get to decide when Marcus was invited to involve himself in helping us and when he must stand by—when Marcus could show concern for my wellbeing and when he couldn't. As if I needed more proof to my screw-up of acting like I had a right to dictate his feelings, his expression revealed a flash of anger, dissipating his concern, and then nothing, as though a switch had been flipped to turn his emotions off altogether.

* * *

After flying back to Portland, the incubus Aleksander had met us at
the arrivals sidewalk of the airport in a shiny new black Escalade. The
late afternoon sun hid behind thick layers of clouds. We had no
luggage to throw into the back, only one small bag for all of us, so we
piled in and set off for the yellow rental house.

"How was your trip?" Heather's incubus asked politely. Aleksander
had sent the same young incubus he'd sent yesterday...or was it the day
before...to let us know the succubi had been captured. The whirlwind
trip messed up my sense of time and date.

"Any new news on the succubi galere?" Celeste asked, ignoring
politeness and getting straight to the point. She sat in the front
passenger seat, so the incubus had no chance of ignoring her.

"No, nothing," the man said, solemnly.

"Thank you," Celeste paused. "I'm sorry, I forgot your name."

"I'm sorry I don't have better news to report," he replied, turning
to share a weary smile. "It's Mason, like the jar." Mason continued,
"We've been keeping an eye on their apartment while ya'll have been
gone. Nothing new to report there either. Everything's been quiet."

"Too quiet," Marcus commented, in thought.

Mason caught Marcus's gaze in the rearview mirror. Unlike his
disdain for Aleksander, Marcus didn't seem to hate this incubus. He'd
stopped shutting me out too, somewhere over the Midwest. My
sincere apology whispered into his ear during take-off had a little
something to do with it.

"You think the Hunters are planning something else?" I asked the
large, dark-haired ex-Hunter sitting beside me, his hand on my thigh. I
made a mental note to be more careful with his feelings. The
patriarchal culture of the Hunters didn't only demonize us Wilds, it
also implied the big, strong males were made of logic and brute,
leaving no room for actual emotions. While neither of us were human,
the roles we were both placed in by the Hunters dehumanized us,
stripped us from acknowledging what lived beneath the surface of one
another. Marcus had proven his ability to see past my huldra exterior

and into me. I needed to remember to do the same, to look past the warrior and into his heart.

Marcus didn't pull his gaze from Mason, but rubbed my thigh as he answered, "I do think the Hunters are planning something else."

"So Mason," he called to our driver who currently negotiated the streets of Portland. "How long have you been an incubus?"

Mason shot a gaze back to the rearview mirror and narrowed his eyes for half a second. "Only forty-five years, Marcus," he answered robotically.

I watched the two men, their tight expressions. Marcus crossed his arms over his wide chest. Definitely the larger of the two males.

Minutes later, Mason continued, his tone more conversational, like before. "Why do you ask?"

"Oh, I don't know," Marcus answered, uncrossing his arms and putting his left hand back on my thigh.

In that moment, I would have given anything to read his thoughts.

But then Marcus opened his mouth again, and becoming a mind-reader was no longer necessary. "I'm interested in the process of becoming an incubus."

I shot him a questioning glare. Mason noticed it too, from his rearview mirror, probably even felt my energy shift from curious to what-the-fuck-are-you-thinking. Marcus glanced at me with a placating smile and returned his attention to the incubus.

What the hell was going on with everyone? Celeste was clearly falling in love with a succubus and now Marcus wanted to be an incubus/Hunter hybrid? I rubbed my temples and looked around the car. My coterie members were too exhausted and weary to take part in the males' conversation or even to know how out of place it was.

Mason gave a nod, his attention set on the road. "It is a topic I don't mind discussing, but not in the presence of females."

"Why?" I asked, my irritation rising. "Because we're too simple-minded or because we're easily grossed out?"

The incubus raised an eyebrow in confusion. "Neither," he said after his bout of confusion passed and he realized I was being sarcastic. "Because females cannot, in any circumstance, become incubi. So it stands to reason that if you cannot join us, then you are more plausible to try to beat us. Sharing the process of changing would be essentially giving you detailed information as to the best time to attack our kind." He looked at me from the rearview mirror and looked back at the road. "I am no fool, Faline."

I didn't like that his answer made complete sense. It occurred to me that Marcus may have been planning on telling me the information once he received it. Yeah, I needed a nap. That took way too long for me to figure out. Feeling stupid, I nuzzled closer to Marcus and rested my head against his bicep.

* * *

We arrived at the split-level rental too soon for me to relax enough to fall asleep on Marcus. By the time we all eased from the Escalade in search of a comfortable place to sleep, I wanted nothing more than to feel Marcus's body beside mine as I drifted off to dream land. But when Celeste jumped from her seat and headed into the house, Marcus gave me a tight squeeze and planted his lips on mine.

He pulled away from my embrace leaving me more than a little confused. "I need the extra key to the house. I'm going to go with him. I've got my new cell on me if you need anything." He hopped into the front passenger seat.

"Wait, why now?" I asked, too confused for the amount of exhaustion that lured my mind to a place of rest and not a place of puzzle solving.

Marcus gave a reassuring smile that failed to reassure me. "I've just got a few questions I want answered. Don't worry, I'll be okay."

I watched the black Escalade drive away as my stomach tightened into a heavy lump of anxiety. I didn't know how many more times I had it in me to stand there while someone I cared about disappeared from my protective grasp, from my sight. More often than not lately, saying goodbye for now meant possibly saying goodbye forever. And if I were a betting woman, I'd wager my bad luck was about to get a whole lot worse.

TWENTY-ONE

THE ANTICLIMACTIC HOMECOMING to our temporary abode involved seven huldra shuffling down the halls and some down the stairs, in search of their claimed beds. My partner sister followed me to my queen-sized bed. Shawna tossed and turned, trying to get comfortable on the mattress we shared, and only settled once she reached a hand to rest on my arm.

She was definitely improving, but her need to touch someone in order to fall asleep, especially when she was so drained, concerned me. As I dozed off, I thought about Marie's explanation of Shawna's post-traumatic stress disorder and how the succubi can't heal my sister, only make her feel better in the moment. I wondered if the incubi had the same limitations.

* * *

"Faline," the male's voice called, interrupting me from my rest, pulling me from blissful sleep. I considered rolling over and ignoring whatever the voice wanted. But then I remembered where I was and whose voice it was that spoke to me.

I peeked one eye open to focus on Marcus's square jaw and

smiling lips. He ran the back of his knuckles along my temple. I closed my eyes at the sensation, and thanked Freyja for returning him to me, for not letting yesterday be the last day I got to hold him.

"I'm back from visiting Aleksander and I think we should talk," Marcus whispered. A new layer of realization struck me like a frigid wind and I opened the other eye.

Shawna, still touching my arm, twitched, but didn't wake. I slowly moved her hand from my arm and slithered out of bed. Marcus and I crept from the room and out to the back deck.

Once the sliding glass door closed behind us, I gave him a once-over. "You're not an incubus now, are you?" I asked, unsure how I'd be able to tell if he'd changed.

He gave a deep chuckle. "No," he said, placing his hands gently on my shoulders and kissing my forehead. "I am not."

"Good." I tilted my face up to get a kiss on the lips.

We sat across from each other on the wrought iron patio chairs and leaned our arms on the matching table. The peaceful quiet of darkness covered the backyard as a fall breeze ruffled my hair.

Marcus took no time in getting to the point. "I can't stand Aleksander," he started.

"So then it makes perfect sense you'd go hang with him," I countered, joking, but also urging an answer to my unasked question.

"He's cocky," Marcus continued.

"Also true," I said.

"But he has good reason to be cocky," Marcus explained. "Dude is old as dirt. He was changed around 900 years ago, Faline. He's had that many years to hone his incubus skills and recruit an army."

"A passive army," I added, unable to wrap my head around the idea that someone could live that long without warring.

"They refuse to involve themselves in other people's battles," he said. "Aleksander apparently created the first incubi hoard, not to fight wars, but to defend their way of life. Normally incubi live by themselves, sexual nomads, basically. Aleksander got tired of that life, and of seeing others like him be picked off. So he found a way for them to all come together."

"Yeah, but how can he keep all that testosterone in one place, under control?" I asked.

Marcus reached toward me and cupped my hands in his, the hard, slightly rusted metal beneath our fingers. "Faline," he said, his tone changing from informative to heart-felt. "The incubi aren't Wild Women, but they're a lot closer to your kind than Hunters are."

"So you're considering having Aleksander change you?" I said.

Marcus only looked into my eyes for a long breath. "If it worked, I'd have my Hunter abilities and incubus abilities. I wouldn't have to pretend to align with the Hunters anymore; I could cut myself free and belong to another brotherhood."

His brotherhood—this hadn't occurred to me. But of course, he missed being a part of a brotherhood. I wouldn't want to live without my sisterhood, my community of like-minded females that both supported me and helped me grow. The unconditional love. How much of a struggle must it be for Marcus to love the Hunters like brothers—because I had no doubt he felt unconditional love for those Hunters he'd grown up with—and yet absolutely disagree with their life decisions? Deplore their choices, even?

The next obvious question popped into my head. "And if it doesn't work?"

"He's never changed a Hunter," Marcus answered. "Hunters don't get along well with other supernatural beings; they kind of have a god complex when it comes to that stuff."

"Wait," I interrupted. "Can you unpack that?" It was obvious that Hunters had a god complex with Wild Women, but I wanted to know how that varied with other supernatural males.

"The council of Nicaea was a group of influential men, rich and powerful," Marcus explained. "One of those men, whose name was removed from the official record of attending those meetings and helping to decide which books made it into the Bible, disagreed with the direction those leaders intended for the church. He left the conventional church of the time and took his religious servants, men later called monks in our Hunter history, with him, to follow the path he believed was the more righteous one."

Just hearing such words as church and righteous caused my muscles to tense. The fear ran deep, the history of persecution and the stories whispered by my mother that told of the burnings of midwives and herbalists. The Hunters' constant teachings covering the inherent evil of Wild Women and their inability to find righteousness didn't help. Marcus's history, his present, and his future, were worth the discomfort, though. He needed to talk about this and since leaving his brotherhood, I was all he had. I knew this was a decision he'd made freely, but I still felt guilt over it.

"They built the first monastery that passed as something else," he went on. "It's not even in history books, I don't think. Because to the world at the time, it was nothing special. They didn't even have monasteries for the mainstream church until much later. But it was the home of the first Hunter complex."

"How did he create Hunters, though?" I asked, my gaze bouncing to the intricate tattoos standing out against his skin in the dark, along his smooth, muscular bicep. "You aren't a human male."

"We kept records for everything, except that," he answered. "If there are no records on how we were made, there will be no way to find out how to unmake us."

"Makes sense," I said, assuming the Goddesses and their priestesses kept no records of how we were made either.

"But what I'm trying to get to," he continued, "is that we were created in response to supernatural beings. There are holy texts that refer to supernatural beings. Most weren't included into today's holy scriptures because of the man who created us, he wanted all non-humans stricken from people's minds, and eventually he obtained his goal, or at least his descendants did. Like thieves in the night, we removed your kind from power, and then from history, and almost from folklore. We believed that we were created by God himself to govern and kill your kind. Think of it as the right hand of the creator."

"Well," I said. "You and I have different ideas of who created the world and everyone in it." I paused for effect. "And why she did it."

Marcus's seriousness finally melted and he cracked a smile. "True. But I'm answering your question about why Hunters don't get along well with other supernaturals. We believe our whole existence hinges on protecting humans from them. Kind of like the way bleach would feel about E. coli."

"But they're wrong. So very wrong," Marcus said deeply before leaning across the table to kiss me just as deeply.

I could have easily gotten swept away in the moment and stood from the chair to trail the sexy man into the quilted bedroom and have my way with him. Unfortunately, something else nagged at the fringes of my mind.

"If Hunters are really so set apart, then it stands to reason that whatever incubi do to change human men could interact with your Hunter genes and kill you," I stated.

"Or maim me," he corrected.

I had no idea what my face looked like at the moment, but apparently the word "concern" was written in my eyebrows because Marcus stood to pull me up and closer to him. "Babe," he rumbled into my ear. "I haven't made the decision yet. I'm only gathering information."

"And from what you've gathered so far?" I asked, my cheek pressed against the soft cotton covering his chest.

"I'm not gonna lie, there are more pros than cons."

I huffed. "What other pros can there be?" I asked, only counting two: more abilities and being accepted as my mate. Oh, and the third of belonging to a brotherhood.

"Aleksander will stop pursuing you," Marcus said as though his statement was as normal as letting me know he picked up peas from the grocery store for dinner.

I pulled away to stare at him. "You don't have to worry about him. I'll never choose him over you," I assured the male who'd risked life and limb for me, the man whose touch melted me.

"The reason I couldn't stand him in the beginning is the same reason I can't fault him now," Marcus said, again too calm for the topic. "He's an incubus, Faline. They rarely find a life mate to lock onto, and when they do, there's no unlocking their intentions. He's old and he can manipulate your energy and mine, make us feel and think things. He's assured me that he's not that type of man, under oath, which is the only reason I didn't slit his throat. But I'm not dumb."

"How do you know he wasn't shifting your energy to feel things about him, your trust of him, when you saw him?" I asked.

"Because." Marcus pulled a Hunter's dagger from a sheath tucked beneath his pant leg. I cringed at the sight "He gave me this as a show of good faith." Marcus tapped the red stone in the dagger's hilt. "And this right here weakens the abilities of supernaturals, just as much as it enhances mine."

"How did he get that?" I said on an inhale.

Marcus grew serious again. "I told you Aleksander's powerful, Faline. Too powerful to be underestimated."

TWENTY-TWO

THE THOUGHT of Aleksander pursuing me certainly wasn't what turned me on, I swear. But something about embracing Marcus, his words forcing me to see his heart behind them, his intention to stay with me at any cost and his place in all of this at the same time, turned me on like a light switch. The nap earlier did a lot to help, too.

Marcus kissed his way from my mouth to my jaw and down my neck. My breath hitched when he pulled my shirt over my head so that his lips could more easily reach their destination. I arched my back giving his hands more room to unbutton my jeans. When his mouth found mine again I stood in front of him while he sat on the iron chair and shimmied my jeans to the wooden slats of the deck to step out of them. There was no way I'd give Marcus the show of my nakedness without getting one from him in return. Our kisses paused enough for me to pull his shirt over his head and expose his swollen muscles, art-filled chest, back, shoulders, and arms.

He reached for me with need and intensity, his supernatural strength meeting its match in mine. I straddled him, positioning myself just right when...my pants pocket vibrated along the deck.

We reluctantly paused.

It vibrated again, the muffled noise distinct against the otherwise silent night.

"Goddam it," Marcus growled. He released his firm hold on me. I climbed off of him and the chair, grumbling my own obscenities at the phone and its fabulous timing.

One day the Wilds wouldn't be fighting for their lives and freedoms and maybe then Marcus and I would be free to ignore late-at-night phone calls from unknown numbers. Unfortunately, we still fought for those things and tonight was not that night.

"The phone number isn't American," I said to Marcus before swiping to answer.

He sat up taller.

"This is Janice," I answered. Since we'd taken down the Hunter complex I'd used burner phones, but as an added precaution I'd also answered the phone with another name if an unrecognizable number popped up. My coterie and Marcus had grown used to my extra step of precaution, making a joke about which name I'd pick next. This caller, however, did not find my precaution so endearing.

"Faline Frey?" the woman asked in a British accent.

"This is Janice," I corrected, waiting for more information before the charade led to honesty.

"The rusalka told me you'd give a false name," she stated curtly.

How did the rusalki know I'd been doing this? It wasn't like they'd called me since everything went down. Then again, when it came to the rusalki, after seeing what I saw under their lake, nothing out of the ordinary should shock me.

"Faline," the woman stated. "This is Anwen of the nagin group. We understand our distant sisters are in trouble and we'd like to help."

I gave Marcus a quizzical look before returning to the phone call. "Thank you, Anwen." My mouth caught up to my brain and the next part of the conversation finally presented itself. "Yes, uh, the succubi galere led by—" I stopped abruptly. I'd assumed the woman at the other end of this phone call was who she said she was. How stupid of me.

"Which rusalka told you to call me? What was her name and what did she look like?" I asked, knowing the Hunters probably knew our names by now. Still, I hoped they didn't know them well enough to spot one from a particular group within a second's notice.

"The rusalka, Drosera," she answered without hesitation. "She has green eyes and auburn hair. Her voice reminds me of a mix between a breeze and a fairy."

Well, she'd passed the test and her explanation of Drosera's voice was spot on.

"Thank you," I said. "We can't be too careful right now, with everything going on."

"I've heard rumors that America still had its Hunters, but I had no idea the Wild Women still answered to them. We were absolutely shocked to hear about Marie and her people."

So many questions bloomed from those two sentences, but I let them grow while she finished her spiel.

"We didn't know Marie," Anwen continued. "Hadn't heard of her or her sisters until today, really. But no snake daughter should be forced into confinement; like she who created us, we must be free to grow, to stretch, and to shed." Her words made no sense to me, at least not the shedding part.

"So are you offering to come help us?" I asked.

I thought back to my mother's stories. She'd told of the daughters of Lilith, of course, but also the scaled ones, and once she'd even mentioned a great and ancient cobra goddess and her many daughters from all over the world, some of which appointed the pharaohs themselves. I'd never heard mention of the nagin group, though. Now I wished I'd taken my mother's stories seriously as a kid. I wished I'd read up on these women of folklore, these goddesses of old. If I'd spent hours in my local library, scouring the books, I'd actually be prepared to meet these strange Wilds. As it was, I planned to do enough googling the moment we ended the call to put a nervous, end-of-the-quarter college student to shame.

"We are offering to help the succubi," she clarified. "Once we make contact with their leader, Marie, and learn their agendas, then we will know more."

I let out a sigh and rolled my eyes. Marcus stood and placed his hand on my back, watching my every expression as though each bite to my inner cheek and each scowl I gave were part of a coded message.

"Do you mind if I ask the size of your group?" I said.

"I've met your kind, huldra," the nagin said. "And I was impressed, so please don't take this poorly, but a captive Wild Woman may pose risks that we'd rather assess in person. You understand."

I didn't, but it wasn't like I had much of a choice.

"Fair enough," I said, deciding a general response was better than my true thoughts and more preferable to a lie that yes, I did understand her concern. I had no clue what a nagin was, or if they could detect lies. I didn't want to start what could become an allied friendship off on a lie. "So then you will be flying here? Are other groups joining you?" I needed to know which other types of Wilds I should research.

"Yes, we will be flying into the Portland International Airport," she said. "If you'll please send the location of the succubi's building to the number I called from?"

"We aren't there," I said. "We're currently staying at a safer location, but I'll send you the address."

"And as far as other groups joining us..." She let that last part ease from her mouth as though she considered her next words. "The echidnas and the shés will be meeting us there as well. That's why I'll need your address, because I don't expect you have a vehicle that can fit all of us." She added just in case I hadn't caught her drift, "A vehicle to pick us up with."

"No, I don't expect we do," I confirmed, repeating in my mind the Wild groups she'd just listed, hoping I could find information about them online, with at least a little portion that was semi-accurate.

"Fabulous," Anwen said. "We'll see you tomorrow then."

She ended the call and I lowered the phone from my cheek, my mind spinning.

"What is it?" Marcus finally allowed himself to ask.

"Three Wild groups are on their way, all connected to a snake goddess, I think." I peered around the deck and down below to the back yard. "We're going to need to find enough computers in this building, one for each of us. We've got until tomorrow to figure out what kind of Wilds we're dealing with."

TWENTY-THREE

FREYJA, known by her Nordic name, is not an old Goddess compared to the many who came before her. The story of the creation of Wild Women speaks of Goddesses breathing their life force into their highest priestesses as patriarchy ravaged their temples and their people's way of life. But some Goddesses, like Freyja, weren't known to dwell in temples made from human hands. And others were worshipped, and their temples destroyed, far before Freyja's name entered the mouths of humans.

But is a deity ever born? Or have they always existed, serving different societies, receiving different names according to which ways they've best helped the people who've named them?

I pondered these questions as I searched the internet for information on the snake goddesses of the world. Olivia and Celeste looked for nagin facts in particular, and the rest of us scoured the digital highways for any nuggets of truth we could extract from the pile of unknowns and speculation we found ourselves dealing with.

As it turned out, the quilter's haven we holed up in was fairly connected to the digital times. We found one laptop on top of the dressers in each room, all connected to strong Wi-Fi signal throughout the building; more than enough to aid in our search. We congregated in the large living room, using the couch and the coffee table, and at the dining table in the adjoining kitchen.

Our main goal was to find out about the Wild Women connected to snake Goddesses. The major snag we knew we'd hit before we even powered up the laptops was the lack of public knowledge concerning Wilds. We could easily find folkloric tales of the nagin, but to really know what these women were capable of, we'd have to learn which Goddess had created them and what her role was in the society in which she was said to have created them from.

For instance, Freyja is a Nordic Goddess. If one was to only go by what the humans said about huldra, that our backs were hollowed out bark and tails grew from our tailbone—they'd be highly misled. But to research the Norse stories of Freyja, her connection to nature, her protectiveness of her people, then one could begin to put the pieces together to create a more actualized idea of the huldra. We are connected to nature, we once protected the forests, and our ability to see in the dark, to grow bark and vines, are displayed in these attributes.

Connected dots like those weren't an exact science, but they were better than getting caught up in things over our heads.

"Okay, so the nagin," Olivia spoke from the dark-wood kitchen table. She and Celeste sat at the oval table, discussing websites and possible matches. "Are from India mostly. The word is Sanskrit for deity or entity in the form of a very great snake. Think cobra."

Shawna, who sat across from me at the coffee table, paused and shared a look with me. Goddess, I hoped these women didn't turn into cobras. Well, if they were on our side against the Hunters, then yes, that'd be fabulous. If they weren't, then no cobras, please.

"Does it mention what form they take?" Shawna asked while I pictured a cobra slithering into my bed at night and wrapping itself around my neck.

"Yeah. According to this, they can look human, half human and half snake, or full snake," Olivia answered as though she were reading directly from the website.

Full snake. Lovely. I shivered at the thought.

"They're mentioned in the myths of neighboring countries too," Olivia continued. "So they seem to travel."

"Well, she had a British accent," I reminded.

"About that," Celeste added. "I looked up Anwen's name. It's Welsh for beauty." Wow, my sisters were digging deep. I hadn't thought to look up name meanings. But it made sense. In naming me Faline, my mother gave a nod to felines, which were known favorites of Freyja.

"So then, maybe we should search for cobra Goddesses," Shawna suggested.

My computer must have been newer than Shawna's because the results popped up on mine while hers was still processing the request.

"Dammit," I said under my breath, massaging my temples. "I think I found their Goddess."

"What?" Shawna glimpsed my screen. "Oh."

"What is it?" Celeste yelled from the bedroom.

"The whole first page of results for a cobra Goddess is of one deity," I said.

"And?" Celeste prodded.

I sighed. "And she's Egyptian. Like, early Egypt."

"What's wrong with that?" Marcus asked, looking up from the pink laptop sitting on his knees, dwarfed by his size.

"You weren't taught about Wild Women who came from the more ancient Goddesses?" Patricia asked the ex-Hunter.

"I was, briefly," Marcus assured her. "But, to be fair, the harpies were created by Inanna, who comes from a more ancient civilization than Egypt, and you aren't worried about them."

"The Wild you know is better than the Wild you don't know," I said. Marcus's comment registered in my mind. "Wait. The Hunters teach their trainees about Goddess beliefs and history?"

Marcus chuckled, peering back at the laptop, while sitting on the flower-printed chair. "Not at all. I don't even think I heard them mutter the word 'Goddess.' That'd be acknowledging the possibility of a divine female." He shook his head while his finger moved around the mousepad. "In matters of Goddess spirituality, I'm self-taught."

If that declaration didn't make me want to grab him right then and there...

Aunt Patricia answered Marcus's earlier question regarding our distrust of Egyptian Wilds from the flower-print chair in the living room. "Wild Women created by Egyptian Goddesses are rumored to have been the driving force behind more than a handful of secret underground cults. At least that's what I overheard as a child from our grandmothers."

"Humans call them cults," Olivia added. "Any belief system that isn't widely held and doesn't feature a male at the top is referred to as a cult. Gets on my last nerve."

"Huh." Marcus paused from working. "That's true." After a few moments of thought he responded to Patricia, who sat on a chair across from him in the living room. "What's wrong with taking part in secret groups? That's essentially what you guys are, a secret group who worships a being not widely venerated. You even claim to have received your abilities from said being."

Patricia searched Marcus's eyes for a moment. I wondered what exactly she saw—the man behind the Hunter or the Hunter behind the man. "When you belong to an old Wild Women group who've planned underground ceremonies and revolts, we can only assume you've been raised to believe traits such as sneakiness and rebelliousness are acceptable, honorable even. Plus," she added in a lighter tone, "they're more likely to have connections and alliances with unsavory types."

The room quieted for a few breaths before everyone went back to their work. Or at least we went back to work for a few minutes.

I hadn't noticed Aunt Renee place the black Dell laptop she'd been using on the table beside her chair until she moved toward the closed sliding glass doors separating the living room from the deck.

"I heard something," she said when the rest of us watched her look out the window to the deck and yard below. "Someone's snooping around the house."

"Did the Hunters find us?" Shawna asked, slapping her laptop shut and standing in a hurry.

Patricia joined Renee beside the glass doors. "Speak of the devil. Who invited the harpies?"

"The harpies are here?" I asked, jumping up from the floor to get a look.

Sure enough, three tall, lean women made their way from the back yard and up the wooden steps to the deck in long strides. Their heads made quick, jerky movements as they took in their surroundings.

"I'll invite them in," Patricia said, sliding the glass door open and making her way onto the deck to meet the tall Wilds.

"I'll join you," Renee said, following her sister.

It didn't take long before the two huldra and three harpies stood in the living room. "They weren't followed, as far as we could tell," Renee whispered into my ear as she passed by me and took a seat on the couch.

True to form for the harpies, no hugs were given or friendly salutations repeated. The three women stood in a half circle, the coffee table separating them from the couch. They craned their necks in sharp movements, their eyes following, as they took in the Airbnb home.

"What brings you here?" I asked, standing behind the couch. I leaned on the back of the furniture, mere feet above my aunt's head.

They zeroed in on me.

"We were summoned," Eonza answered. Golden feathers hung from her blonde ponytail.

"By whom?" I said, reliving flashbacks of the first time I met the harpy outside a golf course restaurant where she'd been trying to pick up the bartender she had no interest in. I didn't take what appeared to be aloofness as an offense. Harpies often kept to themselves and lacked the desire to appear human. Either that or they kept to themselves because they weren't able to appear human. I hadn't quite figured them out. Hell, I'd spent the most time with the succubi and they still confused me to no end. I thought to add another question because Goddess knew Eonza wouldn't offer the information without my asking. "And why'd they send you?"

Eonza cocked her head slightly and narrowed her eyes. Not being rude, just trying to gauge the meaning of my question. Huh, the fact that I knew that much meant I'd picked up a little knowledge about this flock.

"A rusalka appeared beside our pool as soon as the sun set," Eonza began. "She told us the succubi galere had been detained by the

Hunters and the huldra would need help retrieving them. We flew through the night and day to reach you. Before we reached the apartment complex, we were told to adjust course to this location."

I cleared my throat as my eyes filled with tears. The support from a known Wild group hit me in the heart and filled me with a deep gratitude from out of nowhere. I thought better of asking if I could give her a hug—when they'd stayed at our common house I'd noticed the harpies weren't much for physical contact. They just dropped everything to come help us, to come help the succubi, to assist their fellow Wild Women. I hadn't been giving these women enough credit, but that was changing now.

"We really appreciate you coming. I mean that," I said with as much inflection as I felt, which was a lot.

"We are tired," Lapis announced. Her square shoulders released their flex and bent forward.

"And hungry," the third harpy, Salis, said as she turned to view the kitchen.

"By all means," I said, motioning to the refrigerator. "There's a few condiments and sandwich fixings in the fridge and also some non-perishables in the cabinet, but whatever is there you can take."

The three harpies wasted no time in raiding the fridge and cabinets. Abigale cleared the laptops from the dining table, giving the harpies a place to sit and set their food. Harpies did not eat like birds. The women shoveled cold cuts and cheddar cheese slices into their mouths—a deconstructed sandwich.

"I wonder how many calories it took them to fly all the way here?" Renee, ever the nurse, asked. "How many calories they'll need to consume to make up for that."

"It took us over thirty-five hours to travel here from our home in North Carolina," Eonza said between bites of meat and cheese. "And that is not including rest stops."

Marcus said, "Wow," on a breath and the three faces, full of food, jerked to peer at him sitting on a chair pushed to the far corner of the living room.

They had to have seen him when they came in, but now they watched him as though they'd just noticed his presence.

"I see the Hunter still resides with the huldra," Lapis said, returning to her meal. Her sisters resumed eating, too.

The tone of her statement didn't request an answer.

Eonza answered her sister anyway. "I am not interested in mating with a Hunter, but I would like to discuss a possible mating agreement with the incubus."

"Excuse me?" I asked, trying not to laugh at the harpy's insistence on getting pregnant. Before she'd left my house after we'd rescued Shawna, she'd assured me she'd wait to conceive a little harpy until after the Hunter complexes, all of them in the United States, were destroyed.

Eonza looked up at me. "Any will do. I'm not particular."

Her sister Lapis added, "She's volunteered to make the sacrifice for us. She has every right to decide who she will mate with. And if we can form an alliance through this, it will be more beneficial for our flock."

My coterie watched for my response. Celeste suppressed a laugh.

I had so many questions, but one kept pushing its way to the front. "Why the incubi, though?"

Lapis fielded this one. "We are small among the Wild Women groups," she started. "Our daughters will need any advantages we can bestow upon them. To have the protection and possibly the abilities of an incubus only seems logical. Our ancestors were logical in choosing with whom they mated. We should be as well."

I couldn't fault them there. But a small part of me broke for their logic. They may not have realized it, but they were forming a back-up plan, in case the Wilds weren't successful and their small group needed protection. I wondered if this had anything to do with the weak state we'd recently found ourselves in. Would it become a situation of each Wild group for themselves, as it had in the past?

That one strategy of theirs brought forth the tornado of self-doubt I'd been trying to hold back through research and creating new plans. Plain and simple, I wasn't adequate for the job. And the harpies, the most direct Wilds of the bunch, knew it.

I glanced to Marcus. Is that why he was considering being changed to an incubus, to be able to better protect me because I was too weak and unable to protect myself and my coterie? Did he want Aleksander to change him because of me? Maybe his explanation to be changed so that Aleksander will no longer pursue me held less water than I'd thought. No way was I going to let him go through such an unknown thing because of my inadequacies. First though, I needed to blow the Aleksander-wants-me-as-his-mate excuse out of the water.

"Eonza," I said, still looking at Marcus. "I happen to have the incubi leader's phone number. His name is Aleksander. Fair warning, though. I'm told they can't procreate with humans, not sure if that extends to Wild Women. But if you're going to align with an incubus you may as well do it with an old and powerful one."

"Yes?" she answered.

Marcus tilted his head, just slightly.

"I'll call him and invite him over to meet you. Would you like that?"

Eonza stood so quickly the chair she'd been sitting in scraped along the floor and filled the otherwise silent kitchen. I turned to her. Her blank face reminded me of a woman preparing for battle, steeling away her true feelings of fear and disdain for bloodshed.

"Yes," she said solidly, tilting her chin up in decision. "I will do this for my sisters."

TWENTY-FOUR

Since meeting underwater with the rusalki, my dreams had been more the stuff of enlightenment and less the stuff of odd mental knots unraveling their subconscious selves. Tonight's dream held no difference. I strolled through a temple, its stone walls an orangish color with only candles and moonlight streaming through the narrow openings in the outer walls to light my way.

A woman ran past me, holding the hem of her linen robe to keep from tripping. As she passed, she yelled for me to hurry, they were coming and we didn't have much time. I picked up my pace to follow her. She led me to a small alcove of a room, potted plants lined a round pool in the center, a pool I instinctively knew cleansed away past hurts. I also knew the woman was a high priestess. So was I.

"She Who Is will be here shortly," the high priestess exclaimed, motioning for me to get into the water. "We must prepare ourselves."

"For what?" I asked blankly.

Her brows furrowed as she studied me. "For her breath of life, of course."

A head of auburn hair slowly rose to the surface of the pool. The woman eased her way from the water, pulling her naked body up over the edge. The rusalka Drosera stared at me, her body dripping and her hair long, straight, and clean.

I spun to take everything in and clear up my confusion. "Where are we?" I asked the rusalka. "I thought I was dreaming."

The priestess peered at me like I was crazy, talking to myself.

Before the priestess had a chance to remind me of anything, Drosera answered my questions. Her words whispered into my brain like unspoken outside thoughts. "You are dreaming. And I am here to wake you. My physical form waits outside your door. Now, you will wake in three, two, one!" She clapped, an unearthly sound, and I shot up in bed.

Marcus shifted beside me, but the movement failed to wake him.

I crept from our bed and eased open the bedroom door, expecting an auburn-haired rusalka to be standing naked, dripping wet, waiting for me. The dark upstairs hallway was empty and quiet. I rushed to the front door and unlocked it, swinging it open without worry of waking those of my coterie who slept in the other bedrooms.

A shadow moved, just slightly, under the darkness of the porch steps leading to the walkway and driveway. Yes, I could see in the dark. No, I couldn't see through stairs. I jogged down the five steps and peered around the front yard. "Drosera?" I whispered. "Is that you?"

The rusalka, clothed in animal skins, wearing a crown of woven branches and vines, stepped from under an oak tree in the center of the yard. Her green eyes struck me first, they nearly glowed with light, but not in a radioactive way. She smelled like lake water and birch leaves.

"I am," she responded. "I have come with a message."

I yawned and stretched, no longer on the defense at the idea of dealing with a possible intruder. "Anwen called me," I said. "They should be here tomorrow." I looked back to the closed front door. "Or today; I don't know what time it is." Streetlights nearby poured across the wet grass. Early morning dew settled like a crisp mist above the ground.

"I have come to tell you that we spoke to Marie, the succubi leader," she began.

"How were you able to contact her? You went onto the Oregon Hunter complex grounds?"

She shook her head. "No, we are unable to transport ourselves there for the same reason the succubi are unable to leave."

"Because there are Hunters guarding it?" I asked.

"Our sister, Azalea, has explained to us the red stones used in the Hunter's cabin, the ones lining the steps to the attic where your own sister was kept—these blood stones, the very same stones adorning their daggers, inhibit our abilities. It is why my sister had not been able to use the stairs and rather chose another mode to get into the room with your Shawna, weeks ago. Even from the hall they'd weakened her abilities. They weakened yours as well. It is why you were forced to fully unleash your huldra to fight off the Hunter. It is why you blacked out." Drosera paused and looked to the side of the house. I followed her gaze, but saw nothing.

"Marie has told us that her and her sisters chose to attend check-in because some did not agree with the new decision to hide underground," she continued. "They believed the decision too large to make at such a moment's notice and thought it best to discuss it further. Attending check-in would give them that time."

"The incubus said as much," I told her. "I didn't know whether to trust him or not, though."

"He is trustworthy," she explained, "in the way a housecat can trust a lioness. The two may seem connected, but they come from very different worlds. The house cat is aware of her bondage, the lioness lacks the knowledge that such a thing exists."

"Still," I muttered mostly to myself. "It feels good to know the succubi galere, at least some of them, didn't really want to abandon us. And now they're imprisoned for that choice to hold off on going underground."

Drosera squinted at me. "You take too much into yourself. The decisions of others directly reflect their beliefs about themselves, not their beliefs about you."

I waited for the feeling of a brain massage to enter my skull, but nothing came. "Can you not read minds anymore?" I asked.

"We can, but if unnecessary, it is best that we save our energy. I must finish my message and leave," she said.

I waited for her to continue. After looking around and watching the side of the house again, she spoke. "The succubi believed they would be able to thwart any opposition from the Hunters by using their abilities. They assumed that after helping with the Washington complex, there was a chance that they would not pass check-in."

I almost asked why they hadn't mentioned that to me when we'd discussed the topic, but I let her finish because she seemed as though she were on some sort of timeline. I didn't know much about rusalki ways and figured maybe she lacked the energy to stay very long and still return to her sisters. Also, I appreciated Drosera's forthright explanation. In the past the rusalki would explain concepts with parables. Tonight Drosera seemed to find a way to get to the point.

"However," she continued. "They planned to use their power over energy to persuade the Hunters to allow them to pass through check-in and release them. They did not foresee the Oregon Hunters covering their classroom walls with blood stones."

I closed my eyes and let out a sigh. My stomach twisted. I remembered the way I hadn't been able to smell past the red stones, how I'd felt weaker and unable to grow my bark or vines. The succubi were rendered helpless. And so would any other Wild who entered that complex to retrieve them. The acidic urge to throw up rose from my stomach and I swallowed it down. My knees threatened to give out. I leaned against the outer portion of the stairwell.

"How do we get past them, then?" I asked, a new level of hopelessness carving its way into my heart. I had a whole galere of Wilds needing to be freed, and no way of saving them.

"The blood stones only affect those who bleed monthly, Wild Women who are still in their fertile years."

I jerked up to meet her eyes. "The stones are linked to menstruation? That's why you're calling them blood stones?"

She gave one short nod. "The monthly blood is powerful, potent, and misunderstood. For these reasons it is feared."

My mother had been right when she'd hinted as much in her stories of temple priestesses acting as oracles during their bleeding times each month. Had she known about the blood stones, too?

"So then we have to send in men and children?" I asked. "The incubi have already turned us down and human men aren't strong enough to go against Hunters. Mermaids are the only group who have young children, and we can't get ahold of them. Plus, we'd never ask them to send in their daughters, that'd be wrong on so many levels."

"Gabrielle's death has caused dissension among the mermaid ranks," Drosera said as though she were talking about the weather. Gabrielle's name so casually on her lips still stung to hear. "They have been displaced and split to seek out support. At this time they are unwilling to lend help."

"We're screwed. Why are the nagin even coming, then?" I thought out loud.

"They have sent their elders," the rusalka said. "Those whose experiences no longer bleed from their wombs for the good of their kind, but rather now store up their wisdom within them to guide the younger ones."

Nothing in Anwen's voice led me to believe she'd reached the years past fertility. I questioned my own assumptions of her age and put a pin in it later to ask myself why I assumed strong Wilds were younger Wilds.

"Two members of your coterie are able to assist as well," Drosera reminded me.

My heart nearly seized. My two aunts, Patricia and Abigale, had already gone through menopause. Patricia could hold her own, I had no doubt. But Abigale was still in a fragile state over the trauma of her daughter, Shawna.

I gave a nod. Drosera didn't need to read my mind to know I hesitated at the idea of sending my aunts to face a complex of Hunters alongside Wilds they'd never met. But to ask Wilds from other countries to fight this battle for us, and not include our own warrior women, would be unthinkable. It's not that I feared whether or not my aunts would agree to the task. I knew they would. I didn't want to have to ask them in the first place.

"Tell me," Drosera asked, peering at the side of the house again for a quick second and lowering her voice even more. "Do you believe your aunts incapable of protecting themselves?"

Her question caught me off-guard.

"Of course not," I answered automatically, not sure how much I believed my answer to be true.

"Well," I started, correcting my shoot-from-the-hip remark. "I do worry about them, that they're not as experienced in combat with Hunters." Even that response didn't feel right on my tongue. Hadn't my aunts fought beside me and the rest of the Wilds at the Washington Hunter complex and then again at the Oregon winery? They were just as experienced as my sisters, and yet if my sisters were called on to attack the Hunter complex without me, I'd worry, yeah, but I wouldn't fret the same way.

Drosera didn't dignify my last asinine remark with a response.

So, naturally, I kept going. "They just grew up in a different time, learned to follow more than lead." I could just imagine my inner huldra shaking her head as I spoke. I didn't know how much I disagreed with myself until the words were out of my mouth and had no way of returning. I gave up. "I'm ridiculous," I said. "Of course they're capable. I don't know what I was thinking."

The left corner of the rusalka's lip lifted. "You are the inexperienced one and yet you underestimate those who have experienced harder days, those who have raised daughters in a world full of sons."

I didn't quite catch what she meant by that last part, but I was too ashamed of myself to ask.

"Have you ever taken the time or interest to ask your elders of their struggles?" she asked.

I pursed my lips. Point taken.

"One elder took the time to share her experiences with you, what she'd learned, what she'd believed, what she'd hoped for," Drosera said.

My mind went blank before I realized who she referred to. "My mother."

"Would you not say she is your driving force?" the rusalka asked, urging my thoughts to follow the path of breadcrumbs she lay before me.

I stared at the old oak tree. I hadn't thought of it that way, my mother being my driving force in all of this. I'd just figured Shawna held that title. But Shawna was with us now, safe, and yet I still pushed ahead. I desired freedom not just for Shawna and the Washington Wilds, but for all American Wild Women. I desired justice. The sense of justice my mother knowingly fed to me through bedtime stories and hypothetical questions that it turns out weren't very hypothetical. My mother raised the future liberator of Wild Women, maybe even the future liberator of herself. Had she done it knowingly? And if so, how did she know?

"Do you know if she's still alive, my mother?" I asked, still staring at the tree, deep in thought. In that moment it occurred to me that I'd had two differing sides when it came to hope that my mother lived. One side couldn't wait to find her, rescue her, and make up for lost time. The other side hoped she wasn't still alive, hoped she hadn't gone through years of being a ward of the Hunters. This is why I often reigned in my thoughts when they skirted the territory of dreaming of her rescue, why I tried to shift them to more realistic matters like getting Shawna, and now helping the succubi.

"I do know," Drosera said.

A rustle of movement sounded from the side of the house and Drosera jerked her head to study the area again. "When Anwen arrives, be sure to tell her that I will be back." The rusalka disappeared into thin air as she finished the last word.

I gasped and jumped back, studying my surroundings to see how the hell the rusalka played a trick of the eye so well.

A male ran to the railing of the elevated porch that wrapped around the side and back of the house, and called down to me. "You okay?"

I lifted my eyes to his, to Aleksander's. His disheveled hair hung forward as he gazed down at me. Apparently my lack of an answer concerned him because he jumped over the rail and landed on the soft dirt below with a quickness. When his shoes hit the grass all six-plus feet of him rushed to my protection.

Aleksander stopped short a foot away from me and turned in each direction, searching for the culprit. He paused and looked back to me, standing beneath the hazy glow of the front porch light. "I felt an unknown energy and heard you gasp. But, there's no one here," he said in that accent of his, a little disappointed and a lot confused.

"Except for you," I countered. "Why *are* you here?"

The warmth and protection in his eyes disappeared. He crossed his arms and flashed a slightly mischievous smile. "Why, to protect you, of course," he said as though he spoke a commonly understood fact.

I put my hand out in front of me. "So let me get this straight," I started. "You're a pacifist who refuses to help me get your...cousins... back from the Hunters, and yet you are here to protect me? How? From who?"

Aleksander side-eyed the steps and exhaled. He dropped his flirtatious sing-song way of speaking and leveled with me. "Look, this isn't my idea of a good time either," he said, his voice slightly deeper now.

"Then go home. Why are you here?" I asked for the second time in a handful of minutes. I shifted my balance and waited.

"I've been guarding the house tonight from a lounge chair on the side deck. Can we talk somewhere more private?" he asked, motioning for me to go before him, onto the first step.

My initial response was a hard no, but logic told me to listen to what the incubus had to say. I decided not to go much deeper in my soul-searching as to why I took that first step and then climbed the stairs ahead of him. Halfway to the living room, I wondered if he was enjoying the view, and turned to ask him as much, as a way of letting him know I knew all about his kind. But what I saw was not a male ogling my ass, rather an incubus gazing ahead of us, deep in thought. I'd be lying if I said his lack of ogling didn't pee on my ice cream a little.

Who likes to be wrong about people?

No one.

I didn't like that he closed the front door behind him. He strode past me to sit on the living room couch.

"Please," he said, patting the cushion beside him.

I ran a hand through my hair, figured what the hell, and joined him. We sat awkwardly searching one another for a few breaths before he started the conversation.

"I can imagine being here, alone, with me, is not the most comfortable scenario for you right now, and so I want you to know that I appreciate your allowing me to come here," he said. His eyes smiled and I knew he meant what he said.

I gave a nod.

He leaned into the corner of the couch, facing me.

"Incubi are a walking contradiction," he explained. He paused before continuing and I sensed hesitation, maybe even nervousness. "We deal in matters of energy and excel in sexual energy. Social norms have no bearing as to whom we share our sexual energy with. Yet, when we lock onto our life mate, there is no key to unlock the intense need we have to protect and adore them, to receive the same from them in return."

I looked up at the ceiling fan in thought. A whole galere of succubi were currently being detained at a Hunter's complex. The mermaids were unwilling to come to our aid because their shoal was tearing apart at the seams. Wild Women I'd never met, kinds I didn't even know existed twenty-four hours ago, were on their way to maybe help or maybe complicate matters more. I just found out that only non-menstruating Wilds had a chance at saving the succubi, which cuts our already limited ranks to barely anything. And this incubus wanted me to make his feelings for me a priority in my tornado of a world?

I itched my eyebrow as though any movement was a replacement for words.

Fuck it.

I leveled a gaze at the muscular incubus sitting inches from me. "Marcus, *my boyfriend*, already explained this to me," I said.

Had I actually ever determined Marcus was my boyfriend? I couldn't be sure. But there it was, out in the open, between the incubus and me.

I leaned back, done playing mind games and easing out information that clearly refused to budge. "Look, I'm going to be honest. For all of maybe an hour, I considered pretending to have a thing for you so that you'd help us." I looked him in the eye. "It wasn't my idea and I'm embarrassed that I'd even considering leading someone on, so for that, I'm sorry. But since we're laying our cards on the table, I should tell you that I don't feel that way toward you. I admit it'd probably be easier on me if I did, but I don't."

His expression didn't change even a fraction. He sat there, relaxed, confidently leaning back like he owned the place. Don't ask me how I could tell he was confident. It just poured from him and not always in that cocky way either.

"Well," Aleksander said, inhaling deeply, "I'm sorry to hear that."

He stood and stretched before making his way to the back sliding glass door. He didn't invite me to join him, but he didn't close the door behind him either. The wooden slats beneath him creaked from his weight.

"So, are we done then?" I asked, my confusion with this male growing by the second.

"Done or just begun, the ball's in your court," he responded from the deck.

I stood and started toward the hallway to my room where Marcus slept. I paused again, thoroughly confused when Alek didn't ask me to join him or say goodbye.

"Aleksander?"

"Yes?"

"If you heard and respect what I told you, why are you still staying the night out on the deck?" I asked.

He gave one deep chuckle. "In every aspect of my life I have freewill. Except for this one," he answered. "According to my heart, mind, and body, you're my life mate. I'm not stupid enough to fight it; stronger incubi have gone mad trying such a feat. Please don't take this as offensive or me not respecting your wishes, because believe me, I can't help but care deeply for you and I want whatever will make you happy, which I realize isn't me. But I've locked onto you." He sighed. "I deal in energy, remember? And your energy is that of my life mate. Where my mate's energy goes, so do I."

A thought occurred to me. "If that's the case then why isn't your young incubus at the Oregon Hunter complex trying to get his succubus girlfriend back?" I asked.

Aleksander shifted his weight, still holding the door handle. "He is probably trying as we speak. He's younger, so the necessity to be near her once she left took longer to begin. We've had to lock him in a cell and keep five incubi guarding him at all times."

I willed my brows to unfurrow. "It's that intense?"

The incubi leader nodded and scratched the hint of stubble along his jaw. For the first time since I'd met him, he looked weary. It seemed he really couldn't help being here. He wanted to be back with his hoard.

"If I fought the Hunters, would you join me too, seeing as you're compelled to be near me?" I asked.

In folklore humans are taught that succubi and incubi compel them, bend the human's will to fit the creature's wants and desires. Hell, that's what the Hunters taught us huldra. But in reality, the succubi and incubi were the ones being compelled, the ones forced to absorb the whims of others.

Aleksander's shoulders slumped a little, which was a lot for his confident stature. "I would," he said. "Which would put the men I lead in great danger, not to mention intense turmoil over deciding whether or not to follow me or follow our old ways. I imagine it will ruin our hoard."

I leaned on the edge of the corner of the hall wall. We could really use the help of Aleksander and his hoard, but not at such a high cost as knowingly destroying familial bonds. If I couldn't fathom someone doing that to my coterie, I wouldn't fathom doing that to someone else, especially a group innocent in all of this. "What can I do to break this mate lock thing?" I said. I thought to offer a harpy replacement, but since I hadn't clearly gotten the okay from Eonza to share her plan of seducing him, I decided to keep that to myself.

Aleksander's heavy lids opened and his gaze pierced my own. "Either change your mind about me, or let me change your Hunter."

My answer flowed from my lips in one decisive move. "If I agree to consider those two options would you be honest about what all they entail?" I said.

"What do you want to know?" he asked. He made his way to the couch again, closing the glass door.

"Everything," I answered. "I want to know everything."

TWENTY-FIVE

I woke in Marcus's arms after a fitful night of incubi dreams. Marcus couldn't have known the process of being changed to an incubus. He couldn't have, or else he wouldn't be entertaining the idea.

His broad chest rose and fell in even breaths as I twisted my body to study his peaceful face. I couldn't imagine him agreeing to the process of becoming an incubus, a sexual ritual to transfer a key component of Aleksander's energy, the part that made him immortal and powerful, to Marcus. Last night Aleksander had assured me that he was only able to create other incubi at such a rate as he created them because of his long time spent as an incubus himself—his experience as an incubus grew so much that he had enough energy to share to create new brothers. Normally, he'd told me, an incubus can change one man in his lifetime, maybe two. But this could be because traditionally incubi didn't tend to travel in groups; to travel to new areas with other incubi meant fewer lovers for each and sharing wasn't typically their style. Neither was celibacy. So changing one or two men helped to keep the species going without overpopulation.

Aleksander saw it differently. He believed the humans were increasing in population, so why shouldn't the incubi? And being the first incubus to create a hoard gave him a safety net, in case the incubi followed in the footsteps of other supernaturals—created groups and then warred to extinction with other, more powerful groups. Aleksander didn't see his kind as dominant or territorial, but they also weren't the types to roll over and show their bellies either. They wouldn't go looking for a fight, but if one was brought to them, one that jeopardized their brotherhood, Aleksander wished to be prepared.

Shockingly, I respected him more once we parted ways last night, once I'd learned everything there was to know about being a life mate to an incubus as well as the process of changing a man into an incubus. Doesn't mean I wanted any part of either. And yet, to hold up my end of the bargain, I lay beside my Hunter of a man, considering both avenues, racking my brain for a third, hidden option. I imagined him being turned and the feeling of jealousy, a feeling I hadn't much felt before, swelled within me. Ultimately, it was Marcus's decision to be turned or not. But if he decided to go ahead with it, I'd want to be the female vessel that the ritual called for when turning a straight male.

Aleksander assured me that the female benefited greatly from the exchange of incubi energy in the turning ritual between two straight men. Most came away having achieved what perfect bliss feels like and are placed on which life path, which changes they need to make, to achieve their own personal blissful fulfilment. Not that I was questioning my purpose or anything. I only questioned their method, why it sounded like the woman was being used...yet again...for man's gain. Knowing the woman gained as well and was in full knowledge of what she was contributing to, helped to keep me from making the incubi my second worst enemies, right behind the Hunters.

"What are you thinking about?" Marcus asked, stirring beside me. He cracked an eye open and turned on his side to pull me into a horizontal hug.

My cheek nestled between his bare pecs and I breathed in his clean, masculine scent, like soap and faint traces of crisp cologne. I exhaled. "I learned a lot last night and I'm processing it all," I said.

Marcus yawned and his chest expanded enough to push me backwards on the bed. He pulled me to him again and I gladly accepted the nearness. "Was it a dream?"

"No, more like a rusalka waking me in my mind and then waiting for me out front, and then an incubi leader lurking on the side porch to add another layer of knotted intel for me to work through," I explained. Really though, despite the fact that they decided to impart this information in the middle of the night and pull me out of bed for it, I was grateful.

Marcus released me from his hold and sat up. "Why is Aleksander here?"

I pulled myself to an upright sitting position and faced him. "Because I'm his apparent life mate."

Marcus flexed his jaw. "He's pushing it," he nearly growled.

I thought to remind him of Aleksander's insistence that he can't help his need to protect me, but I'd just be telling Marcus what he already knew. So I got to the point instead. "If you decide to be changed, I want to be the woman used for the energy exchange. I know it's immature and territorial, but I just can't see you with another woman—even if it's strictly for business reasons." I hated feeling this... this...claim to a male. It was unfamiliar and uncomfortable and so very not huldra-like.

Marcus ground his teeth and looked to the ceiling before meeting my gaze again to speak. "Was that his idea? Because we can't trust him, we barely know him. What if once he has sex with his life-mate the bond is sealed and felt by both parties? What if he transfers his mate energy rather than his incubus energy, or alongside it, and you all of a sudden want to be with him?"

I cocked my head and studied him. "If you can't trust him, and don't want me involved because you worry this is some sort of trap, why the hell are you considering joining his brotherhood?" I asked.

Marcus exhaled and rubbed the blanket over his legs. "I don't know."

But he did. I could see it in the way he pinched his brows that he was holding something back, hiding something from me. "Yes, you do know why. It's not like you to make rash decisions like this. You've thought this through and mentally weighed the pros and cons."

Marcus leveled a blank gaze at me. "It's what you want. Deep down, I know it's what you want."

I almost jumped off the bed in response. "Excuse me? Since when did you start reading minds?"

He shook his head. "I'm not saying I can read your mind, but I just know..."

"Um, no you don't know," I blurted. I slid from the bed and stood a safe distance. Nothing pissed me off more than someone telling me what I was thinking, unless it was the rusalki of course.

"Really?" Marcus said, his voice getting louder. He stood from the bed and crossed his arms over his chest. "You want to explain to me, then, the growing distance between us? Your refusal to admit that we're anything more than for-now friends with benefits to your coterie? Give me a good reason for your constant reminder to me that huldra don't have long term relationships or marry? From my vantage point, you're dropping hints left and right and I'm doing my best to pick them up and figure out what the hell you want from me."

Goddess, how could I be pissed and heart-broken at the same damn time? What kind of sorcery was love to do such things to the heart and mind? I thought of what Marie had said about the love she felt swirling within me. I thought of her and Celeste, how quick and easy they seemed to act on desires of the heart, and how controlled and reluctant I'd been.

I stared at the beige carpet long enough to pull together enough courage to say how I really felt. I wasn't sure if there was such a thing, enough courage, but I pushed forward anyhow. "You being a Hunter complicates things, yes," I admitted. "And I don't mean to add salt to your wound, but huldra *don't* marry, they spend their days and raise their kids with their partner sisters." I wondered how much thought Celeste had given to this fact and if she'd discussed any of this with Olivia, her partner sister. I wished I'd had the foresight to ask my sisters before diving into this heated conversation with Marcus.

"It would be easier if I were an incubus," he said plainly. He wasn't wrong.

But easy was a relative term and if I'd learned anything these last few weeks, it was that change brings about its own difficulties, new hurdles to jump, most of which we don't see until they're scraping the fronts of our thighs.

"Maybe so," I said quietly, still concentrating on the carpet. "But you wouldn't be you, and I'm in love with you, the way you are, right now."

I looked up to the ex-Hunter standing across from me and waited for an indication on how my secret, one I'd even kept from myself, was received. The man took two long strides and wrapped me up in his arms, my feet dangling from the ground.

"Faline Frey," he said with more bass in his voice than usual, "you've just made me the happiest man on earth."

He pressed his lips to mine and I wrapped my legs around his midsection, eager to be as close to this man as physically possible. He placed my hair at my back and kissed the exposed skin of my neck.

Before things got hot and heavy past the point of return, I had one more thing to mention and I knew before even opening my mouth that I'd kick myself for it.

"One more thing," I said between heavy breaths.

"Oh? What's that?" he asked, and it sounded as though he spoke through a smile, but I wouldn't know because his lips were grazing across my chest, stretching the V-neck on my night shirt lower than it was made to go.

"I think I've come up with a third option in this whole incubus thing," I answered in-between kisses on his forehead as I thread my fingers through his thick, dark hair.

"Okay," he said past his tongue as it trailed lower.

I reconsidered my thoughts before I spoke. If we pretended to agree to Aleksander changing Marcus, but instead of Aleksander shifting his incubus energy to me through sex and then me shifting it to Marcus, I simply kept it for myself, then I could use it to get past the blood stones at the Hunter complex and rescue the succubi galere. Of course, I'd hinted at a similar situation to Aleksander and he'd shot it down saying the incubus energy is highly masculine and unsafe to harbor in a female host for too long, just long enough to transfer. Still, I figured being a Wild, my body was well acquainted with supernatural attributes and probably able to handle the raw energy of an incubus.

Marcus laid me backwards onto the bed and all thoughts of a night with Aleksander for the good of the succubi melted from my mind as Marcus's weight on top of me melted my body.

It didn't take long before our proclamations of love ended in love making. And maybe it was just in my head, but it felt like the man on top of me was fixed on proving his worth as a lover, what the strength of a Hunter could bring to the bed as opposed to an incubus.

His mouth tugged on my breast at my moment of climax, the very same moment I arched my back and suppressed a scream of delight, the very same moment my body disappeared from underneath the six-foot-two, tan muscled man and reappeared on a damp forest floor, pine needles poking into my bare back.

TWENTY-SIX

"THANK YOU FOR COMING," Drosera said dryly as she stared down at me.

I blinked twice and took in my surroundings. Once I realized I was naked and laying on the forest floor, still half writhing in pleasure, I jumped up and hurried to smooth the pine needles from my hair.

Drosera's welcome struck me as a possible double entendre, but then again, it was a rusalka who'd said it, so maybe not.

"How did I get here?" I asked, looking around. "And where is here? What did you do?"

"We are in Forest Park of the Tualatin Mountains," Drosera answered. "It is not ideal, as we're essentially in a public park west of Portland, but I hadn't enough energy to transport you much farther than this."

I noticed a narrow dirt walking trail and listened for humans. I heard none. It was probably too early in the morning and too cold for them to venture out into nature. "Is your kind able to teleport people?" I asked.

Drosera didn't so much as crack a smile, for good or for bad. She only stared at me. "No."

Ah, so the comparably chatty rusalka that was her under the oak tree last night had been just a fluke. Made more sense that way. I took another approach. "Then would you mind explaining why I'm here and why you took me...when you did?"

I would assume she'd frozen in place, glitched, if it weren't for her rising and falling chest.

"The snake women are landing in Oregon momentarily." She paused.

"The harpies have already arrived," I said, updating her on a fact I assumed she already knew.

"Yes," she responded. "We sent them before settling on our new plan. They will still be of help, though."

Awkward silence hung between us as I waited for her to finish. It was odd to have to speak my questions rather than her read my mind. For instance, at this moment I wondered what she was mulling over, if she was deciding how much to tell me. I'd grown to trust the wisdom of the rusalki, and I appreciated their kind. That didn't mean I adored their communication skills, though.

"My sisters and I have spoken and realized a different path for you," she continued. "One walked through trees with deep roots rather than city streets and Hunter complexes."

Experience had taught me to be patient in waiting for a rusalka to express herself. Sometimes, dancing around the point gave it a sharper edge when it finally pricked. At least I assumed the rusalki thought so.

"Despite your connecting us to our Goddess, Mokosh, our energy stores are low, limiting our abilities," she explained. "An orgasm carries with it heightened energy, the burst of which I needed to transport you here." She unfroze and walked to a nearby plant. She squatted to stroke its leaves. "Do you know the meaning of my name?"

"No," I said as I made my way over to her.

"I am named after a carnivorous plant," she said, as if she were speaking to the plant. "Each rusalka in my coven was named after poisonous and medicinal plants."

The plant stood about five feet tall, looking as though it were somewhere between a bush and a flower, with branch-like stems and little white petals alongside thin, green, curved leaves.

"Death leads to birth, which leads to death, as a cycle of nature,"

Drosera went on. "Both cause new beginnings and both bring about change. One is not possible without the other."

Her gaze shot to a different plant with tiny, dark green leaves and beautiful white flowers streaked with red on the insides. "Azalea, the plant for which my sister was named, grows in Oregon, did you know?"

"I didn't know that." I took a solemn minute, missing her sister. When Drosera's attention fell back to the plant she knelt beside, I continued. "But what does the cycle of nature have to do with the snake Wilds?" I asked, incredibly confused.

A stiff wind blew past me and I covered my skin in a bark façade to keep warm.

"The snake Wild Women are sending their elders, those who no longer bleed," Drosera answered. "This, we have discussed, but my sisters believe we can offer more assistance. We have spent time consulting our ancestors in spirit, daughters of Mokosh." Mokosh was the rusalki Goddess, also known as Moist Mother Earth. "And they have told of the old huldras, those who aged with the trees until they too bore branches and hosted squirrels and birds."

An image and the piece of a story entered my mind, and at first I assumed it'd come from Drosera, but I quickly realized I was remembering a story spoken from my mother's lips. *"Long ago,"* my *mother had said one night as she tucked me into bed. "Our grandmothers aged gracefully."* I remembered now, my own grandmother, my mother's mother, had left our coterie early one morning and never returned. She'd kissed me goodbye and told me to watch over my mother. She then held my mother tight, so tightly and mournfully that as a small child I knew something was wrong. Proving my worry to be true, tears rolled down both of their faces as they whispered into each other's ears and kissed one another what was to be one last time. Two days later I noticed a new, freshly dug grave in our private graveyard back in the woods behind our tree homes. That was the night I'd asked my mother where grandmother had gone.

"When huldra aged gracefully, they had time to find their connections, to locate the tree in which they would live out eternity," my mother had said. "Young huldra didn't have to say goodbye to their grandmothers, or even their great-grandmothers."

"Grandmothers lived in tree houses back then too?" my young self had asked.

My mother had chuckled. "No, darling, they became the tree. Picture a great oak opening her trunk, pulling back her bark like curtains, and inviting a huldra inside. The aged Wild Woman would enter, when her time as a huldra came to an end, and she would become one with the tree, her memories sinking into the roots and her personality bursting up from the bark. For a huldra to visit her ancestors, all she had to do was grow her roots deep into the earth, right beside the tree that ancestor had become, and connect her roots to the tree's."

"That's how they talked?" I'd asked.

"Yes," she'd answered. "That's how trees communicate. And we can too. At least we could. In that way, the huldra were able to learn the wisdom of the ages and seek direction and counsel from souls much older than the living huldra."

For weeks I'd believed my mother's story as truth. But when new graves began showing up in our graveyard—the grandmothers of my sisters—and I'd overheard my aunts explaining to their daughters that huldra lives are short due to the difficult lifestyle and that it is natural and normal for a huldra grandmother to know when her time is up and breathe her last breaths alone, among the trees on our property, I'd just assumed my mother had told me another fairytale to ease the pain we both felt at the loss of her mother.

Drosera and the plant she knelt beside came back into focus. And for the first time I figured I understood why the rusalki spoke so little and took long pauses in between their words. It was as if they were giving our minds time to reach deep within our souls and dislodge memories, old knowings we'd long since forgotten.

"Drosera, are you going to help me seek wisdom from an ancestor of mine?" I asked. I peered at the trees around me, wondering which held my huldra kin.

"I am not," she answered, focusing on the plant. "Huldra did not grace this land back during the times they stepped into trees." She waited. "But you will use your ability to grow your roots and connect them with roots of others, much in the way we helped you to do in our lake dome. You will connect to the roots of this plant."

I knelt beside her to get a closer look at the plant.

"Those who fear nature fight it," Drosera started. "Nature is change. They fight change. Nature is death and rebirth. They fight death and rebirth. Nature is predictable in that it is unpredictable; they demand rules and order, predictability. Hunters fear nature. It is why they hate the snake Wilds so, for the snake sheds her skin and still she lives."

I finally understood. "It's why their blood stone debilitates menstruating Wilds," I said. "Because by the very definition, we are able to create life and yet when we bleed monthly we are actualizing death. It scares them."

Drosera paused from petting the plant and turned to look at me. "It terrifies them."

I continued explaining, mostly to myself. "So they find a stone that's from nature, but pulled out of its element so that it never changes. And they use it against those of us who personify nature in every way, menstruating Wilds, which, because they've stolen our wild nature, many of us don't live much past the post-menopausal age anyway. They've pulled us out of our element." The realization hit me like a swift punch to the gut. Tears welled in my eyes and I blinked them back.

The rusalka only nodded and gazed back at the plant as though it brought about a trance state.

I quickly moved on to the next thought. Sitting with that last one had the power to take me to dark places that I didn't currently have the time or emotional energy to visit. "But I'm of menstruating age. How will connecting with this plant help me to fight the Hunters and get the succubi galere back?"

"This plant," Drosera began, "is a poison hemlock. Its roots carry most of the poison, a deadly substance that you, being huldra, are immune to. It is a battle trick your ancestors used, one forgotten in time. I am told some of your ancestors harvested the poison for female human healers to use against those who sought to hang them for their gender."

I didn't waste any time in asking further questions. Drosera said I was immune, and that was all I needed to know. I stood, closed my eyes, breathed three deep breaths in and out, and willed roots to shoot from the soles of my bare feet, into the earth, toward the base of the poison hemlock. I wasn't sure how to communicate with the plant, or how to absorb its poison into me, but within seconds I felt my roots connect with others and less than a second later a feeling of acceptance filled me. Suddenly, a thick, cold substance absorbed into my roots and rushed up to my feet, settling in my torso and spreading through my body to pool in my fingertips and the palms of my hands.

Drosera nodded, taking in the sight of me standing among the forest, naked, and in the power of my ancestors. "You must remember not to fall back on your huldra abilities when you retrieve the succubi. With the hemlock in your system, those will not work and the Hunters will cut you down. As the hemlock is a plant, your huldra abilities that you share with a plant will be within your grasp. Those not in common with a plant, seeing in the dark and elevated scent, will be suppressed by the hemlock. But pressing poison into flesh, this will be deadly. Over time the poison will fade from your system. You are made of the stuff of plants, but not fully plant. The hemlock knows this and will seek to get out."

She turned and began walking away.

I pulled my roots up from the earth and chased after her. "Aren't you going to take me home?" I asked. The power of my ancestors I'd just felt covering me now dissipated with the thought of wandering the Portland streets in broad daylight, naked.

She didn't turn to answer. "I have not the energy for another transport, not with you—"

I cut her off, sure of where she was going with that. "How will I get back to the house then? You said the snake Wilds are on their way." Funny how one can go from I shall smite my enemies to please take me home in the blink of an eye.

"I will send your partner sister to retrieve you," she said, gaining distance on me somehow.

"Shawna?" I asked. "She may not be up for it, she's—"

But before I finished my sentence, the rusalka disappeared like mist on a sudden breeze, and I stood in a public park amidst birds singing their morning hellos, greeting the sun rising in the sky. Rather than waste my time standing around, waiting, I went to work connecting to different roots, asking for their guidance, and receiving whatever they were kind enough to offer.

TWENTY-SEVEN

SHAWNA BOUNDED UP THE HILL, past evergreens, ferns, and wild ginger. "Are you okay?" she said on bated breath as she ran, her dreads smacking against her cheeks. The reusable shopping bag she carried, with what I assumed were my clothes, bopped the side of her leg with each stride she took. "I came as soon as Drosera told me where to find you." A fresh dirt mark covered the right knee on her jeans, causing me to assume she'd fallen at least once in her search for me.

She reached me and checked me over before resting her hands on her knees to catch her breath. "I'm so out of shape," she panted. "I need to do more physical activities."

I almost corrected her, reminded her that we'd just fought a complex full of Hunters a week and a half ago. But then I remembered and shifted my point mid-sentence. "No, you fought the Hunters...at the winery."

"Yeah, no," she said, standing up straight and throwing the bag of clothes to me. "That wasn't endurance. That was pure revenge keeping me swinging."

I caught the grocery bag and pulled out a pair of jeans and a dark grey sweatshirt. I shook the clothing before putting it on, in search of underwear, but she hadn't brought any, it seemed. Commando it'd be.

"Hey," I said to change the subject as I dressed and also to share my newest major revelation with my partner sister. "Drosera told me about this cool thing our ancestors used to do. Want to try it?" I played it down, but not on purpose.

Shawna smiled. "I don't know; does it involve sacrificing children?"

I laughed with my partner sister for the first time in what felt like forever. When the joking stopped, I showed her how to grow her roots into the earth and connect to other roots. I thought to hold her hand after she'd taken off her shoes and socks and allow roots to grow into the ground. I wanted to know if the roots reacted differently, more intensely, to two bonded huldras. But I didn't want to risk pushing the poison into her, not that it'd hurt her. I just knew I had to hold onto the stuff until I met a Hunter who got in my way of rescuing succubi.

Another idea appeared in my mind. "Are you connected?" I asked as she stood beside an evergreen. I hadn't suggested she absorb poison hemlock because I didn't intend on bringing her to the Oregon complex, which, I fully realized was my plan—to accompany the snake Wilds to the complex and release the succubi.

"I am," Shawna said in a whimsical voice.

Yeah, she was feeling it.

"Okay, stay connected and I'll try to connect to the same tree, see if it'll link in to us both at the same time," I said, already closing my eyes and concentrating on growing roots from the soles of my feet.

We each stood on opposite sides of the mid-sized evergreen. For living in a park, it was big. But compared to those I'd tree-jumped deep in forests full of old growth, this one was young. Its russet bark matched my own and a tiny smile pulled at my lips.

It being her first time, I assumed Shawna's roots would connect with the evergreen's slightly below the surface, so I pushed mine a bit deeper. Moist earth moved out of the way as my roots bore deeper; a sense of energy filled me as though the soil's nutrients absorbed into my body and fed me. My roots found their target and wound around the much thicker tree roots. A shot of energy coursed through my veins. I shuddered.

With us both connected, the intense exchange between the three of us transcended words. Shawna's emotions spoke to me as though they were my own. I suddenly longed for my "old self" back, for the days I had been ignorant to the darker things in life. A cloud of heavy worry caused my shoulders to slump forward and yet the fire to overcome raged in my heart. It felt like a necessary anger, the kind that creates steps to help you ascend the pit of despair and show you what you're made of.

"I am like a great evergreen," Shawna whispered as though she answered my concern for her after learning what stirred in the depths of her heart. "Winds may try to beat me down, Faline, but my roots will keep me from falling."

"Our ancestors are older than the Hunters," I whispered in return, my confidence bolstered by her own. "The trees and the huldra. If we trust, in ourselves and our heritage, the Hunters trying to control us will look as silly as a human running full force into an evergreen and expecting the evergreen to be the injured party."

Shawna responded, "Ask her a question, this tree."

"How?" I asked.

Through your roots, was the answer, though not with words. A knowing simply popped into my head.

I couldn't tell if the response came from Shawna or the tree, but I was in awe.

Why is Marcus such a comfort to you? I found my mind asking through the roots—a question I'd been secretly wrestling with since we'd rescued her. *Why at the Hunter complex and after, did you reach for him and not me?*

My embarrassing inner struggles with my sister, my hidden hurt feelings, had betrayed me. My eyes fluttered open to see if she was giving me the death stare, because of course she couldn't help who she reached for in her moment of need. Of course it had nothing to do with our bond. She had every right to be insulted by my question.

Shawna only stood in front of me, eyes closed, a relaxed smile pulling her lips slightly upward.

I closed my eyes, too.

I saw only monsters in the room that day, Shawna answered through the roots, her words finding their way to my mind, leaving her voice behind. *I had never seen a huldra in full force, and yours was shocking, how you tore into my captor. I'd assumed Marcus was just another Hunter, until the rusalka Azalea showed herself and calmed me. She assured me he was safe. I grabbed onto him, and I don't know, I feel safe now whenever he's near.*

Her explanation crushed me. Guilt for my sudden jealousy that she saw Marcus as her safe person quickly followed, and mixed with shame for scaring my sister, for the monster she saw me to be.

"We should be heading back now," Shawna said, abruptly, stiffly.

She disconnected from the roots, leaving my soul with a sudden emptiness I hadn't noticed before. I flung my eyes open to see her watching me.

"Is something the matter?" I asked.

"I know you could you feel me," she said. "Through the roots."

I nodded.

"I could feel you too." She waited a breath. "You love him."

I searched her eyes for a hint of opinion on the matter, but she gave none.

"I won't leave you, Shawna," I heard myself proclaiming. And I meant every word with all of my being. "I still want to grow old with you, raise our daughters together."

I thought of what came after bringing a new generation of huldra into the world. "Mourn our mothers together," I finally said, hoping my mother still lived. My heart broke a little more when I realized that even if my mother lived, even if I rescued her, I'd only have a few years left with her before she went the way of her mother.

"How, though, if you stay with him?" Shawna asked. She bit her bottom lip and I wondered if she was holding tears back. I wondered if she'd felt abandoned at the Hunter's cabin, if she feared I'd never come for her. Questions I should have asked her when we were connected through the roots.

"I'll never let you go, Shawna," I declared, my voice serious. "You're my partner sister until the day we die. No male will change that, whether I love him or not."

Her sullen face cheered. "Do I need to make you pinky-swear?" she asked with a hesitant laugh.

"Better than that," I said. "I'll root swear."

* * *

Shawna and I hadn't made it to the first cement step on the yellow house's front porch before Marcus swung the door open and rushed out to greet us.

"Faline Frey!" he said, standing with legs spread apart, blocking our path into the home. "You scared the shit out of me. I woke up, and no one could find you. We've been out looking."

Shawna disregarded his intensity by swatting at the air in front of her. "Please, I told the others when Drosera summoned me. They knew Faline was safe."

Olivia peeked her head around the corner of the hall on the main level and directly in front of us. She snickered and Marcus turned to see who laughed at him.

"You knew?" he asked her, throwing his hands in the air. "But you were looking for her too."

She burst out laughing and nodded, revealing herself. "I told them when we got to the convenience store, while you were on the next street over," she said after she took a breath.

"Damn," he said under his breath. "That's fucked up." He shook his head.

Marcus moved to stand at my side and put his arm over my shoulders. I kept hold of Shawna's hand as the three of us walked toward the door together.

"It is," I answered, not even trying to whisper because if Marcus could hear it, my coterie could too. I patted his butt with my free hand. "But think of it this way. Olivia wouldn't joke with you if she disliked you."

Right before I parted ways with him so we could single-file through the door, he whispered, "So they're on joking terms with me now?"

I thought to ask him why he was whispering around a bunch of huldra, but my sister beat me to it, in a roundabout way.

"Only when the joke is on you," Olivia yelled, hopping over the back of the couch to sit on its cushions.

Observing the two supernaturals, the ex-Hunter and the huldra, trying to navigate the foreign terrain of a peaceful relationship made me wonder how well we'd get along with the new Wilds headed our way. Did they have a sense of humor? Or would trusting these women leave us worse off and feeling like someone had played a cruel joke at our expense?

TWENTY-EIGHT

IF ASKED a month ago to tell everything I knew about the snake Wild Women and their Goddesses, I probably would have talked for all of three seconds, maybe five. As far as I knew, the snake Wilds were succubi and the Goddess who created them was Lilith. Yeah, I would have listed the few details I'd learned about the succubi from our teachers, the Hunters. But all-in-all, I had been clueless.

Lately, though, my mother's stories were rising up within me. As though, like sediment, they rested at the bottom of my subconscious until life came and stirred it all up. Now her words made their way into my dreams and random thoughts. The snake Wilds had the most to prove, she'd remind me, as they were the most demonized of us all.

Snakes were once regarded as sacred beings, able to shed their skin and live, able to access underground, under rocks, explore the unseen, the darker parts of life. *"It is this reason,"* my mother would whisper while pushing strands of my red hair from my face, *"that the snake itself was identified as evil incarnate, because men could not understand its movements or its ways, but most importantly, because throughout ancient belief systems, the snake and the Goddess, the snake and women, were one in the same."*

That memory blossomed to another. *"You know,"* she'd once said, her own mind in a far off place, *"some ancients believed the soul lived in the gut, and*

I wonder if references to the snake's belly upon the ground meant the soul was nearer the earth, or if it meant the soul was tainted with earth."

I paced the living room pondering that exact question. I had only just realized it, but my mother had left me with more questions than answers. Had she unraveled them all, only to place the knots before me to unravel as I grew? Or had she just begun the mission of finding our truth and hoped I would complete it?

I jumped in place when a car door slammed shut. They were here, the snake Wild Women. My stomach twisted and I caught myself wringing my hands. My sisters jumped up to flank me. My aunts went out front to greet the foreign Wilds as almost a planned welcome of dignitaries, being that they were of similar ages. Most of the Wild Women currently exchanging pleasantries would fight the Hunters alongside one another, as post-menopausal women.

Marcus kept quietly occupied in the great room downstairs. We figured he should stay out of this all. And of course, Aleksander, visiting again, stayed with him. Part of me waited for a blow-up from downstairs, the likes of which would blow the door off the place and expose two supernatural males at each other's throats. But, if all went as planned, the two would stay out of the way until we felt the snake Wilds were ready to make their acquaintance. Past experiences made me assume they'd welcome the incubus much more than the ex-Hunter.

"It'll be okay," Shawna offered quietly along with a side-glance. "They're here to help."

Shawna's voice, not her words, reminded me of our morning in the woods, of grounding deep enough to access the wisdom of the tree. I'm not sure when I'd gotten it in my head that I was always inferior, but in that moment, I realized I was an equal to the Wilds now tromping up the porch steps, chatting.

I'd never learned "my place" from my mother or my aunts. But my first check-in at the Hunter complex, complete with receiving an unwanted thigh tattoo of my five-digit identification number and hours of introductory indoctrination, slapped me with a high dose of reality. I'd turned fifteen (I was a late bloomer) and started my period, absolutely thrilled to be a woman. Maybe it was my mother's stories, or maybe it was the way Freyja moved me during my quiet reflection times, but even as a young girl I looked forward to menstruation as though I were about to take part in the most sacred of rites. And that's how I saw it too, as utterly sacred.

Until, of course, the month following my first period, when I attended my first check-in at the Hunter's complex. I remember wishing my aunts and older sisters had prepared me for what I'd walked into, for the way the Hunters would, layer by layer, peel back my dignity and shine a light on my vulnerability. My back had been investigated under a surgical light as though they were inspecting my biggest fault of all, my huldra, my Wild nature. Next was their use of needles to force ink under my skin without my consent, to mar my body, and eventually control it. And last, I was made to sit, sore and broken, as John stood before me, explaining the rules and conduct of a Wild Woman in Washington State.

It had been traumatic, I now realized, and the root of my constant inferiority complex.

The front door swung open and my aunt Renee walked through. She stepped just inside as a tall, striking woman with long black and silver hair and darkly tanned skin stood in the doorframe behind her.

"Faline, this is Anwen," Renee said in a strong voice. "And Anwen, this is my niece, Faline Frey."

Anwen eyed me before closing the gap between us and wrapping her arms around my shoulders in an embrace. It took me a second to catch up before I hugged her back. She smelled of tea tree oil and sand. She wore a bright Indian-inspired top and dark blue jeans with sandals. An Egyptian-looking tattoo of an eye covered the back of her right hand.

"Thank you for coming," I said into her ear with absolute gratitude.

"It is my pleasure," she said, pulling away to look me over.

"You huldra aren't very tall, are you?" she laughed. I shot a look to my aunts who were laughing too. Clearly this had already been discussed outside, probably in relation to trees being our strongest connection to nature.

I had no response for that one, other than waving the others to come in.

When the others entered the kitchen, leading to the living room, and my aunt Patricia shut the door behind them, I counted seven new Wild Women. Seven. That was all the rusalki sent?

"I sense fear rising up in you, an emotion that was not present when I arrived," Anwen said, tilting her head in confusion. "What is it about us that unnerves you so?"

I inhaled deeply and then exhaled, to calm myself. My statement sounded more dignified than I felt. "There are only seven of you and so many more Hunters. We have only two members of our coterie who are post-menopausal, who can join you. That's not enough." I shook my head and sat on the couch to keep from pacing.

"Allow me to introduce those who will be aiding you on this mission before you dismiss their contributions," Anwen said matter-of-factly.

Yup, I'd known this Wild not even ten minutes and I'd already offended her. An ambassador, I was not.

I placed my hands open on my lap as a show of acceptance. If my words offended them, hopefully my body language wouldn't. "I'm sorry," I corrected myself. "Yes, please, introduce yourselves."

Anwen's smile showed glimpses of her wisdom, in the knowing twinkle of her dark irises and the creases framing her eyes and mouth. I wasn't sure how her kind, the nagin, aged, but to me she looked to be in her mid to late fifties.

She stood proud and tall in the middle of the room, addressing the huldra who stood behind and beside me. "My name is Anwen of the nagin group. The Egyptian Goddess, Wadjet created us and moves through us in the form of a cobra. We believe she moves through each living being as a snake, which some call kundalini."

Another woman with blonde and silver hair, who looked slightly older than Anwen stepped forward and gave a quick chin tilt. "I am also nagin, sister to Anwen, and my name is Berwyn." Her somewhat faded eye tattoo covered a two inch by two inch area of her chest, right above her line of cleavage.

The two nagin women stood in the center of the room and a third woman joined them. She looked older than the first two, maybe in her upper sixties. She wore her silver hair in a crown atop her head and moved with the grace of a serpent. "I am Eta," the woman said with pride and power. "I am the elder of my two sisters here today, Anwen and Berwyn. And I am pleased to make your acquaintance. It has been some time since we've heard from our American Wild Women sisters. While I was not yet alive when the succubi ancestors chose to cross the ocean to the new world, as a child, I heard stories of the painful goodbyes between my nagin ancestors and the ancestors of the succubi."

"I'm eager to hear those stories," I said, wishing my mother were here as well to soak up our Wild history.

Eta's smiled slipped slowly across her lips, lit up her eyes, and then eased away. She ran a finger through her bangs, exposing a small eye tattoo at her hairline on the center of her forehead. She and her sisters stepped aside for the next group to move forward.

Two Chinese women stepped to the center of the living room. Petite in size, they both wore their silver and black hair cropped short with brightly colored scarves over their tops and slacks. The woman on the right spoke, eyeing each huldra for a second before moving on to the next. "Hello, my name is Chen and my sister's name is Fan. We hail from China, where our Goddess Nü Gua breathed her essence into her highest priestesses long ago and created our kind, the shé."

The shé Wilds moved aside and the last two newcomers stepped to the center, in front of the couch I sat on, on the other side of the coffee table.

None of these new-to-me women showed signs of feathers or scales. Anwen's explanation gave me a hint of what the nagin capabilities held; with my aunt Patricia being an acupuncturist I was familiar with the belief of kundalini energy—a female energy residing in all genders, believed to lie coiled at the base of the spine with the abilities to rise up the spine, bringing the body spiritual enlightenment and the ability to connect with other dimensions. But I still couldn't figure out what that had to do with the nagin, how they used that to help or hurt others.

The two Wild Women who now stood before me were most certainly of Greek descent. In a way, they looked similar to Marcus; the tan skin, dark hair, and how their foreheads were broader than some, but fit their noses and faces perfectly.

"My name is Calle," one of the women said with an accent. "It is Greek for free woman."

"And I am Gerda," said the other. "It means strong like a spear in Greek. We come from the Wild Woman group called echidna, created by the great snake Goddess of Crete, whose name we do not utter to outsiders." Gerda bowed to me, but not as though she was at my service, no. She bowed as a sign of respect, from one formidable ally to another.

I stood, and not knowing what to do with my hands, I clasped them in thanksgiving to my seven new friends. "I appreciate you coming from so far away," I started. "And I assume you're hungry and tired. We've got rooms ready for you; it'll be cramped, but hopefully it will suffice. There's food in the refrigerator and cabinets, but if you don't see anything you like, just let me know and one of us can run to the store." I looked out the window to see the sun high in the sky. "How about you rest up until nightfall, then we can plan our attack for tomorrow morning. Does that timeline work for all of you?"

I yearned to sit and talk with these women. What were their abilities? How did they use them? And what about their history had my mother so convinced that the snake Wilds would be the ones who tied us all together?

A few of them nodded as we shuffled toward the vacant rooms on the bottom floor. Thankfully I'd heard the men exit the great room through the double doors on the first level, so I knew they wouldn't be noticed. The shé spoke in Chinese to one another as the echidna followed the shé quietly down the steps. Eta slowed her pace until she walked in step with me, bringing up the rear as my aunts led the way.

The older woman lightly placed her hand on my shoulder and smiled as she inhaled. "Your inner snake is coiled tight, ready to attack," she uttered.

"How do I have a snake when I'm huldra?" I asked, already trusting this woman I'd just met. To me she felt like the grandmother I barely remembered, the one who kissed me goodbye one day and was buried in the plot behind our tree homes the next. Her hair had barely any silver streaks when she'd left us.

"This is the great mystery," she answered with a wink. "Some say it is merely the power of nature we each carry, while others link it back to the creation of the world, and still others believe it represents the spirit realm's energy."

"Which do you believe?" I asked, almost ready to agree with whatever she suggested. I'd been around elder Wild Women on the mermaid island, but that seemed more unique a situation. Now, I was inviting elder Wilds to come fight with us, *asking* them to come fight with us, and only meeting the different Wild groups by way of their elders. It brought up a sense of longing I hadn't realized before—the longing of the wisdom and guidance, the confidence and courage of my grandmother as well as my mother.

She shrugged and said in a British accent, "Who's to say?"

The other Wild guests, with bags in tow, found their temporary sleeping quarters. My aunts showed the nagin to their rooms as I stood back beside Eta. Although my heart wanted to connect with this Wild, who for some reason reminded me of who my grandmother may have been if she'd lived long enough to become her, I did not know this woman. And to pretend I did would be a mistake. But, I couldn't keep from asking one more question before heading outside to Marcus and Aleksander.

"Eta," I said, leaning forward and placing my hands on her worn hands. "Thank you for sharing what you saw with me, for confirming that my inner snake is coiled and ready to attack."

Her eyes softened. She slowly shook her head, and my smile faded.

"Oh, no, my darling, what I shared was not a praise nor a confirmation." Eta pulled her hands out from under mine and began to leave my side. Her soft gaze stayed locked on mine. "T'was a warning."

TWENTY-NINE

"IT'LL BE EASIER for you to do your thing if we're out of the way," Marcus said to me as he kissed me awake. He'd crept into bed hours earlier while I slept, and taken a nap with me. The other Wilds slept too, unsure if we'd get any rest between devising our plan of attack and actually attacking. Plus, our new guests needed to sleep off their jet lag.

I kept hold of his arm as he stood from the bed. "Will I see you again before the morning?" I asked. It hadn't been discussed yet, but in my mind the best time for retrieving the succubi was while the Hunters slept, right as the sun came up, or maybe an hour before.

"That's actually why I'm leaving, to figure that out," he answered.

When I lifted my eyebrow he gave the information I'd been wordlessly asking for.

"Last night," he said, "while you were upstairs with the snake Wilds, Aleksander and I left to meet with the Washington Hunter who'd paid me a visit at my apartment a few days ago. You know of him, he's the buddy of mine from the Mill Creek precinct whose promotion party we attended for our second date at the Westin in Bellevue."

Ah, that buddy, I thought. *The one from my night of hell. Makes sense he was a Hunter. Hunters tend to be nearby when my life is going to shit.*

"He'd agreed to meet me here in Portland," Marcus continued. "But we didn't let him know why we were here or that we had any connection to the succubi. Aleksander wanted to get a read on him."

"And?" I asked.

"And Aleksander said the guy's not a spy—he's genuinely left the brotherhood. To prove his stance in all of this, he gave us intel on the local Hunter complex."

I sat up in bed and watched as Marcus pulled on his jeans in the dim light of our temporary shared bedroom. "So are the incubi opening their doors to wayward Hunters now too? And how would he know you'd want that kind of intel?"

This whole set-up seemed a little fishy to me. We took down the Washington complex, and then out of the blue a Hunter from that complex decided he was ready to give up his dagger and sought out Marcus? Marcus, who, by any knowledge of the Washington Hunters, had been reinstated shortly before the Wild Women attacked. Why would a supposed ex-Hunter go to a supposed current Hunter for help on leaving the brotherhood?

"He didn't know. He offered it up as a show of trust, proof of where his loyalties don't lie. I assume he figured since I showed up with an incubus, I'm not towing the Hunter line either." Marcus paused, his shirt in his hands and not yet covering his tattooed chest. "If you want me to keep him away from you, just say the words and it'll be done."

"The Hunter?" I asked. "What's his name anyway? I feel like we're talking code here or something."

"Rod," he answered. "And yeah, him."

Now that he mentioned it, I didn't much care for the idea of meeting the man. That thought brought about another. He was male and able-bodied, yet I hadn't wondered about the possibility of the guy helping us to get the succubi back...because I hadn't wanted his help. I didn't like him and wanted nothing to do with him. My dislike of him smacked with double standard.

"Why would you keep him away from me?" I asked, curious as to what Marcus's take on all this was.

Marcus sat on the edge of the bed, beside me. "He was an active

Hunter at the same complex your sister was held against her will and drugged, as a substitute for you."

He hit the nail on the head. Of course, the current uncertainty of the fate of all US Wild Women reigned supreme in my head, much higher than sifting through my feelings about a Hunter I'd never met, so I wasn't too upset that Marcus unraveled my own thoughts before me. I had more important things to think about. But still, Marcus's statement made me hate Rod more.

I was pretty sure he read my expression, because he quickly continued explaining, "But you should know he was on vacation when your sister was taken, and when you attacked his complex. He'd taken a month off to go on a cruise and do some soul-searching. When he came back, he returned to email and voice message in-boxes full of demands that he return home, threatening to demote him for being out of range of John's communication methods. He said he'd almost been relieved when he'd heard those messages, figured they'd kicked him out and he wouldn't have to make the tough decision to quit. But seeing as the Wild Women had killed most of the Washington Hunters, the ones that remained are coveted resources now."

"Then what's he doing down here?" I asked, dragging myself from bed.

Marcus stood and stretched his shirt on over his head.

I pulled my jeans on.

"He's here to talk." Marcus wrapped his arms around me. "But I think he assumes I'm re-thinking the whole Hunter thing since the complex attack and I'm staying with the incubi. I think this meeting will be more about two guys from the brotherhood sharing stories. Aleksander may even suggest changing Rod."

"No, he can't," I insisted. "If Rod becomes an incubi, he'll be privy to their information, which means he'll know about us being down here. He could go back to the Hunters and give us all away."

"I'm not sure it works like that, especially since Aleksander let it slip that he's been thinking of a way to help without anyone knowing of his involvement. Or more likely, he pretended to let it slip," he said, his breath warm and sweet on my lips, before pressing his mouth onto mine.

His kiss brought my thoughts to him, to us, to tonight and tomorrow morning, to the realization that that exact moment could be the last I'd ever see of Marcus. In a matter of hours I would storm the Oregon Hunter complex with what felt like a handful of other Wilds I barely knew. And fuck it all if that was the best plan at my disposal.

"And how will the great Alek help without being seen?" I asked between kisses.

"By planting explosives on the complex grounds and detonating them from afar once you've gotten all the Wilds out."

I pulled my face away to study Marcus's eyes. "Seriously? How does that fit in with his pacifist nature?"

He shrugged. "Apparently, an incubus who believes he's met his mate isn't opposed to allowing his cloak of pacifism to drop long enough to expose a weapon or two, if it's to protect the one he thinks he loves." Marcus shook his head. "To be honest, every bit of this whole mated thing pisses me off, but I'm trying to rise above it, not act like a jealous lover."

"Well," I sighed. "You're rising higher than I think I'd be able to if the tables were turned."

"It's not over yet," Marcus said with a dark laugh. "I may fall from that level I've risen to, and strangle the guy." He ran his fingers through his hair and finished answering my earlier question about Aleksander and the explosives. "He knows a guy who can hook him up with what he needs. It's genius, actually. Since this time around our army of Wild Women is so small, it makes sense that you concentrate your efforts on getting the succubi out, and from behind the scenes, we can make sure you aren't followed by blowing the place up."

"But," I started, searching his eyes for a flicker of doubt. I didn't want Marcus doing anything he'd later regret. "You didn't like my kind killing your brothers at the last complex. You said some were innocent and may change their minds about following their orders."

Marcus smoothed my hair and looked past me in thought. "That was before they imprisoned a whole galere of innocent succubi. With your sister, I was almost sure only a handful of Hunters knew about her capture, had anything to do with her being holed up in the cabin. But a whole galere? That sort of thing doesn't go unnoticed. Rod told us he'd had a tryst with a Hunter from the Oregon complex, until the guy's shame caused him to renounce his sexual desires and threaten Rod to do the same or he'd out him to the Hunter officials. Rod called him on speaker phone with us listening. The guy boasted about their capture and invited Rod to come see for himself. Said the Oregon brotherhood has now proven their strength and ability to lead the US Hunters to victory against the Wild Women. He rubbed it in that Rod's brotherhood weren't able to control their huldra like the Oregon Hunters could control their succubi."

"Just hearing that makes me sick to my stomach," I groaned.

"I hate that it has to be this way," Marcus said, holding me tighter and kissing me on the forehead. "But it is, and not by our choice, but theirs."

Twice now, he'd said "our" and applied it to him and the Wild Women rather than him and the Hunters. Who knew a simple word could have such a huge impact on my heart, now beating more wildly for his act of loyalty to me and mine.

I wrapped my arms around his thick back and pulled him into me, as tight and as close to me as I could get him. I wished he'd come along on this fight too, not hiding on the outskirts, but standing beside me in battle. He wished the same thing, and had even tried to figure out ways to join me. In the end, though, it wouldn't work. The Oregon Hunters, if any got away, might recognize him as a Washington Hunter, and his inclusion in the brotherhood was still a wildcard we needed to save for later use. Yeah, it was possible Clarisse spilled the beans about Marcus working with us when we attacked the Washington complex, but he highly doubted that. They'd never said as much, never "coincidentally" saw him wherever he happened to be out in public. Marcus figured Clarisse still wanted out of the Hunter lifestyle, still wanted to be "changed" somehow, and would use his big secret as a bargaining chip to get just that.

The east coast complexes were larger and more manned than those on the west coast, and my mother was probably being held at one of them. If Marcus outed himself to his brotherhood by fighting alongside Wild Women, we preferred he do it fighting the east coast complexes. Not that I didn't still wish he and my sisters were joining me. If I died, I'd wanted to at least say goodbye to them in my last moments.

He pulled back and studied my eyes.

"What's going on in your head right now?" he asked on a deep whisper.

"If I die, you won't just abandon my coterie, right?" I said, worried my coterie may be short three members after tomorrow morning. The men's idea to blow the complex up after we left worked fine for me, but what if we weren't able to leave? What if we died there?

Marcus ran his fingers through my hair, from my forehead, down the side of my head, and across my jawbone. "They'd be all I'd have left of you. Of course I wouldn't abandon them."

He leveled his gaze with mine. "But don't make me live without you."

"I wish I could make that promise," I whispered. Fear had been rolling likes waves throughout me for days. One moment I'd feel totally in control and ready to show the Hunters what the Wilds were made of, and the next I'd just know we were stepping into a losing battle. This wasn't like last time. We didn't have an army of women backing us. We didn't have the ability to get to know one another beforehand, to have some sort of feel for how the others fought. I was heading into battle against known warriors with women who appeared more wise than strong, women whose muscles and bones had known better days.

"Answer me one thing, then," he said quietly.

I gave an unsure nod.

"What's your motivation, for tomorrow?" he asked.

"To rescue the succubi," I answered. Easy.

"Yeah, but what else? What's the bigger picture motivation? Why them? Why the Hunters? Why now?" he prodded.

The answer popped into my head and bark tingled across my naked shoulders, ready to spring forth at my approval. "Because we deserve to be free." I reached deeper into my heart. "I'm tired of feeling inept just because a lie someone forced into my subconscious is ingrained so deeply that it's become part of my root system. And it's something I have to fight before any actual battles; it's exhausting and not right, and not something my daughters and nieces should have to deal with." I locked eyes with the man who'd held me tight. "I will not stop until every American Wild Woman is free to be herself."

Marcus gave a nod. The right side of his lips curved upwards.

"Now," he said, "let me tell you what's driving them to fight: orders. For most of them, that's it. And others, more loyal Hunters, are fighting for what they fear they'll lose, something they already have. But you, you're fighting for a need, not a want or a fear. Your fire is bigger than theirs, just remember that."

I mulled over his words in slow agreement.

"Well, in that case," I said flirtatiously, running my fingers down his back and squeezing his butt. "Don't let Aleksander talk you into becoming an incubus while I'm gone. I may have more fire than the Hunters, but it's not enough to win a battle and then deal with an incubus changing ritual. It may be too much pleasure in one day for this Wild."

"Trust me," Marcus said before giving me one last kiss. "When I do get you to the point of your pleasure limit, Aleksander will have nothing to do with it."

Then to my delight, he did his best to prove his point.

* * *

"We will simply walk onto the complex grounds and demand our sisters back," Eta said over a cup of tea. She sat at the oval dining table, sipping tea and adding her two cents every now and again.

Crazy how an opinion about a person can swing so drastically from one moment to the next. Last night, up until the warning comment she'd given about my inner snake coiled and ready to attack, I'd thought Eta was kind and wise. Now, I watched her, wondering what the hell she meant by giving me a warning. What kind of warning didn't actually include the part where the person is warned?

Cryptic as that was, it was Marcus's words that kept rolling through my mind while Eta sipped tea and waxed about the simplicities of our situation. I wondered, as my body still buzzed from my time with Marcus, if there was such a thing as a pleasure threshold and if so, did two supernaturals have the ability to take one another to that point?

"Did you hear what she said?" Patricia asked, clearing her voice. "Faline?"

I snapped out of it. "I'm sorry, what was that?"

"Your aunt was just saying you have information about the Oregon Hunters you'd like to share," Anwen, a nagin, stated.

"Yes." I perked up. "The Hunters specialize in dealing with the Wild Women of their territories," I started. "So the Oregon Hunters are well versed in succubi abilities and how to combat them, but not at all in the abilities of other Wilds. They will be ready for energy control, as they've already shown by detaining the succubi using their blood stones. But they'll have had no real training in fighting women of our abilities."

I unrolled the notebook paper Marcus had left for me, the blue college-rule lines covered over with Rod's rough pencil sketch of the Oregon complex. At least the driveway and entrance to the main building where the succubi were being detained.

"Okay," I started and tapped the four corners of the main building. "The men on our side," which was an easier way of saying two ex-Hunters and a few incubi, "will be placing their explosives at these locations and throughout the complex while we're distracting the Hunters by storming into the main building. Once we leave, they'll activate the explosives from a remote location in the woods surrounding the complex."

I looked around the table at the older Wilds who sat in chairs, sipping tea and drinking coffee. One shé munched on a banana. Those who weren't heading out to the Oregon Hunter complex in a few hours, my sisters, one aunt, and the harpy flock, sat on the couch and chairs in the living room, listening and adding their thoughts every now and again.

"What are your abilities, by the way?" I asked. "We don't have the privacy or time to go outside and practice, but we still need to know how the other works so we can make quick decisions that'll benefit everyone's fighting style."

Anwen set her tea down softly and stood. Her two sisters rose from their chairs and stayed in place beside the table. Each of the three nagin stood tall with shoulders back, one with black and silver hair, one with blonde and silver, and one full silver.

"The nagin have not had to battle in generations," Anwen said with a look of great pride. "But we have never stopped training for the possibility of needing to fight for our place in this world." She closed her eyes and slowed her breathing. When she opened them again, her dark irises turned yellow and her pupils resembled those of a snake rather than those of a human. "The snake energy within all living beings desires to be loose, relaxed, and open to the changes of life. We desire that as well, for all, but in battle we must simply call to the snake within others and it will become our ally, foe to whomever it dwells within."

"And what does that look like?" I asked, playing different possible scenarios through my mind. "Does your victim need to be able to hear your call for it to work? Will you need quiet or close proximity?"

"We would show you now, but we refuse to use a person's inner serpent unless necessary," Anwen's blonde sister, Berwyn replied.

"It looks like stomach pain at first," Eta answered. She picked up her tea and took a sip before setting it back down on the table and continuing. "And then it transcends to nerve pain. Think of a serpent living in the core of your body, sinking its angry teeth into every major nerve, sending pain ricocheting through each limb, each muscle. In the end, it looks like someone writhing on the floor, screaming."

Mental note taken: never piss off a nagin.

"Okay," I said, happy to have them on my side.

I turned to the two shé sitting close enough that their elbows touched. "What about you?"

The sisters turned to one another before looking at me. The moment both their eyes locked onto me, scales burst over their faces, necks, and arms, sluffing off skin in their wake. Chen reached over her left shoulder and grabbed a small wooden string instrument from the carrier on her back, what looked like a miniature *ruan*. Her scaled fingers plucked each string thoughtfully as a slight smirk lifted her lips.

"Oh, wow," my aunt Renee gasped.

I whipped my head back toward the living room to make sure my aunt was all right. My sister's mother stood in one jerk of her body and then faced Chen, who continued to strum her instrument ever so gently. Still, Chen watched Renee from beneath her lowered brows. Renee's hands, through what looked like no decision of her own, rested, palms flat, on her abdomen. When Chen's music changed just slightly, Renee's hands eased upwards until they cupped her breasts over her button-up top.

I whipped my gaze back to Chen, not sure if I wanted to see what my aunt did next. "I get it," I said, acting the least bit impressed only because I was pretty sure I saw my aunt begin to pivot her hips as I looked away.

Chen responded with something between a smile and a smirk. She raised her hand from her instrument and in one fluid movement, returned the piece to its holding place on her back. I heard my aunt take a seat and exhale with a laugh. Chen kept her gaze on Renee.

I switched my focus to the two echidna, Calle and Gerda. They must have felt my gaze because they nodded to one another and turned their attention to me.

"The people of Crete have one of the most intact Goddess temples from ancient days in all the world," Calle started. "This is because patriarchy took its time coming to our island, and as such, we also still hold to our ancient beliefs and ways."

"One such practice is to be reborn from the Great Mother," Gerda finished.

Both echidnas flexed and stretched their necks and backs as they took turns speaking. Obviously they were preparing to show me their abilities. Thinking it'd be awkward to just wait and watch them pop their spines, I filled the pause with a question.

"How does one go about being reborn?"

Gerda flashed a quick smile. "Some of our caves include labyrinths deep within their bellies. It's where the original Ariadne's Thread myth originated," she added, as though it were a side note. "Only, the original had been more about a powerful woman than a princess vying for the affections of a man."

Gerda shook her head and continued, "Every life has points of transition, when old ways die and new ways must be made. As part of the process, we delve deep into the depths of a cave, into the darkness where we are alone with our thoughts and our Goddess. We seek her wisdom for what we are to embark on, and when she is ready to release us, she shows us the way out of the cave to be born once again."

"That's beautiful," I said in awe. When this was all over and done with, when the Hunters were no more than supernatural males living their own lives and leaving us alone, I wanted to visit Crete and meet Freyja in the depths of a sacred cave. I wanted to be reborn a new, free huldra.

Gerda's eyes flashed from human-looking to snake eyes and then back again. She stood and backed away from the table. Her sister followed. Silver strands wove through their dark brownish-black hair, which they'd tied into a long braid down each of their backs. Their skirts weren't identical, but similar in that each had a mandala print of deep oranges, greens, and yellows against a dark background color.

"Our Goddess, may she be forever honored," Gerda started to say.

"May she be forever honored," Calle whispered in agreement.

"Is mother of the snake women, echidna," Gerda continued. "She whose name must not rest on the ears or lips of outsiders."

Calle closed her eyes and swayed back and forth slowly, her skirt swishing along the tile kitchen floor.

"She is able to slide into unseen places, see unseen things, able to visit the depths of the very earth who bore us," Gerda said, closing her eyes. "She does not need feet, for her whole self kisses the sacred earth mother."

Gerda quieted and swayed in motion with Calle. As their movements picked up speed, their skirts both swinging across the tile, their eyes moved rapidly beneath their lids. With a loud exhale they both stopped in place and their eyes sprang open.

The two advanced on me and before I had the time to stand, they were within inches from where I sat. That was nothing compared to what they did next. In another quick movement Calle lifted her skirt to where her knees should be. Except they weren't there.

I gasped and nearly fell backwards in my chair. "Holy shit!"

THIRTY

"THAT'S AMAZING!" I exclaimed, scrambling out of my chair and backing up to keep a safe distance. I'd only seen Wilds don tails in the water, never on land...in a kitchen.

Each echidna boasted a thick snake tail from the waist down. I restrained myself from getting too close; I didn't know these women well enough to put myself within harm's grasp, or should I say, within their tail's reach. I was learning by the second, though. For instance, Calle's tail, leaner and longer than her sister's, snapped back and forth at the tip and resembled the color of a deep green fern. Whereas the tip of Gerda's tail waved back and forth slowly and its color reminded me of an oak leaf in the early fall, transitioning from green to brown.

Their tails seemed so much longer than their legs, which confused me. I'd seen a mermaid change, how her legs fused together and created a tail. Clearly that wasn't the case for the echidna.

"How does it work?" I asked, barely making eye contact with Gerda before bouncing my gaze back to her tail.

Her greenish-brown scaled tail slunk closer to my foot and I took two steps back.

"The length helps us to entrap our prey," she answered.

I nodded. "I can see that, but how does it get so much longer than your legs?"

Calle piped in, "Our legs fuse together and then shift, one on top of the other. Essentially, our tail is as long as our lower torso and both our legs."

Okay, I could see that now, how that'd work. My bounty hunter brain kicked on and more questions came to mind, pushing out the list of other, non-necessary questions about their island and if the humans inhabiting it knew about them and their snake tails.

"So, to do any damage to your foe, you have to get within tail's reach, right?" I asked.

Gerda looked to her sister and then back at me. "Yes."

"Are Hunters wise to this ability of yours? Have you ever used it against a Hunter?" I wondered if their tails were stronger than a Hunter's supernatural strength, than a Hunter's ability to tear an entwining echidna's tail from the Hunter's body.

"We've never met a Hunter," Calle said as though her statement was no big deal.

It was a huge deal to me.

"Are you in hiding, living off the grid like the mermaids were, before the Hunters located them?" I still wondered if Gabrielle had anything to do with the males knowing where the mermaids resided. I had to believe she didn't, had to believe she'd never had led them to her sisters.

"No hiding," Calle said. "We live near our sisters; some of us even share homes. But our homes are in the same vicinity of the homes of humans."

"The humans do not know that we are echidna," Gerda added. "It is none of their concern. To them we are descendants of the old ones, the earliest people on our island, and because of that they respect our privacy, keep their distance."

"But what about the Hunters?" I asked as though my mind could not compute their idyllic existence. Were there actual Wild Women who'd never attended a check-in in their lives and who didn't have to hide under a grassy roof on an island in the middle of a tumultuous ocean to keep it that way?

"What *about* the Hunters?" Gerda asked me back.

"They just let you live among humans with no consequences? Do they not have a presence on Crete at all, or a nearby place? How have you never met one?" I said. Maybe it seemed a simple fact to them, but I couldn't wrap my head around a life without the Hunters doling out commandments for how to live, which job to pursue, and which abilities to suppress.

The sisters slithered to be near one another. They eyed me and cocked their heads. "Do you not know?" Calle asked.

"No," said Anwen, the nagin from the United Kingdom. "I don't think she does."

"Know what?" my aunt Patricia asked.

An unease filled the air around us as my coterie and I waited for the revelation we'd apparently not been privy to that these other Wilds had known all along. I wasn't sure if these non-American Wild Women were waiting to tell us because what they had to say would rock our world, or if they weren't sure it'd be safe for us to know. Either way, someone needed to come out with it already.

Eta, another nagin, pushed her chair away from the table and stood. She made her way to me and placed a soft hand on my forearm. "Darling," she said in a motherly tone. "None of us answer to Hunters. They still run a few pockets in more controlled lands, but for the most part, they were run out of many parts of the world a long time ago."

My knees weakened and Eta gripped my other arm too, allowing me her strength to stay standing. How had I not known this? How had the mermaids not known this when they seemed to know so much more than the controlled Wilds of the States? Had the mermaids known this? Is that where they were right now, why they couldn't help us get the succubi back? Had the mermaids fled to a Hunter-free part of the world?

My stomach felt as though a void lived within it and my head felt as though it floated. I blinked and found focus on my partner sister who stood from the red couch. "Shawna," I said. "How did we not know this?"

Olivia shook her head. "I've never come across anything suggesting this in all my research on Wild Women."

"But you wouldn't, would you?" Celeste countered. "Clearly, even the free Wild Women don't flaunt the reality of who they are to humans. And most humans tend to dismiss the supernatural. So why would they know and believe Wilds exist enough to put that information online?"

As each coterie member added her two cents, I stared at them blankly, my gaze shifting from one to the next. My logical side scrambled for a thread of thoughts that made sense, but only my emotional side made itself known with a stab of betrayal.

I turned to look at Eta. "Why hadn't you helped us earlier? Why hadn't you free Wilds reached out to your trapped sisters?"

Her eyes softened and the wrinkles around her lids deepened. She released her grasp of my arms, and despite my weak legs, I stayed standing.

"For generations we've been oppressed by the Hunters." I said, bitterness rising up within me and filling my voice. "We've lost our roots, literally and figuratively. We've been conditioned to fit a mold so much so that since some of us have broken that mold we don't even know the first thing about recrafting ourselves. We were so cut off from our nature that we don't even know how to find it enough to connect with it once again."

I thought back to the rusalka in the park and how she taught me to connect to the roots of plants. How much more was missing from my life? How empty had I been this whole time, without a clue of the fulfillment buried within my own bones? How different would my life have been if free Wild Women had teamed up to defeat the Hunters of the States and my mother had been raised free, if I'd been raised free?

"My sincerest apologizes, young huldra, but we hadn't a clue you existed." Eta's words dripped with genuine regret and I believed her.

I believed her because I knew how hard the Hunters worked to suppress us, to hide us away, to create incorrect folklore that either erased us or demonized us.

"The strongest form of manipulation, of control, is the withholding of information," Eta spoke softly. "Information about your kinds here, about the Hunters' reign on this land, has been withheld."

The blank stares on the faces of my sisters and aunts had to mirror my own.

"There were no stories, handed down, of the Wild Women who migrated to the Americas or the Hunters?" my aunt Renee asked.

Anwen spoke up. "Yes, from northern Europe there are stories of huldra and other Wild Women migrating to the Americas to liberate themselves from the Hunters' tyranny, before the Hunters in most of Europe were overthrown. But these are old and speculative stories, changed over the years, I'd presume."

"And we knew the Hunters lived in the States as well," Anwen's sister, Berwyn, continued. "But we'd figured, I think, that it was a situation much like ours. Hunters reside all over the world, but only in the same way other supernatural beings live—they rarely have complexes and if they do, it's not to rule over Wild Women anymore."

"Do you answer to Hunters?" I asked the shé sisters, Chen and Fan. Both shook their heads, looking apologetic.

I found myself void of a response. I stared off into nothingness. My mind only spun around this fact, searching for a foothold, something to process or decide. It came up empty time and time again.

Seconds of silence turned to minutes.

Eta's clear, strong voice broke the quiet. "We are here now. That's what matters. We can't change what we didn't know. No one can. But we're here now."

I blinked as her words slowly permeated my mind, pushed past the fact-searching and foothold-grasping. "Okay," was all I could say at first. I swallowed and breathed in deeply. I gave a heavy exhale. My eyes focused in the direction I'd been staring off into, the above-stove microwave. The time read three o'clock in the morning in green numbers. "Okay, if you're offering to help us not only retrieve the succubi, but fight to regain our freedom, then I for one accept your offer."

Eta smiled, as did her sisters. Chen and Fan smirked as their eyes flashed with snake pupils. Gerda and Calle gave dignified nods.

"If we're going to rescue the succubi and be out of the Oregon complex before sunrise, we'd better head out soon," Abigale spoke up. She'd been fairly quiet this whole morning and I'd wondered if her silence was due to fear, but I threw that assumption out. No, Abigale had more reason to attack the Hunters, more venom for their establishment, than any other Wild Woman planning on fighting tonight. I made a mental note to stay out of her way when we got to the complex; she was a woman on a mission.

"Did you all want to at least practice before you headed out?" Olivia asked.

"We don't have the time," I responded. "I just needed to know their abilities and I do now."

"The rusalka told me about yours," Anwen said.

The other Wild Women agreed that they too had been told about us by the rusalki.

"Then let's go get our succubi sisters back, ladies," I said, leading the others as I made my way to the front door.

Did I wish we could spar with one another to practice or at least warm up? Absolutely. But in this case, time was of the essence. And anyway, the Hunters we were about to go up against knew nothing of how to fight a huldra, a shé, a nagin, or an echidna. They probably assumed they'd already won the war by capturing the biggest oppressed Wild group, and that the rest of us would wave the white flag as a result.

If that was the case, they assumed wrong.

I held the front door open for the Wilds joining me on this battle to pass through. They headed down the porch steps ahead of me.

"Wait, Faline," Celeste said, the last Wild still standing in the kitchen. "Shawna told me about the hemlock in your system, and I trust the rusalki, but what if it doesn't work? You're just as susceptible to the blood stones as we are."

I grabbed my sister's hand and gave it a squeeze of reassurance. "The rusalki seem to know the abilities of our kind more than we do. And plus, if the hemlock wears off or doesn't do its job at keeping up my strength against the stones, the other Wilds I'm going with are more than capable of getting me out of there."

Celeste gave a squeeze and released my hand. Still, her shoulders slumped.

"I'll get her back," I assured my sister. "Don't worry, Marie will come back to you."

Celeste bit her lower lip and nodded. She swallowed hard and wrapped her arms around my shoulders. "Please come back, and bring our mothers back with you." I knew what she meant, and didn't fault her for her words, but so very much I wished my mother was among those we planned to rescue today.

THIRTY-ONE

WE PILED into the black Mercedes Benz passenger van our new Wild Women friends had rented to get them from the airport to our Airbnb. My aunts, Patricia and Abigale, sat on each side of me on the second row of the vehicle while the two shé took the front two seats and the three nagin and the two echidna occupied the rows behind us.

Chen drove and Fan acted as her sister's navigator, studying the car's GPS device, and giving directions in Chinese. I'd only ever visited one Hunter complex, before it became the charred memory of what it once was. From what I'd seen of the map Rod drew, the Oregon complex had the same layout. I could assume the others did too which would give me another foothold when we advanced on the two remaining Hunter complexes after this one. I had to think like that, plan for my future rather than negotiate whether or not I'd have a future after today. There was too much on the line, too much to lose if I failed.

I studied the women in the van with me, my chin lowered to keep them from knowing I watched them. I'd never felt so unsure of what I was going into. These other Wilds had never dealt with Hunters before. Had they ever fought? Did they know how to fight?

I scolded myself for not asking those important questions before stuffing myself and my aunts in a van with them on our way to fight our biggest enemies. It was too late now. I'd look as though I didn't trust them, which could possibly lower my aunts' confidence in them and their confidence in us. And lowered confidence translates to lowered fighting effectiveness.

A hand with an eye tattoo covering most of the back of it tapped my shoulder from behind. Anwen's hand.

I turned in my seat. "Yeah?"

"You're beginning to work yourself up and I don't want that energy to spread," the nagin stated.

Goddess, was anything private among Wild Women?

"I'm only working out an attack plan in my head," I half-lied and then realized she may be able to tell if I was lying too, so I gave in and shut up.

I needed to trust in the rusalki, their guidance and insistence that we had what it took to liberate the succubi. I wished I'd shown my aunts how to access and store the good stuff from the poison hemlock plant, given them more to work with. But no, that would mean they wouldn't be able to use their Goddess-given abilities. I was the only Wild in this van who couldn't. No wonder the others seemed more confident than me. They were.

My phone vibrated in my back pocket, shocking me out of my spiraling self-doubt and borrowed bravado. I viewed the screen and saw Marcus's most recent cell number—I'd stopped inputting names and contacts into my throw-away phones.

"Succubi rescue service, how may I direct your call?" I answered.

"Cute," Marcus responded. "But I've got a young buck on the phone with Aleksander, who's received permission from his incubi leader to help rescue Heather, the love of his life. I wanted to check-in with you before I gave him the address."

"Mason wants to help get Heather out," I repeated, partially to confirm and partially to announce it to the others in the van with me whose hearing may not be as sharp as a huldra's. "Drosera did say the Hunters' blood stones don't affect males, and we could use the added help."

The other Wilds said nothing, so I mulled it over and found no down side to accepting the offer of a forlorn incubus. Isn't love grand?

"I thought Aleksander said he didn't want his incubi fighting the Hunters, in case a Hunter got away and told the higher ups," I reminded.

"Yeah," Marcus confirmed. "He stands firm on that and doesn't want to bring Mason with us onto the complex to set up the explosives either. Thinks it'll be too risky, allowing him to get so close to his captured love. So Aleksander said Mason can help by driving the leader's fastest get-away cars, meet you all after you've left the complex. Mason has agreed to control himself until then."

"That's fine, as long as he doesn't get near the complex before we arrive," I said. "And stays in his car while he waits."

Marcus repeated the address and directions to the Oregon Hunter complex, right outside of Portland, so Aleksander could repeat it to Mason. "We're on our way too, but we plan on approaching the back way, through the woods. The bed of my truck is full of things that go boom."

"Wait," I added. "If Mason is allowed to help us get away, why isn't Aleksander chomping at the bit to follow me into battle? He's honestly all right with his one true mate battling a group of supernatural men while he hides in the forest, waiting to detonate explosives?"

Marcus gave a curt laugh, one that showed his lack of enthusiasm on the topic. "First, we're not hiding in the forest. And second, Aleksander has given his next in command instructions to take him underground and place him on lock-down in a detainment chamber built to house unruly incubi the moment he starts acting weird. And I'll carry out the plan on my own. So to answer your question, no, he's not all right watching from afar. But if he follows you into a Hunter complex he'll be putting his whole hoard in jeopardy and possibly positioning them for outside attacks from other groups of supernaturals. That's why if he loses his shit, he'll do it from behind iron bars and locked doors."

I knew it was cruel, but I laughed anyway.

"It's also why he agreed to allow Mason to meet up with you," Marcus said. "If one incubus is noticed, others won't assume he's with a hoard, which makes him less threatening. And he was given the directive to bring you back alive. From both Aleksander and me."

I grumbled.

"Sorry, babe," he added. "I have no doubt you've got this in the bag, but a little added insurance never hurt anyone."

"That's how I know I'm living in a man's world," I said, only partially joking. "I've got a group of men trying to control me and other men trying to protect me."

"Speaking of the men trying to control you," Marcus said, his tone a tad more ominous than his last statement.

"What now?" I groaned. Good Goddess, I was tired of this tug-of-war shit. I doubted the nagin sitting behind me had to deal with this crap on a daily basis. They probably had lower blood pressure too.

"Rod has new information," Marcus started.

"Yeah?"

"And he says there's been a new development with the Oregon Hunters."

"Dammit," I exhaled. "What now?"

"My dad and John have teamed up and they're in Oregon," he said, his voice low and angry.

"It's a good thing you're not in the van with me, then. They'll recognize you," I stated, skirting around the blaring warnings in my head. "Maybe you shouldn't be a part of the crew placing the explosives at the complex."

"I'm going to do this. I don't care if they recognize me," he nearly growled.

"Well I do," I assured him. "I need your connections more to help take down the east coast complexes, full of trained Hunters whose roots are much deeper into their old ways than the west coast guys."

Of course, it was only a matter of seconds before Marcus put voice to my new worries. "My dad and John have got to be there to help the Oregon complex, help prepare them to know what's coming. Why else would they have left their posts? That means the Oregon Hunters will have been trained in fighting huldra, Faline. They may even have combined their armies after pushing your aunts and sisters out of their homes."

Hello, worst case scenario, welcome to my life. And please don't cause my death.

"Well," I said after a couple breaths and a little prayer to Freyja. "We're not turning this van around."

"No, I wouldn't think you would," he responded. "The same way I'm not letting this stop me from doing what needs to be done. Just come back to me in one piece." That last part sounded more like a plea than a command.

I wanted to make him laugh, loosen the tension in the van and on the other side of the phone call, so I joked. "I will, but if I don't, do me a favor. Set Aleksander free on the Oregon complex. If I go down, I'd love to know a pissed off incubi leader was hot on my heels to slaughter a whole complex of Hunters with the power of non-stop, brain-bursting orgasms, or whatever incubi do to seek vengeance on their foes."

I could almost hear Marcus rolling his eyes. "Very funny, Faline," he said dryly. "But if you don't come back, I'll reach the inner complex before Aleksander's first tear shed hits the forest floor." There wasn't an ounce of joking in his voice.

Chen turned the van off of a dirt road and drove it deep enough into the woods that it wouldn't be easily noticed from the road. She put the vehicle in park and killed the engine. Everyone unbuckled their seat belts. Chen and her sister grabbed their instruments from the space between their two bucket seats and positioned them on their backs.

"It's time," I whispered to Marcus, despite the fact that they could all hear me. "I've got to go."

Marcus let out a long exhale, probably praying to his God for our safety. "All right. Well, Aleksander and I will meet you back at the house when everything's done. You guys leave as soon as possible, we'll stay behind to make sure the place blows up before they can rush to their trucks and follow you," he said. "And Faline, you know how I feel."

That was our new code for "I love you," a decision we both made after exchanging the sentiments for the first time and realizing doing so around the other Wild Women would probably shake things up a bit more than we'd preferred for the time being.

"Thank you," I responded. "I feel the same way. See you soon."

I returned my cell to my back pocket as I shuffled out of the van and stretched. My aunts and I removed our shoes and placed them on the floor of the van beside the echidna's shoes. After locking up the vehicle, the ten of us silently walked through the woods, heading for the Oregon Hunter complex. We planned to come at it from the front, while the men waited for us to enter the building before trespassing from the back of the property.

The sun showed no signs of rising, and only a sliver of moon lit our way, which wasn't a problem because clearly the snake women had night vision too. With my huldra abilities suppressed, I followed the others. Wet ferns brushed our knees. Damp pine needles poked at our bare feet. Owls hooted and small animals scurried out of our path. I missed the peace of the forest at night. It energized me, reminded me what I was made of: wildness. I'd nearly forgotten that, trapped in a city full of man-made things.

Eta put a hand out to motion that we had made it. We viewed the wrought iron fence from the forest. It stood tall and commanding in the night, with bright flood lamps pointing in all directions. Like the Washington complex, what looked like the tips of iron daggers pointed up at the sky from the top of the fence. I also spotted a camera and a speaker box positioned outside the gate. We'd expected as much and planned for it too.

Each Wild Woman crouched, positioning herself to jet out of the line of trees and hit the gate at a run, enough to jump over the thing and storm into the main building where the rusalki had told me the succubi were being kept.

With her hand still held up, Eta counted down from four... three...two...ONE.

THIRTY-TWO

THE TEN of us scaled the fence with no problem. Fan even managed to kick the security camera into pieces on her way over. With everything we had, we raced along the lamp-lit cement path to the double doors of what looked to be the main building from Rod's map. So far the complex layout was nearly identical to the Washington one.

With gusto we swung both doors open and stormed into the main building, filled with fury and vengeance, ready to kill any Hunter who got between us and our succubi sisters.

Except, there were no Hunters.

The eerily empty main floor was ours for the taking. We froze in a horizontal line in the middle of the open floorplan and took turns spinning in place, taking it all in. None of us caught more than the faint linger of a Hunter's scent, heard a Hunter's breath, or felt the emotions of a Hunter, other than what was left behind by the men.

Anwen rested her hands on her hips and shrugged her shoulders.

Calle jerked her head toward a hallway at the far corner of the space. "Our sisters are that way, down below." Exactly where Rod said they'd be.

I hadn't noticed when she'd changed, but those weren't legs

carrying her across the finished cement flooring so quickly. Gerda kept up with her sister and the rest of us followed.

"Can you sense them too?" I whispered to Abigale.

She nodded.

Damn hemlock blocking my abilities.

Calle and Gerda led us to the hallway filled with what looked like office doors on both our left and our right. They stopped in front of the center door on our right, a door that looked like all the rest—beige with a silver knob. Breaking the powerful lock, Calle swung the door open so hard it popped off its hinges and fell sideways, smashing a hole in the wall on its way down and landing in the now-open entry, its end hovering over the first step of many leading deep under the main building.

The two Wilds with snake tails glided down the stairs while the rest of us followed as quietly as possible. Chen and Fan pulled their instruments from their carrying cases at their backs and held their fingers over the strings at the ready.

Blood stones of all different shapes and sizes covered the walls, and suddenly instead of damning the hemlock, I found myself thanking it. A layer of soot darkened some of the stones and my stomach heaved at the sight of them, the very stones taken from my sister's prison. John had brought these, the evil male. I hoped I saw him soon; I yearned to pump poison into his veins and roots into his heart. The hemlock may have been restricting most of my Wild abilities, but thankfully it supported my ability to grow roots, something the plant and I had in common. I caught my aunt Abigale running a finger along a blackened red stone, a look of sadness in her eyes, and I urged her forward. She shot me a look filled with venom and I prayed to Freyja my aunt could soon know the sweet relief of revenge for her daughter's pain.

The cement stairs and blood-stone-covered walls curved in a spiral until we came to the dark bottom and an even darker hallway. Thankfully, the other Wilds joining me on this rescue mission weren't thwarted by poison running through their veins and caught the scent of the succubi galere from behind the door at the end of the hallway.

Gerda broke the steel door from its lock and hinges.

Bars separated us from a group of women from which a combined gasp escaped. Blood stones littered the walls in here too, but I didn't need my nose to tell me. Marie and her succubi galere stood at once, shocked to see familiar and unfamiliar faces.

I rushed ahead and stopped not even an inch from the bars.

"You came!" Marie exclaimed, clinging to the bars that stood between me and her. "But how did you get past the Hunters?"

"They're gone," I answered, knowing full well we may have just walked into a trap. The sooner we freed our Wild sisters, the better. The possibility that we'd need to fight our way out any minute bore heavy on me. "How do we get you out?" I searched for a key hanging somewhere or a keypad on or around the barred door. Rod hadn't gone so far as to explain exactly how the succubi were being detained, just where.

"Did you bring food?" Heather whined, standing from a wooden bench in the large cell. "They haven't fed us and we're so hungry."

"Let's concentrate on getting home first," Marie said to Heather, patting the younger succubus on the shoulder. The succubi leader shifted her attention back to me. "The way to open the cell door is there." She pointed to what looked like a metal box hanging on the wall. "Though I don't know the code. I tried to watch them input it, but they noticed and covered it with their free hand."

Patricia walked to the metal box and tried to open it. "Hold on, it's locked," she said right before she pulled the thing from the wall, exposing a small square of backlit buttons.

"I've got this," Anwen said. "Everything is energy." She held her tattooed hand over the buttons and closed her eyes. Her breathing slowed as her hand shook so quickly it seemed to vibrate.

The holding cell door clicked open and Marie rushed through, wrapping her arms around me. "You don't know how glad we are to see you all!" Marie looked to the nagin, shé, and echidna Wild Women. "Thank you for trusting our rusalki friends and coming to our aide, sisters." She pulled away from me and took turns hugging her new snake sisters. "There were more Hunters than usual, when we came in for our check-in," she said over her shoulder to me.

"Let's get out of here," I said, motioning to the dark hall. "We can compare notes back at the house."

"They drugged our older members," Marie said, motioning to the younger women to help the older Wilds stand from the benches they rested on, and walk. "They separated us from them in the beginning, and then after they enclosed us in here, they brought back our older members, groggy and weak."

"They knew the older succubi were probably post-menopausal and wouldn't be affected by the blood stones. They had to drug them to keep control," I said. Who the hell told them, though?

Thankfully none of their elders were in the same shape I'd found Shawna after she'd been drugged by a Hunter.

The succubi followed my aunts and me, with the other snake Wilds bringing up the rear, just in case we were attacked from the front or from behind. Out of all of us, the succubi were currently the weakest, having spent time confined among blood stones and without food. Yet, when we made it to the main floor and out of the building, no one stopped us. We weren't powerful sonars or Dopplers, but I trusted the fact that we didn't sense one Hunter or human on the premises. It also worried me—not enough to slow our pace, though. I hoped Marcus and Aleksander had been able to get in, set the explosives, and get out because I didn't sense them either. Although, the hemlock still pumped through my body, so maybe that's why.

Once they were away from the blood stone, the succubi regained a bit of their lost strength and scaled the iron fence with the rest of us.

"Heather," I said under my breath as we raced through the trees and ferns.

"Yeah?" she asked, picking up her pace to run beside me.

"We don't have room in the van for all of us, so Mason should be here to offer a ride," I said through a mouthful of hair my ponytail gladly supplied to my open mouth. As I briefed Heather and her succubi sisters on how we were going to get them away from the complex, I listened for an explosion behind us. Each second of silence ticking by amped up my worry for Marcus. If it didn't happen by the time I made it to the cars, I decided to double back and look for the ex-Hunter and the incubus.

"Other than the succubi, the snake women will return without the van," Chen inserted herself into the conversation.

"We huldra can go with Mason, too," I said, holding my ponytail to keep it from finding its way into my mouth again. "The succubi will still have to squish in and forgo the whole seatbelt thing, but it'll give them more room."

Chen gave a nod and sped forward.

The sound of gravel crunching beneath car tires caught my attention and I raced for the road leading to the Hunter complex, declaring that whoever is catching a ride with Mason needed to follow me. I spotted a lone incubus, hurrying up the road to save his love.

I jumped into a nearby evergreen and bounded from one of its sturdy branches to the branch of the next evergreen until I stood in the last tree lining the gravel road. A huge explosion shook the earth and rattled my head, knocking me from the branch and onto the hood of the incubus's candy apple red Tesla Roadster. I peered into the car through the glass roof. Mason slammed on the brakes and I thought quick enough to use the momentum to back-flip onto the ground in front of the car.

"Holy shit!" he exclaimed "Did you hear that?" He rushed from the car to where I stood.

We turned toward the blast and peered down the gravel road. Orange flames licked the dark sky and illuminated everything around the complex. Billows of smoke rose; tiny embers twinkled like stars in the dark tendrils. The wrought iron gate with its daggers pointing to the sky, looked to hold back evil incarnate...or at least the fire that would burn all the evilness down. I thought of the soot on the blood stones, the ones taken from the last Hunter complex fire I'd walked away from. Hopefully the blast blew the stones to smithereens.

"Yes" I said on a breath of relief. "They did it."

After our little group pulled ourselves from the bewitching scene before us, Mason made sure I was okay from nearly being hit, which of course I was fine, if not a little sore. He looked at the hood. "This is Aleksander's. He's going to kill me for that dent."

I ran my hand over the hood and felt a definite dip in the red aluminum. I wiped the dust from my hand onto my jeans. "Just tell him I did it," I said with a smile.

"Did I miss everything?" he asked, peering towards the complex.

"Everyone got out okay, I assume?" He looked toward the direction I came from. "Where's Heather?"

If I wasn't so paranoid about the Hunters not being at their complex to greet us, and so awestruck with how the flames lit the dark early morning surroundings, I would have laughed at the way Mason changed subjects at the speed of light.

"You missed nothing. They weren't there," I answered. "And Heather is..." I turned to point toward the woods we came from, and stopped mid-sentence when the young succubus ran from the tree line and straight into the arms of her incubus.

He picked her up and spun her around, showering kisses on her exposed skin from her neck up.

My aunts paused to smile at the display of young love. I smiled too. Ah, romance between two supernaturals, accepted for who their hearts beat for. Must have been nice. I scolded myself for the bitter reaction. Still, it had to be nice to not have to use code phrases to say they loved each other or only kiss when no one was looking.

I snapped out of my moment of self-pity. We had a job to finish.

"Come on," I said, motioning to Aleksander's damaged car. "You two can kiss all you want in the backseat. We need to get out of here."

The two lovebirds ran hand-in-hand and slid into the back of the car, where they did, in fact, continue kissing.

My aunts and Eta squeezed into the small car with me and the intertwined young ones. Eta sat in the backseat and my aunts shared the front seat, Patricia sitting on Abigale's lap.

We only drove down the road for a couple minutes before the black van full of succubi barreled out of the woods. The echidna followed closely behind them, some on foot, some on tail. They slowed and let me go in front. I hit the gas as the van kept steady in my rearview mirror.

"I assume this is your leader's nicest car?" I asked the only male in the vehicle.

Mason pulled his mouth away from Heather, who sat on his lap, for all of two seconds. "This is his fastest car, tops out at 250 miles per hour. He wanted to make sure I got you out of here in time." Aleksander didn't think about the van that'd be following us. No way would I push this baby to a speed the others couldn't keep up with.

I eyed Mason in the rearview mirror then returned my gaze to the gravel road.

The Bluetooth in the car rang and I eyed Mason in the rearview mirror again.

"You can answer it; it's just Aleksander," Mason said, before going in for more suck-face time. I felt bad for Eta, who had to witness the whole thing.

I pressed the dash screen. "This is Faline," I announced.

Aleksander's low voice rumbled through the speakers. "Faline? You're safe? The blast didn't get you right? We wanted to give you ample time to move far enough away."

I turned the volume down. "Yes, yes, and yes."

"Then you're on your way back?" he asked with a little less rumble.

"Also yes," I answered.

He sighed. "Good, good. Okay then, we'll be on our way soon. Meet you at the house."

"Wait," I almost yelled into the car's dash. "Can I talk to Marcus?"

Aleksander scoffed as though my request bothered him, which it probably did seeing as he'd proclaimed his undying love and devotion for me and I still chose Marcus instead.

Aleksander spoke to me again, "I'll let him know you'd like to speak with him. See you soon."

The line went dead.

It wasn't five minutes later that my cell vibrated in my back pocket. Marcus!

"Yes?" I answered hurriedly as I turned from the gravel road onto pavement.

"Ah, it's so good to hear your voice," Marcus said on a sigh of relief.

He was rushing to his truck, I could tell by the thuds of his quick footfalls. I was fine, he was fine, everyone was fine. "We got 'em, baby," he said through quick breaths.

"The Hunters weren't there," I said. "I wonder if they captured the succubi to weaken us and then left for the east coast, leaving the succubi to starve to death. Maybe somebody tipped them off that we were planning to head there next." Which I had been, before I'd gotten sidetracked with the whole succubi thing. I couldn't say that though because the sidetrack herself smooched in the backseat.

"Fuck! So we just blew up their building, but not the actual enemy." He shared a few words with Aleksander. "You think the mermaids told them your plan?" he asked me, putting words to the uncomfortable questions in my mind.

Damn, that man got me sometimes.

"It's one theory floating through my head," I said.

"What are the other theories?" he asked.

I hadn't fully fleshed out the others. "Hey, I'm about to merge onto the highway and don't want to get pulled over by a Hunter cop for using a cell phone while driving and having more people than seatbelts in the vehicle. Meet me back at the house to finish this discussion and maybe, if everyone is up for it, plan to leave for the east coast in a day or two?"

For the last few days I'd thought we were screwed, that all our plans were nothing but lost hopes and the reality of being an American Wild Woman came full force as a stinging slap across my face. But it turned out we'd only been derailed by a few days. And now we had more Wild Women to help us and more knowledge on how to overcome our enemies. Thanks to the ex-Hunter and the incubus, our enemies had one less stronghold. Two complexes had gone up in smoke. There were two left to level with flames, or explosives, or whatever else we had at our disposal.

Thank Freyja, this actually worked out for us.

"Sounds good," Marcus replied as he shut a door behind him. "How far out are you?"

"Twenty minutes or so."

"Okay, I'll see you in a little more than twenty," he said. "Oh, and Faline, you don't know how thankful I am that you're all right."

"Me too, Marcus," I said, and thought to add our code phrase. "You know how I feel."

THIRTY-THREE

THE SUN WOKE as we neared the outskirts of Portland. Rays of pink and orange threatened to swallow the dark sky. I took a right and slowed as I neared the yellow house. I parked by the curb closest to the front yard to give the succubi the driveway spot so they'd have less of a walk to the comfort of a safe space.

As I marveled at how easy the Tesla's oh-so-smooth handbrake was to secure into place, my phone vibrated again. I'd set it in the center console, so I only had to glance at it to know Marcus was calling again.

"Hey," I answered. "How many bad guys you think I need to bring in to be able to afford a Tesla?" I ran my fingers along the perfect inner stitching of the black steering wheel.

Marcus laughed, caught off guard. "It depends. How open are you to working for the mob on the side? I'm sure your skills would come in handy in locating snitches."

He joked, of course, but I played along because why not? "Snitches are the worst. Snitches get stiches, I've always said."

"Then you'd make a perfect addition to the mob's illegal payroll and should be driving your own blood-money Tesla in no time. But hey," he said, changing the subject. "I'm calling to let you know we're running behind."

"Okay," I said, stepping from the car with a sad goodbye to the machine. I winced when I caught sight of what I'd done to the hood. "Well, we just got here."

"We're not too far behind," Marcus responded. "Maybe seven minutes or so. There was a cop following our car and we didn't want to stop and wait for him to approach the vehicle to find out if he was a local Hunter or not—two Hunters and incubus may look suspicious. We also didn't want to lead him to you all."

"Rod's with you?" I asked, pressing the lock feature on the key fob and walking up the cement path.

I reached into my pocket for the key to the front entrance, but remembered I'd left it with my sisters. I hoped they hadn't accidently locked us out.

"Yeah," Marcus replied. A turn signal sounded in the background and I looked for signs of the truck of men down the street. Nope, must not have been turning onto our street.

The succubi galere moved a little slower than usual, but they made it up the porch steps soon after I realized the front door wasn't locked.

"All right," I said, walking into the entryway. Marie broke off from the group and headed downstairs, in search of Celeste, no doubt. "That's weird."

"What?" Marcus asked.

"My sisters and Patricia aren't here to greet us." I paused and for the first time, noticed the faint scent of cologne—intruders. "Celeste wouldn't miss seeing Marie for the world; she should have met us in the yard."

I clicked my tongue and each Wild Woman within viewing distance stopped and focused on me. Some stood on the stairs, others in the hall. Everyone froze.

I whispered, knowing my two aunts would hear me, and hoping the succubi and incubus would pick up on it too. "We're not alone."

"Shit," Marcus exclaimed. "Alek, go, go go!"

The car's engine revved on Marcus's side of the phone. I thought to end my call, but opted to keep him on the line, just in case he needed to hear what came next.

A closet door at the beginning of the hallway flung open, smacking a succubus in the head with enough force to drop her to the ground, bleeding. Instantly, bedroom doors opened and Hunters dressed in black shirts and cargo pants rushed us. Screams echoed through the stairwell and hall, making it impossible for me to listen for more hiding men.

Marcus shouted into the phone at me, but I couldn't pay him any attention, I had to keep my sisters safe. A cluster of Wilds turned to run out the way they'd come in, but a handful of black-clad males shoved the front door open and filled the entryway behind us. Another group of Hunters ran up the deck steps and piled through the back sliding glass door. We were trapped, stuck, with every obvious exit blocked by at least two Hunters.

I backed into a wall and flattened myself enough to take in my surroundings and formulate a plan of attack. Bark rose to my skin and I willed tiny branches to grow from my palm, at the ready. The hemlock kept the branches from being very strong, though the fact that I was able to grow even weak branches meant the poison was wearing off. I'd forgotten to ask the rusalka how long the substance would stay in my system. I felt roots push from the tips of my toes and I peered down, thankful I'd forgotten to grab my shoes from the van when we'd gotten back to the house.

Other than the shuffling and yelling in the downstairs great room, I counted nine Hunters on the main floor, grabbing Wilds and throwing them into the bedroom Marcus and I had shared. I assumed the harpies, my sisters, and aunt had been stuffed in there too.

Okay. I took a breath to calm my huldra who wanted blood NOW.

If my coterie and the harpy flock were in my temporary bedroom and unable to get out, I could assume the Hunters had redecorated the quilt-covered walls with blood stones, or maybe just piled the place with them. Which meant me breaking down that door to get to my Wild sisters would result in my capture as well, if the hemlock had lost its strength enough to protect me from the effects of the stone.

"They've got blood stones in my room," I yelled to Patricia and Renee. "And probably the rest of our coterie and the harpies!"

My coterie elders wasted no time. They fought two Hunters who held the arms and legs of a succubus and were attempting to carry her to my room at the end of the hall. I knew the captured succubus used her abilities to change their perception of energy because the two males grimaced in pain as they slowly walked, as though each step caused them agonizing pain.

My aunt Abigale shoved her palm into the face of the Hunter who held the succubi's arms. Before he had time to drop her and push my aunt's hand away, strong branches shot from her palm and bored into his skull through his eyes, causing a quick death. He fell to the floor with a thud, taking the succubus with him. From the floor, the succubus kicked her feet free of the living Hunter and hurried to stand and face him. With her right hand she punched him in his nose, a tactic to hold his attention, while with her left hand she thrust her open palm onto his chest and screamed. The Hunter fell to the floor, dead.

My aunts jumped over the bodies and bounded for my room. I desperately wanted to join them, to make sure they weren't overpowered once they entered, but I'd be more of a hindrance than a help at this point. From the sounds of it, I was needed downstairs. I pushed off from the wall, ready to rush down the narrow stairwell and burst into the great room, when the snake Wilds erupted through the front door singing their ear-piercing war cries as the two shé played their stringed instruments. Calle and Gerda, the echidnas, shot forward, their legs already changed, and thrashed their tails through the air, clotheslining two confused Hunters in the process.

"In here!" Abigale yelled to the newcomers, and the echidnas whipped around to join the elder huldras.

The shés continued playing their instruments, their snake eyes scanning the area, as they followed my aunts down the hall and into my room. The nagin kept close behind, their hands in the air and at the ready to make the Hunters do as they wished. Once I saw that they'd all made it into my room, and heard the terrified screams of males, I flung myself onto the stairwell and nearly flew down the stairs. I landed on the polished cement flooring with barely a thud, and crouched to take in the scene around me.

Two blasts rang out from a gun, but the depth of the sound it made reminded me of the tranquilizers the Hunters had used on the mermaid's island. I paused, ready to spring back upstairs, when the instruments grew louder followed by the unmistakable thumps of bodies hitting the floor above me.

Heather and Mason held their own, working together to force a fighting Hunter up against the great room wall with arms splayed. Against the two of them, he didn't stand a chance, so I let them do their thing.

Every scream I heard, every cry, every roar, I yearned to catapult myself to the main floor and check on my coterie and the harpies. To be away from my coterie killed me, but to be with them could put us all in worse danger. Last time my sister was in trouble and blood stones covered the walls, I had no choice but to let my huldra take complete control. I'd blacked out and came to minutes before my huldra turned her wrath on Marcus. With the hemlock still in my system, but waning, I didn't know how the blood stones would affect my huldra. Who knew who my huldra would hurt today, with no rusalki here to pull me out? Still, I listened for the voices of my coterie, and if any one of them called for me, screw the consequences.

Through the open lower level double doors, I noticed Marie and four succubi standing on the back patio in two lines, their backs to one another, looking out. Each succubus held both hands out in front of her, palms flat and upright, to keep the two rows of Hunters on each side at bay. But that's all they were doing and it seemed the Hunters were waiting for the succubi to weaken before they pounced.

Energy has to come from some place, and without fuel, or food, for the past couple days, the succubi were running on empty.

I, on the other hand, happened to still have a small amount of hemlock poison pulsing through my body.

Before me stood a row of five Hunters with their backs to me, facing the succubi. In front of them stood a row of two succubi who had their back to a row of three succubi who had their hands held out to ward off another row of five Hunters. I thought to take out the row of males with a bowling ball approach, but changed my mind mid-run and decided to go with the money approach. Six steps away from the first row of Hunters, I jumped into the air and spread my legs, willing roots to grow from the soles of my feet—poisonous roots.

Each foot slammed into the back of a Hunter and my roots broke through their black shirts and bore into their tattooed skin. I willed a portion of the poison to release from my body as I wrapped my arms around the neck of the Hunter in the middle of the two screeching out in pain, trying to slice my roots from their backs. Middle Hunter wasted no time pulling his dagger from its sheath. He tried to plummet the thing into my arm, but my thick, russet bark held the blade at bay long enough for me to shove the fingers from my free hand up into the flesh under his chin and shot vines from my fingertips.

I didn't will my fingers to release poison, but the middle Hunter fell seconds after the other two. I had two left. I pulled my vines and roots back into me, and jumped from Middle Hunter's back to crouch behind the row's remaining Hunters.

With me representing the huldra coterie in the best of ways, the two rows of succubi banded together to take down the five Hunters on the other side of them.

The two Hunters in the closest row of five, before I'd whittled their numbers, turned their attention to me. I flashed a smile from where I crouched. I hadn't realized it earlier, but my huldra was antsy and the more the poison left my body, the stronger my huldra became. Letting her come out to play felt pretty damn good.

"So are you two boys from Washington or Oregon?" I asked, which took them off guard.

"Oregon, demon bitch," the one on the right answered. He looked to be near the tender young age of eighteen or nineteen; not even the faint hints of stubble graced his chin.

"Now, now," I chided. "You must be new to the brotherhood, aren't you? Because I'm not a succubus. But hey, real quick, are any of you here from Washington?"

The Hunter on the right spoke again. "They're in that room upstairs."

The Hunter on my left elbowed the younger one and chided him for giving me information. "Shut up."

Huh, so the Washington Hunters were guarding the Washington

Wild Women along with the harpies, which they probably hadn't thought they'd find. I should have assumed as much.

Before I could thank the young Hunter, they unsheathed their daggers and rushed me.

"Faline!" Out of nothing but pure, dumb, reaction, I turned toward the open double doors, toward Marcus's voice.

And paid the price for that costly mistake.

THIRTY-FOUR

"FALINE!" Marcus called for me again as the younger Hunter grabbed my arms and pulled them behind my back, hoisting me up to my feet in the process.

The other Hunter put his dagger to my throat and pushed. The blade hit bark, so he trailed it up my jaw, across my chin, and pushed the tip against my right temple.

I froze.

"You know the one move, the one way to kill anyone?" he whispered into my ear as he brought his face within licking distance to mine. "It's a sharp object to the brain, through that sweet, sensitive spot in the temple. It's a humane death, though, not one fit for a Wild Woman such as yourself. But," he shrugged, "it'll have to do."

"You're not from around here," I said, trying to speak evenly and stay calm despite the fact that one move from him meant certain death for me. If I kept him talking, I kept from dying.

I snuck a quick glance at the succubi who still fought hard with waning strength and had only taken out two Hunters for their troubles.

"Well, you're perceptive," the Hunter answered in his southern accent. "I'm from North Carolina."

If I lived through this, my next stop would be his home complex. I had to keep him talking, so I thought of more questions, ones that wouldn't piss him off enough to drive his dagger through my skull.

"What brought you out west? It couldn't have been the sun," I tried to say jokingly.

He scoffed.

"Don't talk to her," the younger Hunter piped in, still holding my arms behind my back and facing my hands down. "You told me to shut up when I talked to her."

The older Hunter kept his eyes on me, studying my face, as he answered his brother. "This is different, she's about to die."

Well, that didn't sound promising for me.

"The complex got a little too...full," he went on. "So I put in for a transfer."

"Full of Hunters?" I pushed further, just watching and waiting for him to be done with me.

He scoffed again, clearly unhappy with the direction his Hunter organization headed in. "Whores. It's full of whores."

"Dude!" the other Hunter exclaimed with wide eyes.

A wry smile grew on the slightly older Hunter's face and I knew we were done talking. He pressed the dagger's tip harder against my temple. I fought to wriggle away, grew vines to wrap around the younger Hunter's hands and squeeze them to loosen his hold on me, but nothing worked. He only cut my vines with a painful slash of his dagger. The blade's tip bore into my temple. Blood trickled from the wound as the older Hunter pushed slightly harder with each breath, reveling in his slow kill.

When I'd had enough, when I knew I wouldn't make it out of this one, I let go.

And I let my huldra free.

Only this time I didn't black out completely. Like standing in a closet, its door opening and closing quickly, blanketing me in darkness and then showering me in light, my huldra flickered in and out. She moved quicker than I thought possible, slipping from the Hunter's grasp by dropping out from under them. Pain sliced along the side of my face where the dagger cut against my skin, but it was muted and I knew it wouldn't kill me. She killed the older Hunter first, with his own dagger, twisted his arm enough to plunge the dagger's tip into his right temple.

I gave in as she released my inner beast and allowed me to watch from the sidelines. And my inner beast, the suppressed wild part of me? Yeah, she was pissed.

We, my huldra and I, turned our attention to the younger Hunter.

"I'm not a demon, asshole," I heard myself say, but in a guttural voice, animalistic. "I'm a motherfucking huldra!"

I lunged at him and slammed into his brick wall of a chest. He grabbed my ponytail to yank me down to the ground, but I flipped up and kicked him in the groin. Out of what I assumed was instinct, he released his hold on me to cup his jewels.

My huldra and I went in for the kill. And when we were done with him, we helped the succubi finish off the rest of their Hunters too.

Our band of bloodied Wild Women tromped up the stairs to help on the main floor.

They seemed to have everything covered, especially since the succubi's snake Wild sisters were fighting in full force against the few Hunters still standing, so I made my way to my temporary room. My huldra wanted her coterie and as thankful as I was that she was playing nice with me, I wasn't about to try to stop her for reuniting with her family. I passed the front entry. The door had been left open, a Hunter's body lay on the cement porch and two stunned Hunters hung from the old oak tree in the yard. Aleksander stood below them, his arms raised as though he'd flung the men onto the branches with the sheer force of killer energy.

I grabbed the knob to my room and swung the door open, nearly pulling the thing from its hinges. "Shawna!" my huldra called in that animalistic voice. "Shawna!"

"I'm here, Faline! I'm here!"

I caught sight of my sister standing over a dead Hunter, her dreads a mess, her shirt torn, blood streaked across her arms and jeans.

I thought to run to her, to catch her in my arms, to mutter thanks to Freyja for keeping my partner sister safe.

But the sight of Marcus in the middle of a standoff with an older Hunter who resembled him in the eyes and chin, froze me in place.

"I should have known," his father seethed. "You are weak as a sniveling little girl." The man styled his thick, silver hair very much like his son. It was as though I stared at an older version of Marcus. Unlike the other Hunters, a silver dagger emblem attached to a black ribbon, hung around his neck. Marcus's father was a Hunter leader, and from the looks of it, high up in the chain of command.

John scaled from the open bedroom window, making his escape. Marcus's father was the only Hunter left, and surrounded. But Marcus only stared at the man, both with their daggers drawn. My aunts and sisters had already left the room, to check on the other Wilds. Only Shawna, Marcus, and his father remained.

Marcus's father jabbed the dagger forward, shocking his son, and throwing Marcus off balance. Rather than taking a step back, Marcus jumped to the side and hit the dresser with a crack, flinging him back toward his father, toward the dagger. His father's dagger scraped his side before I rushed in between them and pushed Marcus onto the bed, away from the blade. I shot a thin branch from my palm, but his father made quick work of slicing through the plant with his dagger, sending scorching pain up my hand and arm.

"He'll never belong to you," his father jeered. "His Hunter blood will always bring him back to his roots."

I flung my other hand up and shot vines from my fingers, but before they could wrap around the man's neck, he spun on his heel and catapulted himself from the window, landing on his feet and running in the opposite direction of the front yard, where I presumed Aleksander finished off the Hunters in the tree.

Marcus jumped from the bed. "They left!" he yelled, leaning out the open window. He pulled himself back inside. "Damn it!" he punched a hole in the wall. "I let them get away!"

I let my huldra slink back to her resting place, pleased from a job well done as I stood, stunned, beside Shawna. What kind of power did Marcus's father hold over him that he caused his son to freeze up in his presence?

"You let him go," Shawna uttered. Tears filled her eyes. Her hands shook and bark stayed thick across her skin as though it wasn't safe to let her guard down. As though Marcus was no longer safe to her. "You let my captor go."

THIRTY-FIVE

Our total Hunter body count for the day topped out at eighteen. Marie assured us that once she and her sisters had gotten something to eat and drink, they'd dispose of the bodies. Their snake Wild sisters offered to help, and as curious as I was about what they did with dead bodies, I asked no questions. The harpies looked disgusted by the idea and didn't offer to help.

As expected, one of the neighbors called the cops from all the commotion, but Aleksander shifted the energy surrounding the property, settling a peaceful calm over the place, that somehow caused the cop car, its siren blaring, to drive right past.

Marcus only sat on the bed in our room, his head in his hands. After my best efforts to comfort him, and my assurance that he'd done what he could, he'd asked me if he could have some time alone.

My coterie and I, along with the harpies, incubi, and Rod, cleaned and treated gashes for one another and stuffed any blood-stained quilts, wall and bed decorations, into large, black trash bags.

"We'll cover the expense of not only the Airbnb rental, but the damages too," I assured Aleksander as I stood, taking in all the destruction around us. The full trash bag on the ground beside my leg only held a tiny portion of what was left to clean up.

Aleksander shrugged as though whether we paid or not was no big deal to him.

When only morose silence greeted my offer, I thought to bring up another topic, anything to get people talking. "So Rod, how'd the Hunters know we were going to visit them? I mean, it seems perfect timing to me that they came over here during that small window we were at their empty complex."

All eyes swung to me and the claimed ex-Hunter.

I hadn't meant to accuse him—Marcus had assured me Rod was trustworthy. But, the words were out and I couldn't take them back.

"Well," Rod started, calmly, as though he were deescalating a tense situation in a way that only a decorated police officer could. "I think it's safe to assume the Hunters took the succubi galere as bait to draw your group to their complex." He paused. "And from a strategic standpoint, I'd say they were waiting, in their vehicles somewhere, for a lookout to give word that you'd set foot on their complex before entering your temporary home."

"But how did they know where we were staying?" Eonza asked. "They'd snuck in through the doors and windows and blindsided us. We'd tried to fight back, but there were too many of them and we weren't prepared, our guard had been down. They herded us into the bedroom where other Hunters had broken in and already began setting up the red stones. It all happened so fast. How?"

Rod shook his head and exhaled. "Now that one I couldn't tell you. I have no clue how they knew where to find you."

"They've banned together," I said, thinking of the Hunters I'd taken down earlier and what they'd said about the North Carolina complex. "Which means they've got more resources than Rod or Marcus know of, since they're mainly familiar with the Washington Hunter ways and intel."

The room quieted again, as we all went back to work and no-doubt back to considering what exactly it meant for us that the Hunters had banned together.

As I cleaned and made my way back into my room, my mind buzzed with new information.

First, my huldra and I had come to some sort of agreement to work together, which opened new doors for me when it came to fighting—doors to truths I still hadn't quite figured out completely. Second, and the part that made my bounty hunter side the happiest, according to the North Carolina Hunter, the women being stolen from the Seattle area and trafficked were being funneled through the Hunter's North Carolina complex. That had to have been the "whores" he'd referred to.

The Hunters clearly had a detailed system set up of transporting the women for holding and then shipping them off to wherever their buyer lived.

"But it makes no sense," I said to Marcus who'd tired of sitting on our bed and now scrubbed a blood stain on the wooden floor beside the nightstand.

He paused to look up. I eyed his amazing traps through his t-shirt from my vantage point and quickly felt guilty for ogling him when his eyes clearly expressed his inner pain. Although, he didn't want to discuss that pain at the moment. So I changed the subject.

"What doesn't make sense?" he asked.

"If the Hunters value chastity and feminine virtue so much," I said. "That they don't let their betrothed daughter be alone with single Hunters, why would they kidnap women to sell for sex?"

Marcus shook his head and scrubbed harder. "Just the idea of them selling women for sex makes me wish I could attach dynamite to each and every one involved and light them all up like Christmas trees. Makes me sick to call them my brothers." After a few beats of him scrubbing so hard it looked as though he were wearing a hole into the wood, he paused and leaned back to sit on his knees. He exhaled slowly. "But to answer your question, they say their rules are for their women's own good, that the rules protect their virtue, but that has nothing to do with it. To them, women are objects."

"Yeah," I agreed.

"Would you want someone messing around with your new car?" he continued. "Say you were picking it up from the lot, brand new, and you saw that there's already someone else's scent in the car, and coffee stains on the seat. Then you go to drive it and the steering wheel keeps pulling to the right."

"But what does a car have in common with a woman?" I asked, pausing from disinfecting the broken dresser.

"Nothing," Marcus answered gruffly. He returned to his scrubbing, his strong shoulders moving back and forth under the thin layer of cotton. "But to them, everything. No one wants their one and only car to be used, with used car problems. They want brand spankin' new. The fact that they liken cars to women sickens me."

"So, then," I clarified. "You're saying they don't value unvirtuous women because those women are no longer wife material and therefore have no value?"

Marcus nodded. "Disgustingly, yes."

"It's archaic," Aleksander added, striding into our room like he owned the place, which in a rental-agreement way, he kind of did. "Don't worry about that dent, Faline. I know a guy."

"Speaking of worrying," I said to Aleksander. "You were in the front yard. Why didn't you use your energy powers to stop John and Marcus's dad from running away? Couldn't you have forced them to stop and walk back?"

"I had just finished bringing a deservedly slow and painful death to the Hunter's who had tried to follow you down the stairs. The moment their weakness set in and allowed their deaths, I had found myself otherwise occupied, bringing a succubus back from the brink of death," Aleksander replied. "Such a use of energy takes all my concentration. I hadn't noticed the leader Hunters' escape until it was too late."

Wow, so incubi had the ability to bring people back from the brink of death. Good to know.

A toilet flushed and then Rod stood in the doorframe to the bedroom, making the room feel more cramped. He worked his sore and swollen muscles, a side effect for Hunters after being around so many Wild Women, releasing their wildness. I was actually impressed that he'd been able to keep it together and not accidently turn on one of us during the fighting. It was in their genes to want to kill us.

"So, Rod," I said, tying another black bag of bloody items. I wasn't about to try to remove blood from an orange and white mandala quilt, so into the new empty bag it went. "What do you know about the whole human trafficking thing your brothers are involved with?"

Rod sat on the bed and exhaled. "Marcus told you then?"

I shot a questioning glace to Marcus.

He sighed. "No, I haven't had time to tell her. And then today happened, and—"

"Tell me what?" I asked, my interest thoroughly piqued.

Marcus sat back on his knees. "The final straw that made Rod leave the brotherhood, or think about leaving to take a break."

"Well, I'm out now, brother, they saw me," Rod chimed in.

Marcus ignored him. "You remember they'd recently had him promoted in his precinct."

I nodded.

"Well," he continued. "They did that for a reason, in exchange for a favor. Only he didn't learn the favor until after the promotion. They wanted him to talk his golfing buddy, an investigator with Seattle PD, into burying a complaint made against Samuel Woodry, the same guy you brought in the day we had our first date, the guy who'd recently become a runner for the trafficking ring before you caught him."

"Holy shit." I stared off at nothing, compiling my thoughts.

Marcus went on. "The complaint made against him was from the parents of a barista in Seattle. Apparently, the day you brought him in, he'd creeped out their daughter, an eighteen year-old senior about to graduate from high school."

"Wait," I said, holding up my hand. "I think that may be the one I witnessed. Did he just creep her out at the coffee shop, or did he approach her somewhere else before that?"

Somewhere that would give me a hint as to where the Hunters were setting their sights as of late. Maybe they'd had Samuel feeling out a new market for them, a new crop of women, spoiled by the world's evils, to pick off.

"He'd joined their private online group, Witches not Bitches, under an alias, and started sending inappropriate messages to the ladies," Rod answered. "When he ordered his coffee at her shop, he quoted something he'd said to her in one of his messages, about her teacher."

"That's it!" I dropped the trash bag and slapped my thigh. "That's it. They're targeting young pagan women. I remember seeing her wearing a pentagram necklace and she had a tiny crescent moon tattoo on the inside of one of her wrists. But it hadn't occurred to me that he'd been stalking her. I thought he was just jonesing for a fix."

When Clarisse had told me, after she'd killed Azalea, that their plans had already been set into motion because of Samuel, she'd meant that he'd found where they'd locate their newest victims, or commodities as they saw it. Online groups brought in people from all over the country. Of course, they had to move their operation out of Seattle, out of the limelight, and to a broader location. They were gearing up, if they hadn't started already, to target young women from pagan and wiccan online groups, kidnap them or lure them into a trap, funnel them through the North Carolina complex, and sell them to the highest bidder.

My stomach turned in on itself and my huldra stirred from her nap. Marcus caught my gaze with a look that assured me we'd put a stop to this.

* * *

My coterie and I, the three harpies, Marcus, Mason, Aleksander, and the snake foreign Wilds crammed ourselves into the now packed Airbnb living room. I watched Eonza for signs of making advances on Aleksander, but so far she'd only peered in his direction a time or two, quickly looking away when he noticed her watching him.

Celeste sat beside Marie on the flower-print couch, clutching her hand as though she planned to never let it go. Marie stood and Celeste proved my assumption by standing with her.

"Now that we are all here, I have an announcement to make for my galere," Marie started. "We have decided the underground life is not for us."

I gazed around the room to see succubi smiling and Heather crying quietly, tucked under Mason's arm. Even if they interpreted Marie's declaration as the end to their relationship, I had no doubt those two would find a way to be together. But seeing as the two Hunter leaders got away, and probably noticed Aleksander in the process, I assumed the incubi leader's earlier declaration to stay out of the war had gone out the window much like the two Hunters. The fact that he helped to blow up the Oregon Hunter complex only strengthened my assumption.

"Our snake sisters from across the sea have pledged themselves to our cause, and we have pledged ourselves to the huldra's and harpies' cause." Marie paused long enough to find my face among the crowd. A smile lit her eyes and for a second, I thought I saw what Celeste had found and cherished in the succubi leader. "You have our vow; we will assist you in returning your mother, and the mothers and sister of other Wild Women. Together, we will bring freedom to the Wild Women of this land."

The living room filled with cheering and clicking tongues and yipping, as though most of these women weren't covered in bandages and others with their arms in slings. The scene spoke to our resilience and reminded me of what Marcus had said about our fire being bigger than the Hunters'.

When the excitement died down I took the stage, so to speak. "You don't know how happy I am to hear you say that, Marie."

"We aren't safe here," I reminded. "So I say we leave tonight. I know we're battered and bruised, but if we load into rental vans we can take turns driving and sleeping and recoup when we get to the harpies' home. They don't have much space in their house, but they own and rent out vacation homes in the area that they've offered to us for the time being. John knows that the harpies were here with us, and he'll no doubt alert the North Carolina complex, but they assure us that they've already taken steps to keep the Hunters from learning of their properties. Each rental home was purchased under an alias name, and aren't even managed by the same property managers, so there's no connecting them to one owner." I knew the harpies' distrust of all things human would come in handy.

"What do you say, sisters?" Marie canvassed the room with her eyes to ask her fellow succubi. Their answer was a resounding yes.

"The Hunter leaders saw me," Aleksander spoke up. "There's no longer a reason for me to stay out of this. I'll go, and bring Mason with me, as my hoard holds down the fort here in Portland."

Eonza gave a short nod, as though readying herself for her next phase of incubus seduction.

Marcus snuck his hand to mine and squeezed my fingers before releasing it and letting it fall to my side. My heart ached for him. *What inner turmoil must he be feeling?* I wondered. I could only imagine and hoped that when we were finally alone, he'd be willing to open up and share his thoughts.

Mason thanked his leader. Aleksander addressed the young male, who stood beside the fireplace in the center of the room. "It is the least I can do, and I am sure it will keep you and me both sane in a way that holding you back from your mate will not."

Heather clung tighter to her incubus and smiled.

"I have something else to say. An announcement," I said boldly. I grabbed Marcus's hand and held our joined hands above my head. "I'm done watching love blossom between others while I feel forced to hide my own. Marcus has more than proved himself, many times over, so I'm done pretending for the comfort of others." I peered around the room. "I love this male, and he loves me back. And that right there, is enough."

Marcus pulled me into his chest and leaned me backwards, pushing his lips passionately into my own. My huldra stirred again, this time more than content with my choice to declare my lover to the other Wild Women.

Celeste clapped and my coterie joined in, hesitantly at first. But hey, it was a step. And honestly, their acceptance was all I really cared about, even if I'd said I didn't care. Even Shawna gave a smile, although worry settled behind her eyes. Her savior had a chance at killing her captor and didn't take it. My sister had new emotions to work through, and I caught her gaze with mine, sending silent promises to stand beside her every step of the way. A root promise isn't one taken lightly.

"It's settled then," Marie said, above the hesitant laughing and exhaustion-filled conversations. "Everyone gather your things. We'll stop by the incubi's underground to get our stuff and then it's off to North Carolina. We leave in an hour."

With that, Marie and Celeste left into Celeste's room and closed the door behind them.

I grabbed Marcus by the hand and we made our way down the hall. He closed the bedroom door behind me, and before I could ask him how he was doing, he pressed his lips onto mine, shutting us away from the world and our inner battles, if only for an hour.

THE END

Thank you for reading! Did you enjoy?

Please Add Your Review! And turn the page for a sneak peek for ISHTAR'S LEGACY, book 3 in the Wild Women series.

SNEAK PEEK OF ISHTAR'S LEGACY

The moment I set foot on the cement waiting area outside the North Carolina airport, the soles of my feet tingled with the need to push roots into the earth of the east coast. Above us, in large lettering, a sign clung to the cement outer walls of the airport.

Arrivals.

I'd walked through this airport, along the grounds of this part of the country, and this time my heart quickened with a knowing. Only this time, my body insisted on the culmination of the past months, of the fighting and hiding and absolute hell, that I rise like an ocean wave and crash onto the Hunter's shore, wiping them out for good.

Marcus grabbed my hand, pulling me out of my battle fantasy and back into the moment.

"Where were you just now?" he asked with a twinkle of curiosity in his eyes and a smirk on his lips. We had unintentionally matched, both wearing bomber style jackets and jeans with boots. Though, if you asked me, he wore it better.

"I think you already know the answer to that," I teased.

"I know I *know* the answer," he said, squeezing my hand. "But how does it look in your mind?"

I exhaled. My breath, visible in the winter night's frigid air, dissipated before I put words to the images in my mind. "I think you and Aleksander were on to something. I like the idea of blowing the two last complexes up. But this time, with bigger explosions. I want the whole country to feel the fall of our oppressors."

I looked to my partner sister Shawna, who hooked her left arm into mine. She gave an approving nod. We'd planned to drive rental vans to North Carolina, but decided it'd be smarter to fly instead.

"Where are they?" my aunt grumbled. Her feet balanced on the edge of the sidewalk as she leaned into the road to peer left, in the direction our ride should have been visible from by now.

"Be patient," the nagin, Anwen said. She stood tall, her long black and silver hair framing her dark skin and eyes. "They flew here on their own wings, not a machine's."

Renee ignored the British Wild Woman and continued toeing the edge of the sidewalk silently.

We hadn't wasted much time in Oregon after blowing up their Hunter's complex and then coming back to a Hunter ambush at our Airbnb. After collecting our things and trying to clean the place up as much as possible—though our new ally the incubus Aleksander was still going to owe repair charges, which we'd fully reimburse him for—we piled into our vehicles and made for the airport. We couldn't all get on the same flight headed to North Carolina—the flights were too full—so we had opted to use cash and buy tickets to leave the following afternoon. We'd rented hotel rooms under an incubus's name and Aleksander had his incubi bring the succubis' things to pick through at the hotel, deciding which items to leave behind and which to take with them on our little east coast excursion.

The harpies left right away, as soon as we made the decision to fly. Last we talked to them, from our hotel room right before we checked out and left for our flight, they were almost home and stopping at a rental car business to borrow a few passenger vans. Eonza assured us they'd be able to pick us up when our flight landed.

Yet, there we stood, a group of Wild Women, two incubi, and a Hunter. We probably looked like we were visiting for a Bad Ass convention.

"I wish we could call them and see how far out they are," Celeste complained.

Marie kissed her partner's hand and smiled. "Leaving our phones behind was for the best. Now we're untraceable."

"Hey Aleksander," I said, turning to eye him as he sat on a metal bench beneath the overhang as though it were his throne. He looked up from his hands with a questioning gaze. "Can you feel them approaching? What's your energy radius when it comes to that?"

He stood. The incubi leader reached over six-foot-two. A smile crept along his lips as he made his way toward us. His black wool overcoat barely shifted against his dark slacks. He looked like New York in North Carolina. He gave me a nod as he passed and said, "You should know better, Faline, than to ask a man his size, energy, or otherwise."

Marcus stifled a laugh.

I rolled my eyes.

Aleksander stood to the left of my aunt and relaxed his body, his arms falling to his sides. Renee took a few steps back from the curb and joined us in watching the incubus work. My skin tingled in pulses, as though I could feel his energy growing to encompass the surrounding area enough to sense if harpies were nearby. I peered at my sisters and aunts to see if they felt it too. If they did, they didn't show it.

The incubi leader spun on his heel and addressed his audience. "They will be here shortly." He casually returned to his throne of a bench, retrieved his carry on, and made his way to stand patiently at the curb.

He couldn't have seen them when he'd made the announcement, because it was several minutes before the three blue passenger vans stopped at the curb and slid their side doors open.

"Thanks for picking us up," I said to Salis as I filed into the van along with my coterie, Marcus, Aleksander, another incubus. The succubi climbed into the van behind ours, and the shé, echidna, and nagin boarded the last van in the line.

Salis gave a nod, her tawny ponytail only moving enough across her shoulders to readjust the brown feather woven into a small strand of braid among her tresses. With one sharp movement of her lean neck, she turned back toward the road, hitting the gas the moment Aleksander shut the sliding van door. After exiting the airport traffic and making her way over to the carpool lane on the freeway, Salis spoke. "Once we near town, we will break off from the other vans. Each is going to a separate location."

"That won't work," Renee started in before I could ask Salis to explain her plan.

"We don't have cell phones to communicate with one another," Celeste clarified. She probably hadn't yet realized she wouldn't be sharing a bed with Marie during this trip, let alone be unable to talk to the succubus leader, who also happened to be her lover.

Salis only stared forward through the windshield. Both my sister and my aunt made statements, so our Wild cousin didn't respond. She probably assumed the huldras were talking amongst themselves.

I reworded my coterie's concerns and made sure to address the harpy. "Salis, they're worried they won't be able to stay connected to the other Wild Women groups, which is imperative to our mission here. Have you made provisions for this?"

I watched the harpy's expressionless face through the rearview mirror as she spoke.

"Each house has a landline," she said.

I figured the harpies would have already thought of everything we needed in the coming days. Unlike the Wild Women on this trip, other than my huldra coterie, they still had a group member missing. Only, we could all accurately guess where their mother was being held. In the North Carolina Hunter complex. Knowing where my mother was being held was a bit more difficult to pin down.

My mother had gone missing when I was a little girl. Up until recently, I'd always thought she'd been killed by jealous succubi, angry at her for mating with a human male their leader had claimed. Multiple times, Marie had assured me her predecessor, who'd trained her to be a succubi leader, never would have commanded such a thing be done. Succubi healed and helped, they did not hurt and murder.

Through my own bounty hunter research skills and Marcus's gathering of old police documents and Hunter intel, I now knew my mother had been taken by Hunters, along with a handful of other Wild Women, twenty years ago. When the Hunters recently abducted another collection of Wild Women—my partner sister Shawna being one of them—my hunt for the truth began. What I found were answers knotted in oppression masquerading as protection, lies about our kind costumed as history, and the trafficking of women whose humanity had been stripped away and replaced by objectification.

At first I only sought to get my sister back. It was the mermaids who had burned down the Washington Hunter complex. But their pyro tendencies lit a fire within me, an insatiable blaze to destroy each and every Hunter complex in the United States. Not only would I retrieve every Wild held in Hunter captivity, but I'd burn their prisons to the ground in the process.

"Where will we be staying, then, in relation to the succubi galere?" Celeste asked our harpy driver. If, earlier, she hadn't realized she wouldn't be sharing a bed with Marie, according to the need in her voice, she did now.

"Your coterie and the shé will stay in town, in the historical district," Salis answered in her regular emotionless tone. "The succubi galere, will stay at a larger vacation home nearer the mountains. This will keep them away from the human emotions of the town's population, help them to gain their strength for the battles ahead."

Damn, the harpies' preparedness impressed me.

"The phone numbers to the other houses, where your comrades are staying, will be written beside the phone," Salis finished.

Salis exited the freeway and drove down what I remembered as one of the main roads in town, where I had once booked Gabrielle and I a room at the little motel she deemed beneath her. I smiled at the memory of bantering with the mermaid and wished once again that she'd trusted me enough to tell me why she'd felt the need to double cross the Wild Women by working with the Hunters. I refused to believe she was mean-spirited and wanted us to fail. But she would never be able to tell me. She was dead.

"Isn't that the motel?" Marcus whispered into my ear in his low voice as we passed the little red building with white trim.

I suppressed an almost purring tone when I responded, "Yes, it is." with a smile and a wink.

If our fellow passengers knew what we referenced, they didn't make a show of it. This town held good memories as well as hard ones.

"So, Salis," I said, speaking louder and clearer to keep any possible questions about the importance of the motel at bay. "I'm curious, what was your thought process behind which houses you placed us in?" I realized my query could be seen as questioning her decision rather than seeking a deeper understanding of her strategy, so I clarified. "Your flock is quite strategic in all things, and I'm wondering which strategy is at play here."

Salis peered at me through the rearview mirror for a breath, her light eyes studying mine, then returned her gaze to the road. "I have already explained why I placed the succubi galere in the foothills of the mountain."

"True," I responded. "But why put us in the historical district? And where did you place the foreign Wilds?"

"The shé, nagin, and echidna are on their way to a residential home in a newer community," Salis answered. "Not one owned by any of us, but rather an empty rental a business associate has agreed to allow us to access for the time being."

"And the one we're staying in isn't owned by you either?" I asked, judging how easily the Hunters may or may not be able to find us.

"It is indirectly owned by us," she responded. "Passed to us through our flock's paternal grandparents, but left in their family name."

She knew of her parental lineage? And had been given property through the father's line? Her statement brought up a slew of questions I promised myself to ask her later. Unlike my sisters and I, the harpy flock—Eonza, Salis, and Lapis—all had the same mother. Now, I wondered if they had the same father too. They did bear a shocking resemblance to one another, which wasn't something you often found among Wild Women sisters. Did their father know he had mated with a harpy? She'd said the house was from her parental grandparents, so I wasn't sure if that meant from her mother's grandfather or her grandfather.

After a few more turns she slowed the speed of the car. Mature trees lined the quant street, standing between the sidewalks and the well-kept traditionally built homes. Salis pulled into the driveway of a house unseen from the road, with evergreen bushes acting as thick natural privacy fences. She parked in front of a brown detached garage trimmed with beige and merlot.

"Your coterie," she finally continued after turning off the ignition and twisting her tall, lean body in her seat to face me, "were chosen to stay in this home because its historical aspects could be of use to you."

"What does it have?" Olivia joked, "a secret room hidden behind a bookshelf?"

Shawna snickered.

"No," Salis said, unlatching her seatbelt and opening her driver's side door. "For a long while North Carolina was a dry state. And my paternal ancestors were bootleggers."

Shawna quieted.

"We chose this house for you," Salis went on, dead serious, "because it contains a secret underground connected to cursed passageways."

* * *

Don't stop now. Keep reading with your copy of ISHTAR'S LEGACY coming soon.

Don't miss Wild Women with book 3, ISHTAR'S LEGACY and discover more from Rachel Pudelek at www.rachelpudelek.com

* * *

With Wild Women of the snake Goddesses at her back, Faline has two more complexes to take down before her oppressors, the Hunters, are defeated.

But when an ex-lover of a pregnant harpy threatens to out the Wilds, Faline's role as leader of the American Wild revolution goes world-wide and jeopardizes her last battle against the Hunters who are holding her mother hostage.

* * *

Please sign up for the City Owl Press newsletter for chances to win special subscriber-only contests and giveaways as well as receiving information on upcoming releases and special excerpts.

All reviews are **welcome** and **appreciated**. Please consider leaving one on your favorite social media and book buying sites.

For books in the world of romance and speculative fiction that embody Innovation, Creativity, and Affordability, check out City Owl Press at www.cityowlpress.com.

ACKNOWLEDGMENTS

As I birth another book into the world, I have to first thank my book doula, my agent, Jacquie Flynn. Without you, Jacquie, the Wild Women would still be hiding in the trees and seas. And to my book's midwife, my editor, Heather McCorkle, your excitement and support for Faline and me fills me with absolute thankfulness.

To my coterie—Geno, Christany, and Isabel: your support and cheerleading mean the world to me. To my original coterie, my mom, Cathy Sullivan, and my sisters, Wendy Perry, Michaele Trujillo, and Dani Woodruff: you fill my heart with love and acceptance, gifts I do not take lightly.

Thank you to my Wild friends who advise me and champion my work: Amanda Lynn, Rayna Stiner, Rachel Spillane, Sara Wilkerson, Alli Roerden, Lynn Moddejonge, Samantha Heuwagen, Cass Morris, Jody Holford, and Sarah Glenn Marsh.

And to my readers, because of you I can write this acknowledgement page. I am overfilled with appreciation at your willingness to spend time in my Wild world and your eagerness to make it your own. Your messages to me of your favorite Wild group, characters, and scenes make me smile. I hope this book helps you to dive deeper into the minds and hearts of the Wild Women, the Hunters, and the new characters you'll meet. And above all, I hope you're entertained and empowered.

ABOUT THE AUTHOR

RACHEL PUDELEK is a dog-hugger and tree-lover. Growing up with three sisters sparked her passion for both women's history and women's advocacy, which led to her career as a birth doula and childbirth educator. These days she channels those passions into writing fiction. When she's not writing, Rachel enjoys hiking, attempting to grow her own food, or reading.
Rachel lives in Seattle, Washington with her husband, two daughters, two dogs, a cat named Lucifer, and two well-fed guinea pigs. Freyja's Daughter is her debut novel.

www.rachelpudelek.com

facebook.com/AuthorRachelP

twitter.com/rachelpud

instagram.com/rachel_pud

ABOUT THE PUBLISHER

City Owl Press is a cutting edge indie publishing company, bringing the world of romance and speculative fiction to discerning readers.

www.cityowlpress.com